4TH OF JULY

more . . .

3RD DEGREE

2ND CHANCE

1ST TO DIE

"HIS CLEVER TWISTS AND AFFECTING SUBPLOTS
KEEP THE PAGES FLYING."
                    —*People* (Page-Turner of the Week)

"DELIVERS A SHARP PUNCH."
                    —*Chicago Tribune*

"THAT RAPID-FIRE, IN-YOUR-FACE, YOU'D-BETTER-
KEEP-READING-OR-ELSE FORMAT WILL MAKE
YOU FINISH *1ST TO DIE* IN ONE SITTING (BARRING
WORLD WAR III, A 9.1 EARTHQUAKE, OR THE
EBOLA VIRUS)."
                    —*Denver Rocky Mountain News*

ALONG CAME A SPIDER

"JAMES PATTERSON DOES EVERYTHING BUT
STICK OUR FINGER IN A LIGHT SOCKET TO GIVE
US A BUZZ."
                    —*New York Times*

"WHEN IT COMES TO CONSTRUCTING A HAR-
ROWING PLOT, AUTHOR JAMES PATTERSON CAN
TURN A SCREW ALL RIGHT. JAMES PATTERSON IS
TO SUSPENSE WHAT DANIELLE STEEL IS TO
ROMANCE."
                    —*New York Daily News*

KISS THE GIRLS

"TOUGH TO PUT DOWN . . . TICKS LIKE A TIME
BOMB, ALWAYS FULL OF THREAT AND TENSION."
                    —*Los Angeles Times*

more . . .

POP GOES THE WEASEL

ROSES ARE RED

more . . .

LONDON BRIDGES

"ANY THRILLER WRITER, WANNABE OR ACTUAL, WOULD DO WELL TO STUDY [*LONDON BRIDGES*.]"
—*Publishers Weekly*

"AS WITH THE BEST OF PATTERSON'S WORK, IT IS IMPOSSIBLE TO STOP READING THIS BOOK ONCE STARTED."
—**BookReporter.com**

"BRILLIANT . . . ONCE AGAIN PATTERSON BLEW ME OUT OF MY SEAT."
—**RoundTableReviews.com**

The novels of James Patterson

Featuring Alex Cross

The Women's Murder Club

Other Books

For previews of upcoming James Patterson novels and information about the author, visit www.jamespatterson.com.

JAMES PATTERSON
& ANDREW GROSS
LIFEGUARD

GRAND CENTRAL
PUBLISHING

NEW YORK   BOSTON

This book is a work of fiction. Names, characters, places, and incidents are the product of the author's imagination or are used fictitiously. Any resemblance to actual events, locales, or persons, living or dead, is coincidental.

If you purchase this book without a cover you should be aware that this book may have been stolen property and reported as "unsold and destroyed" to the publisher. In such case neither the author nor the publisher has received any payment for this "stripped book."

Grand Central Publishing
Hachette Book Group USA
237 Park Avenue
New York, NY 10017
Visit our Web site at www.HachetteBookGroupUSA.com

Grand Central Publishing is a division of Hachette Book Group USA, Inc. The Grand Central Publishing name and logo is a trademark of Hachette Book Group USA, Inc.

Printed in the United States of America

Originally published in hardcover by Little, Brown and Company
First International Paperback Printing: May 2006
First US Paperback Printing: August 2006

16 15 14 13 12 11 10 9 8 7

Thanks—Sunny and Don Sweeney, natives of Brockton, and friends. Jennifer Genco and the staff of the Breakers in Palm Beach. And Steve Vasblom of Auckland, a crazy Kiwi, but one whose feet get more on the ground with every year.

Part One

THE PERFECT SCORE

Chapter 1

"DON'T MOVE," I said to Tess, sweaty and out of breath. "Don't even blink. If you so much as breathe, I know I'm gonna wake up, and I'll be back lugging chaise longues at poolside, staring at this gorgeous girl that I know something incredible could happen with. This will all have been a dream."

Tess McAuliffe smiled, and in those deep blue eyes I saw what I found so irresistible about her. It wasn't just that she was the proverbial ten and a half. She was more than beautiful. She was lean and athletic with thick auburn hair plaited into a long French braid, and a laugh that made you want to laugh, too. We liked the same movies, *Memento, The Royal Tenenbaums, Casablanca.* We pretty much laughed at the same jokes. Since I'd met her I'd been unable to think about anything else.

Sympathy appeared in Tess's eyes. "Sorry about

the fantasy, Ned, but we'll have to take that chance. You're crushing my arm."

She pushed me, and I rolled onto my back. The sleek cotton sheets in her fancy hotel suite were tousled and wet. My jeans, her leopard-print sarong, and a black bikini bottom were somewhere on the floor. Only half an hour earlier, we had been sitting across from each other at Palm Beach's tony Café Boulud, picking at DB burgers—$30 apiece— ground sirloin stuffed with foie gras and truffles.

At some point her leg brushed against mine. We just made it to the bed.

"Aahhh," Tess sighed, rolling up onto her elbow, "that feels better." Three gold Cartier bracelets jangled loosely on her wrist. "And look who's still here."

I took a breath. I patted the sheets around me. I slapped at my chest and legs, as if to make sure. "Yeah," I said, grinning.

The afternoon sun slanted across the Bogart Suite at the Brazilian Court hotel, a place I could barely have afforded a drink at, forget about the two lavishly appointed rooms overlooking the courtyard that Tess had rented for the past two months.

"I hope you know, Ned, this sort of thing doesn't happen very often," Tess said, a little embarrassed, her chin resting on my chest.

"What sort of thing is that?" I stared into those blue eyes of hers.

"Oh, whatever could I mean? Agreeing to meet someone I'd seen just twice on the beach, for lunch. Coming here with him in the middle of the day."

"Oh, that . . ." I shrugged. "Seems to happen to me at least once a week."

"It does, huh?" She dug her chin sharply into my ribs.

We kissed, and I felt *something* between us begin to rise again. The sweat was warm on Tess's breasts, and delicious, and my palm traveled up her long, smooth legs and over her bottom. Something magical was happening here. I couldn't stop touching Tess. I'd almost forgotten what it was like to feel this way.

Split aces, they call it, back where I'm from. South of Boston, Brockton actually. Taking a doubleheader from the Yankees. Finding a forgotten hundred-dollar bill in an old pair of jeans. Hitting the lottery.

The perfect score.

"You're smiling." Tess looked at me, propped up on an elbow. "Want to let me in on it?"

"It's nothing. Just being *here* with you. You know what they say: for a while now, the only luck I've had has been bad luck."

Tess rocked her hips ever so slightly, and as if we had done this countless times, I found myself smoothly inside her again. I just stared into those baby blues for a second, in this posh suite, in the middle of the day, with this incredible woman who only a few days before hadn't been conceivable in my life.

"Well, congratulations, Ned Kelly." Tess put a finger to my lips. "I think your luck's beginning to change."

Chapter 2

I HAD MET TESS four days before, on a beautiful white sand beach along Palm Beach's North Ocean Boulevard.

"Ned Kelly" is how I always introduced myself. *Like the outlaw.* Sounds good at a bar, with a rowdy bunch crowded around. Except no one but a couple of beer-drinking Aussies and a few Brits really knew whom I was talking about.

That Tuesday I was sitting on the beach wall after cleaning up the cabana and pool at the estate house where I worked. I was the part-time pool guy, part-time errand runner for Mr. Sol Roth—Sollie, to his friends. He had one of those sprawling, Florida-style homes you can see from the beach north of the Breakers and maybe wonder, *Whoa, who owns that?*

I cleaned the pool, polished up his collection of vintage cars from Ragtops, picked up mysteries specially selected for him by his buddies Cheryl

and Julie at the Classic Bookshop, even sometimes played a few games of gin with him around
the pool at the end of the day. He rented me a
room in the carriage house above the garage. Sollie and I met at Ta-boó, where I waited tables on
weekend nights. At the time I was also a part-
time lifeguard at Midtown Beach. Sollie, as he
joked, made me an offer I couldn't refuse.

Once upon a time, I went to college. Tried
"real life." Even taught school for a while back
up North, until that fell apart. It would probably shock my pals here that I was once halfway
to a master's. In social education at BU. "A
master's in *what?*" they'd probably go. "Beach
management?"

So I was sitting on the beach wall that beautiful day. I shot a wave to Miriam, who lived in the
large Mediterranean next door, who was walking
her Yorkies, Nicholas and Alexandra, on the
beach. A couple of kids were surfing about a
hundred yards offshore. I was thinking I'd do a
run-swim-run. Jog about a mile up the beach,
swim back, then run *hard* up and back. All the
while watching the ocean.

Then like some dream—there she was.

In a great blue bikini, ankle-deep in surf. Her
long reddish brown hair knotted up in a twist
with a flutter of tendrils.

Right away, it was as if there was something
sad about her, though. She was staring vacantly
at the horizon. I thought she was dabbing her
eyes.

I had this flash: the beach, the waves, the pretty,

lovelorn girl—like she was going to do something crazy!

On my beach.

So I jogged down to her in the surf. "Hey . . ."

I shielded my eyes and squinted into that gorgeous face. "If you're thinking what I think you are, I wouldn't advise it."

"Thinking what?" She looked up at me, surprised.

"I don't know. I see a beautiful girl on a beach, dabbing her eyes, staring forlornly out to sea. Wasn't there some kind of movie like that?"

She smiled. That's when I could see for sure she'd been crying. "You mean, where the girl on a hot afternoon goes in for an afternoon swim?"

"Yeah," I said with a shrug, suddenly a little embarrassed, "that's the one."

She had a thin gold chain around her neck, and a perfect tan. An accent, maybe English. God, she was a knockout.

"Guess I was just being cautious. Didn't want any accidents on my beach."

"*Your* beach?" she said, glancing up at Sollie's. "Your house, too, I guess?" She smiled, clearly toying with me.

"Sure. You see the window above the garage? Here, you can see it." I shifted her. "Through the palms. If you lean this way . . ."

Like an answer to my prayers, I got her to laugh.

"Ned Kelly." I stuck out my hand.

"Ned Kelly? Like the outlaw?"

I did a double take. No one had ever said that

to me. I just stood there with a dumb-ass, starstruck grin. Don't think I even let go of her hand.

"Sydney. New South Wales," she said, displaying her Aussie "Strine," her accent.

"Boston." I grinned back.

And that was how it started. We chatted a little more, about how she'd been living there for a couple of months and how she'd take long walks on the beach. She said she might come back this way the next day. And I said there was a chance I might be there, too. As I watched her walk away, I figured she was probably laughing at me behind those $400 Chanel sunglasses.

"By the way," she said, suddenly turning, "there *was* a movie. *Humoresque*. With Joan Crawford. You should check it out."

I rented *Humoresque* that night, and it ended with the beautiful heroine drowning herself by walking into the sea.

And on Wednesday Tess came back. Looking even hotter, in this black one-piece suit and a straw hat. She didn't seem sad. We took a swim and I told her I would teach her how to bodysurf and for a while she went along. Then as I let her go she hopped the right wave and crested in like a pro. She laughed at me from the shore. "I'm from Australia, silly. We have our Palm Beach, too. Just past Whale Beach, north of Sydney."

We made a "date" for lunch at the Brazilian Court in two days. That's where she was staying, one of the most fashionable places in town, a few blocks off Worth Avenue. Those two days were like an eternity for me. Every ring of my cell phone I figured was her canceling. But she didn't. We met in Café Boulud, where you have to make a reservation a month in advance unless you're Rod Stewart or someone. I was as nervous as a kid going out on his first date. She was already sitting at the table in a sexy off-the-shoulder dress. I couldn't take my eyes off of her. We never even made it to dessert.

Chapter 3

"SO, I'M THINKING this was one of the top ten afternoons of my life." I folded my arms behind my head and tickled Tess playfully with my toes. Both of us were spread-eagle on the king-size bed in her hotel suite.

"So, you were a lifeguard on Midtown Beach," she was saying. "Before you became a kept man. What does a lifeguard do—in Palm Beach?"

I grinned, because Tess was so obviously tossing me a softball. "A good lifeguard is a true waterman," I said with a twinkle in my eye. "We watch the water. Is it glassy, choppy? Are there riffs? Smooth flashes warning of riptides? We warn the sleepy snowbird to roll over and fry the other side. Douse the occasional jellyfish encounter with a splash of vinegar. Stuff like that."

"But now you're a kept man?" She grinned.

"Maybe I *could* be," I said.

She turned. There was a glimmer in her eye

that was totally earnest. "You know what I said about your luck changing, Ned. Well, maybe I'm starting to feel the same way, too."

I couldn't believe that someone like Tess McAuliffe was actually saying this to me. Everything about her was first-class and refined. I mean, I wasn't exactly Average Joe; I knew if I was on the show, I'd be one of the hunks. But holding her, I couldn't help wondering what in her life had made her so sad. What she was hiding in her eyes that first day on the beach.

My eyes slowly drifted to the antique clock on the fold-out writing desk across from the bed. "Oh, Jesus, Tess!"

It was almost five. The whole afternoon had melted. "I know I'm going to regret these words . . . but I've got to go."

I saw that sad look from the other day come over her face. Then she sighed, "Me, too."

"Look, Tess," I said, putting a leg into my jeans, "I didn't know this was going to happen today, but there's something I have to do. I may not see you for a couple of days. But when I do, things are going to be different."

"Different? *How* different?"

"With me. For starters, I won't have to keep people out of trouble on the beach."

"I like you keeping people out of trouble on the beach." Tess smiled.

"What I mean is, I'll be free. To do anything you want." I started buttoning my shirt and searching around for my shoes. "We could go somewhere. The islands. That sound good?"

"Sure, it sounds good." Tess smiled, a little hesitantly.

I gave her a long kiss. One that said, *Thank you for an amazing afternoon.* Then it took everything I had to get out of there, but people were counting on me.

"Remember what I said. Don't move. Don't even blink. That's exactly how I want to remember you."

"What're you planning to do, Ned Kelly, rob a bank?"

I stood at the door. I took a long look at her. It was actually turning me on that she would even ask something like that. "I dunno," I said, grinning, "but a man's gotta do what a man's gotta do."

Chapter 4

NOT A BANK, I was thinking as I hopped into my old Bonneville convertible and headed onto the bridge to West Palm, floating on cloud nine. But Tess was close. A one-shot, can't-miss deal that was going to change my life.

Like I said, I'm from Brockton. Home of Marvelous Marvin Hagler and Rocky Marciano. Ward Four, Perkins Avenue, across the tracks. *There are neighborhoods,* anyone from Brockton will agree, *and then there's the Bush.*

Growing up, people said Brockton's a quarter black, a quarter Italian, a quarter Irish, a quarter Swedish and Polish, and another "quarter" no one wanted to mess with. Hardscrabble neighborhoods of run-down row houses, churches, the ruins of closed-up factories.

And the Bush was the toughest. We had gangs. We got into fights every day. You didn't even call it a fight unless someone broke a bone. Half the kids I knew ended up in reform schools or juvie detention programs. The good ones took a few courses at the junior college or commuted to Northeastern for a year before they went into their father's restaurant or went to work for the city. Cops and firefighters, that's what Brockton seems to breed. Along with fighters.

Oh yeah, and crooks.

It wasn't like they were bad people. They paid for their homes. They got married and took the family out for birthdays and Communions like everyone else. They owned bars and joined the Rotary. They had barbecues on Sundays and screamed bloody hell for the Sox and the Pats. They just ran some bets at the same time. Or fenced a few stolen cars. Or cracked open some poor sucker's head now and then.

My father was that kind of guy. Spent more time up in the Souz in Shirley than he did around our dinner table. Every Sunday we'd throw on a tie and pile into the Dodge and make the trip up to see him in his orange prison suit. I've known a hundred guys like that. Still do.

Which brings me to Mickey, Bobby, Barney, and Dee.

I'd known them as long as I can remember. We lived within about four blocks of one another. Between Leyden and Edson and Snell. We knew everything about one another. Mickey was my cousin, my uncle Charlie's son. He was built like a wire hanger with curly red hair, but as tough a sonuvabitch as ever came out of Brockton. He was older than me by six weeks but made it seem as if it were six years. Got me into trouble more times than I can count—and got me out of it a whole lot more. Bobby was Mickey's cousin, but not mine. He'd been like a big brother to me, ever since my own big brother died—in a shoot-out. Dee was Bobby's wife, and they'd been together since before anybody could remember. Barney was about the funniest human being I had ever met; he'd also been my protector all through high school.

Every year we'd spend the summer working the Vineyard: tending bar, waiting tables, doing a "job" now and then to pay the bills. Winters, we came down here. We parked cars at the clubs, crewed tourist boats, bellhopped, joined catering teams.

Maybe someone who lived a conventional life would say we were a bad lot. But he'd be wrong. You can't choose your family, people always say, but you can choose the people you love. And they were more of a family to me than my own. Proved it a hundred times.

There are two types of people who come from Brockton. The ones who try to make it by putting away pennies every week. What the government doesn't take, the church will.

And the ones who keep on waiting, watching, keeping their eyes peeled for that one big score.

Once in a while they actually came around. The one you couldn't pass up. The one that could get you out of the life.

And that's where I was headed when I left Tess's suite at the Brazilian Court.

My cousin Mickey had found it.

The perfect score.

Chapter 5

AS SOON AS Ned left, Tess threw herself back on the bed with an exhalation of joy and disbelief. "You must be crazy, Tess! You *are* crazy, Tess."

Crazy, to be opening herself to someone like Ned, especially with everything else going on in her life.

But something about Ned wouldn't let her stop. Maybe his eyes, his charm, his boyish good looks. His innocence. The way he had just come up to her on the beach like that, like she was a damsel in distress. It had been a long time since anyone had treated her that way. *Wanted.* And she liked it. What woman didn't? If only he knew.

She was still cozied up on the sheets, reliving every detail of the delicious afternoon, when she heard the voice.

"Next." He stood there—leaning, smirking—against the bedroom door.

Tess almost jumped out of her skin. She never even heard the key open the door to the suite.

"You scared me," she said, then covered herself up.

"Poor Tess." He shook his head and tossed the room key in an ashtray on the desk. "I can see the lunches at Boulud and Ta-boó have started to bore you. You've taken to going around to the high schools, picking up guys after SAT practice."

"You were watching?" Tess shot up. That would be just like the bastard. Thinking he could do that. "It just happened," she said, backing off, a little ashamed. And a lot ashamed that she had to justify herself. "He thinks I'm something. Not like you . . ."

"Just happened." He stepped into the bedroom and took off his Brioni sport jacket. "Just happened, like, you met on the beach. And then you went back a second time. And you both just happened to meet at lunch at Boulud. A *lifeguard*. How very romantic, Tess."

She sat up, angry. "You were following me? Go fuck yourself."

"I thought you knew," he said, ignoring her response. "I'm the jealous type." He started to remove his polo shirt. Tess's skin broke out in goose bumps. She was sure he could sense her alarm as he began to unbuckle his pants.

"And about fucking *myself*"—he stepped out of his slacks, smiling—"sorry, Tess, not a chance. Why do you think I buy you all that expensive jewelry?"

"Look," Tess said, wrapping herself into the sheet. "Let's not today. Let's just talk. . . ."

"We can talk," he said with a shrug, folding his shirt neatly on the edge of the bed, slipping off his shorts. "That's okay with me. Let's talk about how I treat you like some kind of society princess, how I bought the rings on your fingers, bracelets on your wrist, that diamond lariat around your neck. Hell, I know the girls at Tiffany's by their first names—Carla, Janet, Katy."

"Look . . ." Tess stared at him, nervously. "It just happened. He's a good guy."

"I'm sure he is." He smiled. "It's you I can't figure out. The jewelry and the Mercedes. Then you're like some horny little cotillion bitch, doing it in the parking lot with the guy who parks the cars."

She was starting to get scared. She knew what he was like when he got this way. He moved over to the edge of the bed and sat down. His erection almost made her sick. She pulled away, but he grabbed and squeezed her arm. Then he sort of cradled her diamond lariat. For a second she thought he was going to rip it off her neck. "My turn, cupcake. . . ."

He yanked away the sheet and threw her down on the bed. Then he grabbed her by the ankles and spread her wide. He rolled her back and thrust himself inside. She didn't fight him. She couldn't. Feeling him inside her made her gag. He thought he owned her, and maybe he did. He moved hard against her, the way he always did, something crude and foreign inside her. All she felt was shame. "I'm sorry, Ned," she whispered to herself. She watched him grunt and sweat like some disgusting animal.

He made her do everything he liked—all the things she hated. When he was finished, Tess lay there, feeling so dirty, shivering, as if the room had grown cold. She wanted to cry. She had to end this. Now.

"I need to talk to you," Tess said. He was up and looping his belt through his fancy Italian golf pants.

"Sorry, darling, no time for cuddle talk now. I have to get back."

"Then I'll see you later? At the benefit?"

"Well, that depends." He smoothed his hair in the mirror.

"On what?" She didn't understand.

He smiled, almost pathetically. "Things have gotten very cozy, haven't they, Tess? It must feel just like home, right, since you seem to make a habit of shitting where you sleep. You're very pretty, my love, but you know what I think? The jewelry and the fancy car . . . I'm beginning to think they've made you feel like you really belong." He smiled one more time. "Hope that was as good for you as it was for me."

He turned, tossing the room key in the palm of his hand. "And by the way, you know you really ought to lock the door. You can never tell who might pop in for a quickie."

Chapter 6

IT'S OVER! she screamed to herself.

Tess kicked at the covers in rage. She felt ashamed, angry, weak. *This wasn't going to happen anymore.*

Some stuff that must've fallen out of his pocket jangled on the sheets. Loose change, a golf tee. Tess hurled them with all her might against the wall. It wasn't worth it anymore. Not for anything.

She threw on a robe and ran herself a bath, anything to remove the touch of him. That was the last time she would ever feel his hands on her. It would mean giving this up, but he was more than she could take. Like Ned said, they could go anywhere. Go walkabout. He didn't know just how prophetic he was. A fresh start. Yeah, she'd earned that.

Tess went into the bedroom closet and laid out a long backless Dolce & Gabbana evening gown.

She picked a pair of brown Manolo Blahniks. She would look gorgeous tonight. Give him something to miss for the rest of his life.

Tess knotted up her hair and sank naked into the large tub. The scent of the lavender bath oil made her feel good, clean. She lay back and rested her head on the smooth porcelain rim. The water lapped up over her shoulders. She shut her eyes.

Ned's face and his laugh crept into her mind. Whatever shame she felt, it wasn't enough to erase what had been a very good day. Ned Kelly. *Like the outlaw.* She smiled again. More like the pussycat. It was about time she had a go with someone who treated her well—make that *great*. He actually looked up to her.

She heard the bathroom fan go on. For a second Tess just lay back with her eyes closed. Then she heard humming.

Her eyes bolted open. Someone huge was standing over her. Tess's heart leaped into her throat. "What're you doing here?"

He had a sullen, cold look in his eye, dark hair tied in a ponytail. She thought she'd seen him somewhere before.

"A shame," he said with a shrug.

Suddenly he had Tess by the throat with his thick hands. He forced her head underwater. *What're you doing?*

Tess held her breath as long as possible, but as she opened her mouth, water rushed into her lungs, making her cough and gag, letting more water in. She was thrashing and kicking against the porcelain tub. She tried to force herself up, but Ponytail had her by the shoulders and head. He was incredibly strong, probably outweighed her by a hundred pounds.

Panic took hold, more water pouring into her lungs. She was clawing for the man's face, trying to scratch him, *anything*. Through the soapy water she could see his thick arms holding her down. Too much time going by. She stopped kicking. Stopped flailing. She wasn't coughing anymore. *This can't be happening,* a voice said inside her.

Then another voice, afraid—far more accepting than Tess ever imagined. *Yes, yes, it can. This is what it's like to die.*

Chapter 7

"HEY, OUTLAW!" Bobby exclaimed as I stepped into the kitchen of the run-down, canary yellow house in a seedy area just off 95 in Lake Worth.

"Neddie." Dee got up and came over and gave me a kiss on the cheek. A dream in jeans and long honey blond hair, every time Dee wrapped her arms around me, I flashed to how I'd had a crush on her since I was fifteen. Everyone in the neighborhood did. But she fell for Bobby and his Bon Jovi looks in the ninth grade.

"Where you been?" My cousin Mickey looked up. He was wearing a black T-shirt that read, YOU AIN'T REALLY BAD, TILL YOU BEEN BROCKTON BAD.

"Where do you think he's been?" Barney rolled back in his chair and grinned under the kind of black-framed glasses Elvis Costello wears. "Look at the kid's face. Biggest day of his life, and he's out romancing the ladies."

"Please." Dee scowled at him reprovingly. Then she shrugged with an inquisitive glint. "So?"

"So . . ." I looked around the table. "She showed."

A little cheer went up. "Thank God," said Bobby. "I was wondering how we were going to pull this off with Neddie-boy having a panic attack every five minutes. Here, you deserve this. . . ." He slid me a beer.

"Judging by the time, and that shit-eating grin on your face," Mickey said, looking at his watch, "I'd say it was the best lunch of your life."

"You wouldn't even believe me." I shook my head.

"Hey, we've got all the time in the world," Mickey said, the sarcasm running thick. "What the hell else we have going on here today? Oh, yeah, just that little matter of the five million dollars."

"Relax," Barney said, winking at me, "he's just pissed 'cause the only thing that'll lay down with him just got euthanized by the ASPCA."

Some laughter trickled around the table. Mickey picked up a black canvas bag. He removed five legal-type manila envelopes. "So, what's her name?"

"Tess," I said.

"Tess." Mickey pursed his lips, then curled them into a little smile. "You think this Tess will still love you if you come back with a million bucks?"

Everyone pulled up to the table. Tonight, things were going to change for us. For all of us. It was exhilarating. But it was business, too.

Mickey handed out the envelopes.

Chapter 8

IT WAS MICKEY'S PLAN, down to the last detail. Only he knew it. And how it all fit together.

There was this fabulous house on South Ocean Boulevard. On Billionaire's Row in Palm Beach. It even had a name. Casa Del Océano.

Ocean House.

And in it, 50 to 60 million dollars' worth of world-class art. A Picasso. A Cézanne. A Jackson Pollock. Probably other valuable stuff, too. But Mickey was clear: only these three were to be taken.

There was a mastermind behind the job. Went by the name of Dr. Gachet. Mickey wouldn't tell us who it was. The whipped cream and cherry on top was we didn't even have to fence the stuff. Just a textbook B and E. Our cut was 10 percent in cash. *Five million*. The next day. Just like the old days, split five ways. I was risking everything on this. A clean record. The life I'd been leading, whatever that was.

"Bobby, Barney, and me, we'll be the ones going in," Mickey explained. "Dee's outside on the walkie-talkie. Ned, I've saved the really cushy job for you."

All I had to do was zip around Palm Beach and trigger the alarms in several expensive homes. All the owners would be at some posh charity ball at the Breakers. There were pictures of the houses and a sheet with the addresses. The local police force was small, and with alarms going off all over town, they'd be like the Keystone Kops going in fifteen different directions. Mickey knew how to get into the target house and disable the alarm. There might be a housekeeper or two to worry about, but that was it. The hardest part would be not dropping the paintings when we took them off the walls.

"You're sure?" I flipped through the house photos and turned to Mickey. "You know I'll go in with you."

"You don't have anything to prove," he replied, shaking his head. "You've never been arrested since you were a kid. Besides, for the rest of us, what's a little conviction for grand robbery and interstate traffic of stolen goods gonna matter? If you're caught, whadda they get you for—petty vandalism?"

"If you're caught, don't even come back here." Barney laughed, then downed a swig of beer. "We'll hold back half your stake."

"We all voted," Dee said. "It's not up for discussion. We want to keep you safe and sound. For your little Tess," she giggled.

I looked at the addresses. El Bravo, Clarke, Wells Road. Some of the nicest streets in Palm Beach. The "core people" lived there—the Old Guard.

"We meet back here at half past nine," Mickey said. "We should have the money in our accounts tomorrow. Any questions?"

Mickey looked around the table. The people I'd known all my life, my best friends. He tilted his beer. "This one's *it*. After this, we're done. Dee, you and Bobby can buy that restaurant you're always talking about. Barney's got a car dealership in Natick with his name on it. Neddie, you can go write the Great American Novel or buy a hockey team, whatever. I always told you I'd get you this one chance, and here it is. Five million. I'm happy we're all here to share it. So . . . hands on the table. . . . This is what we've been working for since we were thirteen years old." He looked from face to face. "Last chance to bow out now. Guys . . . Neddie, are we in?"

My stomach was churning. This was bigger than anything I'd ever done before. Truth was, I was actually happy living a regular life down there. But would something like this ever come my way again? Life had taken a few things from me up North. It seemed this was my way of grabbing back a piece.

"In," said Bobby, Barney, Dee.

I took a breath. Five million. I *knew* I was crossing the line. But I wanted this. Like Tess said, maybe my luck was changing. I was starting to dream again, and a million dollars buys a lot of dreams.

I put my hand on top of the pile.

"In," I said.

Chapter 9

IT DOESN'T RAIN in Palm Beach, it Perriers.
Some asshole told me that line once, but there
was an element of truth to it. This was definitely
the place for the perfect score.

An hour and a half after the meeting in Lake
Worth, I parked the Bonneville down the block
from an impressive stucco-and-glass contempo-
rary behind a tall hedge on Wells Road. I was
dressed in a baseball cap and jeans, and a dark
T-shirt that blended into the dusky light.

Reidenouer, the mailbox read. I was wondering if this was the same Reidenouer who'd been
all over the news for running a Florida health-
care company into the ground. If so, it hurt a little less.

A Mercedes SUV was parked in the circular
tiled driveway. I crept around the driveway and
lifted the latch on a metal gate that led to the
back. I was praying that no one was in the house

and that the alarm would be set. The interior was dark, except for a single dim light that seemed to be coming from deep inside. Kitchen, maybe. The Reidenouers were supposed to be at the Breakers. Everything seemed perfect. Except maybe the ten thousand butterflies fluttering in my stomach.

There was a gorgeous lap pool in back, and a pool house in the style of the main building under a canopy of leaning palms. I glanced at my watch: 7:40. The crew would be getting in position, Dee scanning the police frequencies.

Take a deep breath, Neddie. . . . Everything was rolling on this—years of a clean record, the possibility of jail, whatever was going to happen with Tess. I told myself that this one time, it was worth the chance. And that I wasn't doing something I hadn't done a few times before.

I snuck around the side of the pool to the sliding rear doors. A typical latch lock. I could see art on the walls inside. I was sure there was an alarm contact on the door.

I took a metal jimmy from my back pocket and jammed it between the doorframe and the glass slider. I pried at the space. There was a little movement, but the lock would not budge. I wasn't surprised. I wedged it in there again. Suddenly there was the slightest slip. *C'mon, Neddie, hard!*

I felt the glass frame give way. Suddenly, several loud, penetrating beeps resonated around the house. Lights flashed on, and my heart stood still. I looked through the glass and didn't see anyone.

I'd done what I came to do. *I was outta there!*

I hurried out the same way I entered, hugging the hedges until I reached the street. I jumped back in the Bonneville. No one came to the street. I didn't see any lights going on. You could barely hear the alarm sounding behind me. But I knew the police were on their way.

I felt a shot of adrenaline.

One down!

I drove back onto County, reassuring myself that the cops weren't waiting for me at every turn. *Keep cool.* . . . So far, everything was according to plan.

I drove south over to Cocoanut Row, past the Royal Poinciana Plaza. I made a right toward the lake. A street protected by hedges, called Seabreeze. This time, it was an old plantation-style ranch, like from the thirties. I parked half a block away and tried to mosey up to the house as inconspicuously as I could, though I had a timetable to keep.

I saw an ADT security sticker on the front door. *That'll scare off the robbers.* I hung for a second in the hedgerow, took a look around. Down the block a woman was walking her dog, and I gave her a moment to go back inside. 7:58. Clear. I found a rock on the ground. I hurled it as hard as I could at the front window. A shrill alarm sounded and suddenly an automatic light bathed the driveway in unexpected illumination. I heard the high-pitched sound of a dog barking.

I took off, hugging the shadows, my heart beating a mile a minute. *That's two!*

The last one was one of those stately Mizner

mansions on El Bravo off South County below Worth Avenue. It was 8:05. I was right on schedule.

There was a huge boxwood hedge in the shape of an arch, and a heavy iron gate. I figured there must be an army of servants inside. I parked the car a block or so from the house and went around back. I wedged myself through the tall sculptured hedges. This was a house for the ages. Had to belong to some Old Guard family, Lauder or Tisch, or maybe some hotshot Internet billionaire. The glass French doors overlooking the sea were double-sided. I'd never break them.

I hugged the side of the house and came across a regular framed door I assumed led to the kitchen. I looked inside, no light.

I wrapped my hand in a cloth I was carrying and punched through a glass panel in the door. Shit . . . *No sound*.

I glanced at my watch. Mickey and the guys were ready to go in.

I reached inside the door and twisted the knob and let myself in. *Jeez, Louise.* I was in some kind of pantry, leading toward the rear of the house. I saw a sunroom overlooking the lawn. Next to it was a dining room. High ceilings, tapestries on the walls. A couple of candelabra that looked as if they might have belonged to the Romanovs.

God, am I crazy doing this? I knew the place was wired. Clearly the owners or the staff hadn't put on the alarm. I was thinking I could search along the windows for the contact points. 8:10. The crew would be going in at any moment. I had to get this done. My heart was racing.

Suddenly I heard footsteps and I froze. A black woman in a white robe shuffled toward the kitchen. Must be the maid. She looked up and saw me, and I could see by the little gag in her throat, she was more scared than I was.

She didn't scream, her jaw just dropped. My face was hidden under the cap. There was nothing she could identify about me. I just stood there for a second and muttered, "Sorry, ma'am." Then I bolted for the door.

I figured that in two seconds she would be on the phone to the police. That was as good as an alarm.

I ran back through the hedges and hugged the shadows to Ocean Boulevard. I jumped in the Bonneville, slammed it into gear, and drove away at a reasonable speed. I looked back. Everything was dark. No one had come out to get a look at my plates. It was 8:15. Cops were probably crisscrossing all over town, trying to figure out what the hell was going on.

"You're goddamn crazy, Ned Kelly!" I shouted at the top of my lungs.

Three house alarms in record time!

I hit the accelerator and felt the night sea breeze whip my hair. I was alongside the ocean and the moon was lighting it up and I felt an incredible thrill buzzing through my veins. I thought about Tess. How it could be with her. How I'd been marking time down there for a long time, and now I'd made the perfect score.

Chapter 10

SOMETHING DIDN'T FEEL RIGHT. Mickey sensed it as soon as they stepped through the front gates.

He had an inner feeling about these things.

The house was there in front of them. Spectacular, vast. Lit up like this great Italian palace. Pointed Venetian arches and windows with stone balconies. An arched loggia, ringed with bougainvillea, leading around to the sea. The driveway was probably a hundred yards long, every bush and tree perfectly lit. He heard the crunch of pebbles under their heels. They were in stolen police uniforms. Even if someone was around, no one would suspect a thing. Everything was just the way he was told it'd be.

And still he had this bad feeling in his gut.

He looked at Bobby and Barney. He could see they were nervous, too. He knew them well enough to know what they were thinking.

Never been so close to anything this grand.

Casa Del Océano. Ocean House.

Mickey knew everything about the place. He had studied it. Knew it was built by someone named Addison Mizner in 1923. He knew the interior layout, the alarms. How to get in, where the paintings were.

So why did he feel nervous? *C'mon,* he thought, to calm himself, *there's five million bucks inside.*

"So what the hell is *that?*" Barney nudged him with the black satchel containing his tools. At the end of the long pebbled driveway, there was this huge, lit-up marble . . . bowl.

"Birdbath," Mickey answered, and grinned.

"Birdbath?" Barney shrugged and adjusted the brim of his police cap. "More like a fucking pterodactyl!"

Mickey's watch read 8:15. Dee had called in; Ned, as expected, had done his job. Cop cars were probably bouncing all over town right now. He knew there were cameras hidden in the trees, so they kept their faces hidden under their caps. In front of the oak doors, he took a last glance at Bobby and Barney. They were ready. They had waited a long time for this.

Mickey rang the bell, and a minute later a Latino housekeeper answered. Mickey knew there was no one else in the house. He explained how there were disturbances all over town, and an alarm had gone off there, and they were sent to check it out. Maybe she noticed Barney's bag. Maybe she wondered where their car was. But a second later, Bobby whacked her with his Maglite and dragged her into a closet. She never got a decent look. He came back wearing a smirk as wide as the Charles River. A million-dollar smile.

They were in!

Chapter 11

THE FIRST THING WAS to disable the interior alarm. The paintings and sculptures were wired to contact points that would go off if they were lifted. Motion detectors, too. Mickey unfolded a piece of paper he had stuffed in his uniform pocket.

He punched in the numbers on a digital plate: 10-02-85.

This better work. Everything depended on the . . . next . . . couple . . . of . . . seconds.

A green light flashed on. *Systems clear!* For the first time, Mickey's stomach actually relaxed. A grin came over his face. This was going to happen! He winked at Bobby and Barney. "Okay, fellas, the place is ours."

In front of them, a carved mahogany archway led into the large vaulted living room. Spectacular stuff was just about everywhere. Art all over the walls. There was a large stone fireplace and

some scene from Venice over the mantel. A
Canaletto, but he'd been told to leave it. Blue and
white Chinese urns, bronze Brancusis. A chandelier that looked as if it came from a czar. Six
French doors led out to a patio overlooking the
sea.

"I don't know if this is what that guy meant
when he said the rich were different from us,"
Barney said, gawking, "but, uh . . . holy shit."

"Forget it." Mickey grinned excitedly. "This is
cab fare compared with what we've come for!"

He knew where to go. The Cézanne was in the
dining room. That was to the right. Barney took
out a hammer and a file from his black case to
pry the canvases out of their heavy antique
frames.

The dining room had flocked red wallpaper
and a long polished table with giant candelabra.
It looked as though it could seat half the free
world.

Mickey's heart was pounding. *Look for the
Cézanne,* he was saying to himself—*apples and
pears.* On the right-hand wall.

But instead of the $5 million thrill he was ex-
pecting to feel, his insides turned to ice. Cold,
right at the center of his chest.

The wall was empty. There was no still life. No
Cézanne.

The painting wasn't there!

Mickey felt a sharp stab through his heart. For
a second, the three of them stood there, staring at
the empty space. Then he took off, running to the
other side of the house.

The library.

The Picasso was over the fireplace on the wall. Mickey's blood was rushing and hot. Everything had been mapped out. He ran into the book-lined room.

Another chill. No, this was more like a freezer blast.

No Picasso! This wall space was empty, too! Suddenly he felt like vomiting. "What the fuck—?"

Mickey ran like a madman back to the front of the house. He bounded up the large staircase to the second floor. This was their last chance. The bedroom. There was supposed to be a Jackson Pollock on the bedroom wall. They weren't going to lose this. He'd worked too hard. This was their ticket out. He had no idea what the hell was going on.

Mickey got there first, Bobby and Barney right behind him. They stopped and stared at the wall, the same nauseated look on all their faces.

"Sonuvabitch!" Mickey shouted. He smashed his fist through a framed print on the wall, leaving his knuckles bloody.

The Pollock was gone. Just like the Picasso and the Cézanne. He wanted to kill whoever did this—whoever had stolen his dreams.

Someone had set them up!

Chapter 12

SEEMS SILLY NOW . . . an orange martini . . . a sailboat drifting on a blue Caribbean sea . . .

That's what I was thinking when I first got word something had gone wrong.

I was parked on South County Road, across from the Palm Beach firehouse, tracking the cop cars racing by me, lights and sirens blaring. I had done my job really, really well.

I was letting myself think about Tess lying next to me on the deck. In a tight little suit, all gorgeous and tanned. And we were sipping those martinis. Don't know who was making them. Let's throw in a skipper and a crew. But we were somewhere in the Caribbean. And they tasted soooo good.

That's when Dee's voice crackled on the walkie-talkie. "Ned, where are you? *Neddie!*"

Just hearing her voice made me nervous all over again. I wasn't supposed to hear from her until we met back at the house in Lake Worth at 9:30. She sounded scared. I think I knew right then that the scene on the sailboat was never going to happen.

"Ned, something's gone wrong!" Dee shouted. "Get back here, right now!"

I picked up the receiver and pressed the TALK button. "Dee, what do you mean, 'gone wrong'?"

"The job's busted," she said. "It's goddamn over, Ned."

I had known Dee since we were kids. She was always cool. But disappointment and anger were exploding through her voice.

"What do you mean 'busted'?" I said. "Bobby and Mickey, are they all right?"

"Just get back here," she said. "Mickey's contact . . . Gachet. The bastard set us up!"

Chapter 13

MY HEART ALMOST CAME to a full stop at that moment. What did Dee mean, 'set us up'?

My head dropped to rest on the steering wheel. All I knew was a name—Gachet. Mickey never told us any more. But it was clear, the job was gone. My million dollars, too. Then I realized it could get worse. *Much worse.* Mickey, Bobby, and Barney could get nabbed.

I put the car in gear but I wasn't sure where I should go. Back to the safe house? Or to my room at Sollie's, and just stay clear? I suddenly realized that everything was in jeopardy. My job, my place at Sollie's. My whole life. I flashed to Tess. . . . *Everything!*

I started to drive. I made a right onto Royal Palm Way, heading toward the middle bridge over to West Palm.

Suddenly sirens blared all around me. I froze. I looked behind and there were cop cars gaining on me. My heart got a jolt as if I had touched a live wire. I was caught! I slowed, waiting for them to pull me over.

But, incredibly, they raced right by. Two black-and-whites. They weren't looking for me, or even headed in the direction of Ocean House, or of any of the places I'd set off alarms. *Weird*.

Suddenly they turned down Cocoanut Row, the last major street before the bridge. They made a sharp left into traffic, sirens blaring, lights flashing. Didn't make sense at all.

Where could they be headed with all the shit going on all over town? I followed, at least for a couple of blocks. The black-and-whites turned onto Australian Avenue. I saw them come to a stop halfway down the block.

More cop cars. A morgue van, too.

They were pulled up in front of the Brazilian Court. I started to get nervous. That was where Tess lived. What was going on?

I parked the Bonneville at the end of the block and wandered up closer to the hotel. There was a crowd across the street from the entrance. I'd never seen so many cop cars in Palm Beach. This was crazy. We were the ones they ought to be after. I knew I'd better get back to Lake Worth. But Dee's words echoed in my head. *The bastard set us up*. Set up, how?

A ring of onlookers had crowded around the hotel entrance. I eased my way in. I went up to a woman wearing a white sweater over her sun-dress and holding the hand of a young boy. "What's going on?"

"There's been a murder," she answered anxiously. "That's what all those sirens were about."

"Oh," I mumbled.

Now I was really starting to get scared. *Tess lives here.* I pushed out of the crowd, not even thinking about myself. Hotel staff in black uniforms were being ushered outside. I latched onto a desk clerk, a blond woman I recognized from earlier in the day. "Can you tell me what's going on?"

"Someone's been killed." She shook her head, dazed. "*A woman.* In the hotel."

"A woman." I held her eyes. Now I was starting to freak. "You mean a guest?"

"Yes." Then she looked at me funny. I couldn't tell if she remembered me or not. "Room 121," she said.

My world started to spin. I stood there, numb, feeling my lips quiver. I tried to say something, but nothing came out.

Room 121 was the Bogart Suite.

Tess is dead, isn't she?

Chapter 14

I WATCHED just long enough to see the stretcher loaded into the flashing morgue van. That's when I saw Tess's hand, dangling through the body tarp, those three gold bracelets hanging from her wrist.

I backed away from the crowd, feeling as if my chest were going to explode. All I could think was that I had just left her, a few hours before. . . .

I had to get out of there. The Palm Beach police were all around. I was afraid they'd be looking for me, too.

I made it back to my car just as the shakes took over my body. Then this awful knot hurtled up in my throat. I threw up on somebody's manicured lawn.

Tess was dead.

How could that be? I had just left her. I had just spent the most wonderful afternoon of my life with her. The hotel maid said *murdered.* How? Why? Who would kill Tess?

In a daze, I started to fast-forward through the days since we met. How we agreed to see each other again; how the Ocean House job had been set up.

Everything was *separate.* It was just a coincidence. A horrible one. I felt myself fighting back tears.

Then, unable to hold it back any longer, the dam burst.

I hung my head and just stayed there, my face smeared with tears. At some point I realized I had to leave. Someone could have recognized me from that afternoon. That blond desk clerk! I couldn't exactly go to the police and clear myself, not with what had happened tonight. I pulled out from the curb. I didn't know where the hell I was going. *Just away.*

Chapter 15

I MADE A LEFT, then another, found myself back on Royal Palm. My mind was a mess. My clothes were soaked in sweat. I drove the whole way down to Lake Worth in a daze. Everything had just changed. Everything in my life. It had happened once before—in Boston. But this time I wasn't going to be able to put it back together.

I turned off 95 onto Sixth Avenue, the awful image of Tess's dangling wrist and the sound of Dee's freaked-out warning alternating in my head.

Mickey's place wasn't far from the highway. No Breakers on this street. No Bices or Mar-a-Lagos. Just shabby streets of boxy homes and trailers where people drank beer on lawn chairs, with flatbeds and Harleys in their open garages.

A cop car streaked past me, and again I tensed. Then another cruiser. I wondered if somebody knew my car. Maybe I'd been spotted in Palm Beach?

I wound the Bonneville down onto West Road, a couple of blocks from the yellow house Mickey and Bobby had rented.

My stomach almost came up into my throat.

Flashing cop lights everywhere. Just like before. I couldn't believe my eyes. People were crowded all over the front lawns—in tank tops and muscle shirts, looking down the street. What the hell was going on?

Mickey's block was barricaded off. Cops everywhere. Lights flashing like it was a war zone.

A stab of dread. The cops had found us. At first it was just fear. This whole mess was going to be exposed. I deserved it. To have gotten involved in something so stupid.

Then it wasn't just fear. It was more like revulsion. Some of the flashing lights were EMS vans.

And they were right in front of Mickey's house.

Chapter 16

I JUMPED OUT of the Bonneville and pushed my way to the front of the crowd. No way this could be happening again. No way, no way.

I edged up to some old black guy in a janitor's uniform. Never even had to get the words out of my mouth.

"Some kind of mass-a-cree in that house over there." He was shaking his head. "Bunch a white folk. Woman, too."

Everybody was staring at Mickey's house.

Now it was as if I were having a full-out heart attack. Everything in my chest was so tight that I couldn't breathe. I stood in the semidarkness with my lips quivering and tears sliding down my cheeks. They had been alive. Dee had told me to come back. Mickey and Barney and Bobby and Dee. How could they be dead now? It was like some terrifying dream that you wake up from, and it isn't real.

But this was real. I was staring at the yellow house and all those police and EMS people. *Tell me this isn't real!*

I pushed forward, just in time to see the front door open. Medical techs appeared. The crowd started to murmur. They were wheeling out the gurneys.

One of the body covers was open. "White boy," somebody said.

I saw the curly red hair. *Mickey.*

Watching him being wheeled toward the morgue van, I flashed back twenty years. Mickey always used to punch me in the back at school. His twisted way of saying hello. I never saw it coming. I'd just be walking in the hall, between class, and *wham!* And he hit like a sonuvabitch! Then he started making me pay him a quarter not to get punched. He'd just raise his fist with his eyes wide. "Scared?" One day, I just couldn't take it anymore. I didn't care what happened. I charged him and slammed him back against a radiator. Left a welt on his back that I think stayed with him through high school. He got up, picked up his books, and put out a hand to me. In it was about four dollars. In quarters. Everything I had given him. He just grinned at me. "Been waiting for you to do that, Neddie-boy."

That's what flashed through my mind, the whole crazy scene in an instant. Then there were more gurneys. I counted four. My best friends in the world.

I backed away in the crowd. Felt boxed in, trapped. My chest was cramping. I pushed against the tide of people pressing closer for a better look.

And I was blasted with the thought: What good is a lifeguard who can't save lives?

Chapter 17

I DON'T REMEMBER MUCH about what happened next. All I know is that I staggered back to my car—fast—and drove—much faster.

I went through my options. What choices did I have? Turn myself in? *C'mon, Ned, you participated in a robbery. Your friends are dead. Someone's bound to connect you with Tess. They'll pin a murder charge on you.* I wasn't thinking straight, but one thing became shining clear: *My life here is over now.*

I flipped on the radio to a local news channel. Reporters were already at the scenes of the murders. *A young beauty at Palm Beach's posh Brazilian Court. Four unidentified people murdered execution-style in Lake Worth. . . .* And other news. *A daring art heist on the beach. Sixty million in art reported stolen!* So there *was* a theft. But no mention if the police thought any of this was connected. And, thank God, nothing about me!

It was after eleven when I finally crossed the Flagler Bridge back into Palm Beach. Two police cars were parked in the middle of Poinciana, lights flashing, blocking the road. I was sure they were looking for a Bonneville.

"Game's over, Ned!" I said, almost resigned. But I passed right by without a hitch.

The town was quiet up there, considering everything going on. The Palm Beach Grill was still busy. And Cucina. Some tunes coming out of Cucina. But the streets were generally quiet. It reminded me of a joke: there are more lights in downtown Baghdad during an air raid than in Palm Beach after ten o'clock. I hung a right on County and drove down to Seaspray, then hung a left to the beach. I cautiously pulled into number 150, automatically opening the gates. I was praying for no cops. *Please, God, not now.* Sollie's house was dark, the courtyard empty. My prayers were answered. For a little while.

Sollie was either watching TV or asleep. Winnie, the housekeeper, too. I parked in the courtyard and headed up the stairs to my room above the garage. Like I said, my life there was over now.

Here's what I'd learned in Palm Beach. There're thousand-dollar millionaires, the guys who pretend they're rich but really aren't. There are the old rich, and then there are the new rich. Old rich tend to have much better manners, are more attuned to having help around. New rich, which Sollie was, could be trouble—demanding, insulting, their insecurities about their windfall money coming out in abusive ways toward the help. But Sollie was a prince. Turned out he needed me to keep his pool clean, drive his big yellow Lab to the vet, chauffeur him around when he had an occasional date, and keep his cars polished. That turned out to be a joy. Sollie traded in collectible cars at Ragtops in West Palm as frequently as I switched out DVDs at Block-buster. Right now he had a 1970 six-door Mercedes Pullman limo that used to belong to Prince Rainier; a '65 Mustang convertible; a Porsche Carrera for a runaround; and a chocolate Bentley for big events . . . your typical Palm Beach garage stable.

I pulled out two canvas duffels from under the bed and started to throw clothes in them. T-shirts, jeans, a few sweatshirts. The hockey stick signed by Ray Bourque that I'd had since the tenth grade. A couple of paperbacks I always liked. *Gatsby. The Sun Also Rises. Great Expectations.* (I guess I always had a thing for the out-sider bucking the ruling class.)

I scribbled out a quick note to Sollie. An explanation that I had to leave suddenly, and why. I hated to go like this. Sol was like an uncle to me. A really great uncle. He let me live in this great house and all I had to do was keep the pool in order, clean a few of his cars, and do a couple of errands. I felt like a real heel, sneaking away in the dark. But what choice did I have?

I grabbed everything and headed downstairs. I

popped the trunk on the Bonneville and tossed in the duffels. I was just taking a last look and saying good-bye to where I'd lived these past three years when the lights went on.

I spun around, my heart in my throat. Sollie was standing in his bathrobe and slippers, holding a glass of milk. "Jesus, you scared me, Sol."

He glanced at the open trunk and the bags. He had a look of disappointment on his face, putting it together. "So I guess you don't have time for a good-bye game of rummy."

"I left a note," I said a little ashamedly. To have him find me sneaking away like this, and more, for what he was bound to find out in the morning. "Look, Sol, some terrible things have happened. You may hear some stuff. . . . I just want you to know, they're not true. I didn't do it. I didn't do any of it."

He bunched his lips. "It must be bad. C'mon in, kid. Maybe I can help. A man doesn't run off in the middle of the night."

"You can't"—I dropped my head—"help. No one can now." I wanted to run up and give him a hug, but I was so nervous and all mixed up. I had to get out of there. "I want to thank you," I said. I hopped in the Bonneville and turned the ignition. "For trusting me, Sol. For everything . . ."

"Neddie," I heard him call. "Whatever it is, it can't be that bad. No problem is too big to solve. When a man needs friends, that's not the time to run off. . . ."

But I was at the gates before I could hear the

rest. I saw him in the rearview mirror as I swung out of the driveway, driving off.

I was almost crying as I hit the Flagler Bridge. Leaving everything behind. Mickey, my friends, Tess . . .

Poor Tess. It was killing me, just remembering how we'd been together only hours before, when I thought things were finally working out for me. A million dollars and the girl of my dreams.

Your luck's returned, Neddie-boy. I couldn't help but laugh. *The bad luck.*

As I headed toward the Flagler Bridge, I could make out the shining towers of the Breakers lighting up the sky. I figured I had a day at most before my name surfaced. I didn't even know exactly where I was going to go.

Someone had killed my best friends. Dr. Gachet, I don't know what the hell kind of doctor you are, but you can be sure I'm gonna make you pay.

"Split aces," I muttered again grimly as I crossed the bridge, the bright lights of Palm Beach receding away. The perfect score. *Yeah, right.*

Part Two

ELLIE

Chapter 18

ELLIE SHURTLEFF WAS KNEELING in front of the security panel in the basement of Casa Del Océano and shining a light on the clipped coaxial cable in her gloved hand.

Something didn't make sense at this crime scene.

As the special agent in charge of the FBI's new Art Theft and Fraud department for the south Florida region, she'd been waiting a long time for something like this. Sixty million in art reported stolen last night, right in her own backyard. Truth be told, Ellie *was* the department.

Since leaving New York eight months ago— and the assistant curator thing at Sotheby's—Ellie had basically sat around the Miami office, monitoring auction sales and Interpol wires, while other agents hauled in drug traffickers and money launderers. She was slowly starting to wonder, like everyone else in her family, if this had been a career move or a career disaster. Art theft wasn't exactly a glamour assignment down there. Everybody else had law degrees, not MFAs.

Of course, there were benefits, she constantly reminded herself. The little bungalow down by the beach in Delray. Taking her ocean kayak out in the surf—year-round. And surely at the ten-year reunion get-together for the Columbia MFA class of 1996, she'd be the only one packing a Glock.

Ellie finally stood up. At barely five-two and 105 pounds, with her short brown hair and tortoiseshell frames, she knew she didn't look like an agent. At least, not one they let out of the lab much. The joke around the office was that she had to get her FBI windbreaker from the kids' department at Burdines. But she'd been second in her class at Quantico. She'd lit the charts in crime scene management and advanced criminal psychology. She was qualified with the Glock and could disarm somebody a foot taller.

It just happened she also knew a little about the stylistic antecedents of cubism as well.

And a bit about electrical wiring. She stared at the sheared cable. *Okay, Ellie, why?*

The housekeeper had specifically overheard the thieves putting in the alarm code. *But the cable was cut.* Both the interior and outside alarms. If they knew the code, why cut the cable? They had access; the house was shut down. The Palm Beach police seemed to have already made up their minds, and they were very good at this kind of thing. They'd dusted for prints. The thieves had been in the house for only minutes; they'd known exactly what to take. The police declared the three intruders in their stolen police uniforms brazen, professional thieves.

But no matter what the local cops thought, or how that asshole upstairs, Dennis Stratton, was ranting about his irreplaceable loss, two words had begun to worm their way into Ellie's head:

Inside job.

Chapter 19

THE DENNIS STRATTON was sitting, legs crossed, in a well-cushioned wicker chair in the lavish sunroom overlooking the ocean. Multiple calls were lit up on the receiver and a cell phone was stapled to his ear. Vern Lawson, Palm Beach's head of detectives, was hovering close by, along with Stratton's wife, Liz—a tall, attractive blonde in cream slacks and a pale blue cashmere sweater wrapped around her shoulders. A Latino house-maid flitted in and out with a tray of iced tea.

A butler led Ellie into the room. Stratton ignored them both. Ellie was bemused by how the rich lived. The more money they had, the more padding and layers of swaddling they seemed to put between themselves and the rest of us. More insulation in the walls, thicker fortress bulwarks, more distance to the front door.

"Sixty million," Dennis Stratton barked into the phone, "and I want someone down here today. And not some flunky from the local office with an art degree."

He punched off the line. Stratton was short, well built, slightly balding on top, with intense, steely eyes. He was wearing a tight-fitting, sage green T-shirt over white linen pants. Finally he glared at Ellie as though she were some annoying junior accountant with a question about his taxes. "Find everything you need down there, Detective?"

"Special Agent," Ellie said, correcting him.

"*Special Agent.*" Stratton nodded. He craned his neck toward Lawson. "Vern, you want to see if the 'special agent' needs to see any other part of the house."

"I'm fine." Ellie waved off the Palm Beach cop. "But if you don't mind, I'd like to go over the list."

"The list?" Stratton sighed, like, *haven't we already done this three times before?* He slid a sheet of paper across a lacquered Chinese altar table Ellie pegged as early eighteenth century. "Let's start with the Cézanne. *Apples and Pears . . .*"

"Aix-en-Provence," Ellie interjected. "1881."

"You know it?" Stratton came alive. "Good! Maybe you can convince these insurance idiots what it's really worth. Then there's the Picasso flutist, and the large Pollock up in the bedroom. These sons of bitches knew just what they were doing. I paid eleven million for that alone."

Overpaid. Ellie clucked a little. Down there, some people tried to buy their way into the social circuit through their art.

"And don't forget the Gaume. . . ." Stratton started to leaf through some papers on his lap.

"Henri Gaume?" Ellie said. She checked the list. She was surprised to see it there. Gaume was a decent postimpressionist, moderately collectible. But at thirty to forty thousand, a rounding error next to what else had been taken.

"My wife's favorite, right, dear? It was like someone was trying to stab us right through the heart. We have to have it back. Look . . ." Stratton put on a pair of reading glasses, fumbling on Ellie's name.

"Special Agent Shurtleff," Ellie said.

"Agent Shurtleff." Stratton nodded. "I want this perfectly clear. You seem like a thorough sort, and I'm sure it's your job to nose around here a bit, make a few notes, then go back to the office and file some report before you break for the day. . . ."

Ellie felt the blood boil in her veins.

"But I don't want this tossed up the chain of command in a memo that gets dropped on some regional director's desk. *I want my paintings back*. Every single one of them. I want the top people in the department working on this. The money means nothing here. These paintings were insured for sixty million. . . ."

Sixty million? Ellie smiled to herself. *Maybe forty, at the most*. People always have an inflated impression of what they own. The Cézanne still life was ordinary. She'd seen it come up at auctions several times, never commanding more than the reserve. The Picasso was from the Blue Period, when he was turning out paintings just to get laid. The Pollock—well, the Pollock was good, Ellie had to admit. Someone had steered him right there.

"But what they took here is irreplaceable." Stratton kept his eyes on her. "And that includes the Gaume. If the FBI isn't up to it, I'll get my own people involved. I can do that, you understand. Tell that to your superiors. You get the right people on it for me. Can you do that, Agent Shurtleff?"

"I think I have what I need," Ellie said. She folded the inventory into her notes. "Just one thing. Can I ask who set the alarm when you went out last night?"

"The alarm?" Stratton shrugged. He glanced at his wife. "I don't know that we did. Lila was here. Anyway, the interior alarms are always activated. These paintings were connected straight to the local police. We've got motion detection. You saw the setup down there."

Ellie nodded. She packed her notes in her briefcase. "And who else knew the code?"

"Liz. Me. Miguel, our property manager, Lila. Our daughter, Rachel, who's at Princeton."

Ellie looked at him closely. "The interior alarm, I meant."

Stratton tossed down his papers. Ellie saw a wrinkle carved into his brow. "What are you suggesting? That someone knew the code? That that's how they got in here?"

He started to get red in the face. He looked over at Lawson. "What's going on here, Vern? I want qualified people looking into this. Professionals, not some junior agent, making accusations . . . I know the Palm Beach cops are sitting on their hands. Can't we do something about this?"

"Mr. Stratton," the Palm Beach detective said, looking uncomfortable, "it's not like this was the only thing going on last night. Five people were killed."

"Just one more thing," Ellie said, headed for the door. "You mind telling me what the interior alarm code was?"

"The alarm code," Stratton said, his lips tightening. She could see he resented this. Stratton was used to snapping his fingers and seeing people jump. "Ten, oh two, eighty-five," he recited slowly.

"Your daughter's birthday?" Ellie asked, trying a hunch.

Dennis Stratton shook his head. "My first IPO."

Chapter 20

JUNIOR AGENT. Ellie seethed as the butler closed the front door behind her and she stepped onto the long pebbled drive.

She'd seen a lot of big-time houses over the years. Problem was, they were usually filled with big-time assholes. Just like this rich clown. She was reminded that this was what made her want to leave Sotheby's in the first place. Rich prima donnas and jerks like Dennis Stratton.

Ellie climbed into her office Crown Vic and called in to Special Agent in Charge Moretti, her superior at C-6, the Theft and Fraud division. She left word that she was headed to check out some homicides. As Lawson had said, five people were dead. And 60 million in art had disappeared the same night. Or at least 40 . . .

It was only a short drive from Stratton's over to the Brazilian Court. Ellie had actually been there once when she had first moved down, for brunch at the Café Boulud, with her eighty-year-old aunt, Ruthie.

At the hotel, she badged her way past the police and the press vans gathered outside and made her way to room 121 on the first floor. The Bogart Suite. It reminded Ellie that Bogart and Bacall, Cary Grant, Clark Gable, and Garbo had all stayed at this hotel.

A Palm Beach cop was guarding the door. She flashed her FBI ID to the usual look—a long, scrutinizing stare at the photo and then her again—as if the cop were some skeptical bouncer checking fake IDs.

"It's *real*." Ellie let her eyes linger on him, slightly annoyed. "I'm real, too."

Inside, there was a large living room decorated smartly in a sort of a tropical Bombay theme: British Colonial antique furniture, reproduction amaryllis prints, palm trees waving outside every window. A Crime Scene tech was spraying the coffee table, trying to dig up prints.

Ellie's stomach shifted. She hadn't done many homicides. Actually, she hadn't done any—only tagged along as part of her training at Quantico.

She stepped into the bedroom. It didn't matter that her badge said FBI, there was something really creepy about this: the room, completely undisturbed, precisely as it had been at the time of a grisly murder last night. *C'mon, Ellie, you're FBI.*

She panned the room and didn't have even the slightest idea what she was looking for. A sexy backless evening gown was draped across the rumpled bed. Dolce & Gabbana. A pair of expensive heels on the floor. Manolos. The gal had some money—and taste!

Something else caught her eye. Some loose change in a plastic evidence bag, already tagged. Something else—a golf tee. A black one, with gold lettering.

Ellie held the evidence Baggie close. She could make out lettering on the golf tee: Trump International.

"The FBI training tour isn't scheduled for another forty minutes," came a voice from behind, startling her.

Ellie spun around and saw a tan, good-looking guy in a sport jacket with his hands in his pockets, leaning against the bedroom door.

"Carl Breen," the jacket said. "Palm Beach PD. Violent Crimes. Relax," he went on, smiling, "it's a compliment. Most of the feds who come through here look like they were stamped out of officers training school."

"Thanks," Ellie said, smoothing out her pants, adjusting her holster, which was digging into her waist.

"So what brings the FBI to our little playpen? Homicide's still a local statute, isn't it?"

"Actually, I'm looking into a robbery. An art theft, from one of the big estates down the road. *Up* the road, I guess."

"Art detail, huh?" Breen nodded with a kind of a grin. "Just checking up that the local drones are holding up our end?"

"Actually, I was looking to see if any of these murders tied in, in any way," Ellie answered.

Breen took his hands out of his pockets. "Tied in to the art theft. Let's see. . . ." He glanced around. "There's a print over there on the wall. That the kind of thing you're looking for?"

Ellie felt a slap of blood rush to her cheeks. "Not quite, but it's good to know you have an eye for quality, Detective."

The detective grinned to let her know he was just kidding. He had a nice smile, actually. "Now if you said Sex Crimes, we'd be humming. Some Palm Beach social whirl. She's been camped here for a couple of months. People going in and out every day. I'm sure when we find out who's footing the bill, it'll be some trust fund or something."

He led Ellie down the corridor to the bathroom. "You may want to hold your breath. I'm pretty sure van Gogh never painted anything like this."

There was a series of crime-scene photos taped to the tile walls. Horrific ones. The deceased. The poor girl's eyes wide and her cheeks inflated out like tires. Naked. Ellie tried not to wince. *She was very pretty,* she thought. Exceptional. "She was raped?"

"Jury's still out," the Palm Beach cop said, "but see those sheets over there? Those stains don't look like applesauce. And the preliminary on the scene indicates she was dilated like she'd had sex minutes before. Call it a guess, but I'm figuring whoever did this was on some terms with her."

"Yeah." Ellie swallowed. Clearly Breen was right. She was probably wasting her time there.

"The tech on the scene pegged it between five and seven o'clock last night. What time your robbery take place?"

"Eight-fifteen," Ellie said.

"Eight-fifteen, huh?" Breen smiled and elbowed her, friendly, not condescending. "Can't say I'm much of an art expert, Special Agent, but I'm thinking, this tie-in of yours might just be a bit of a reach. What about you?"

Chapter 21

SHE FELT A LITTLE BIT like a jerk. Angry at herself, embarrassed. The Palm Beach detective had actually tried to be helpful.

As Ellie climbed back in her car, her cheeks flushed and grew hot again. *Art detail.* Did it have to be so totally obvious that she was out of her element?

Next was the run-down house in Lake Worth, just off the Interstate, where four people in their twenties and early thirties had been killed, execution-style. This one was a totally different scene. Much worse. A quadruple homicide always got national attention. Press vans and police vehicles still blocked off a two-block radius around the house. It seemed that every cop and Crime Scene tech in south Florida was buzzing inside.

As soon as she stepped inside the yellow shingled house, Ellie had trouble breathing. This was really bad. The outlines of three of the victims were chalked out on the floor of the sparsely furnished bedroom and kitchen. Blotches of blood and stuff Ellie knew was even worse were still sprayed all over the floors and thinly painted walls. A wave of nausea rolled in her stomach. She swallowed. *This is one hell of a long way from an MFA.*

Across the room, she spotted Ralph Woodward from the local office. Ellie went over, glad to find a familiar face.

He seemed surprised to see her. "What're you thinking, Special Agent," he asked, rolling his eyes around the stark room, "slap a few pictures on the walls, a plant here and there, and you'd never know the place, right?"

Ellie was getting tired of hearing this crap. Ralph wasn't such a bad guy really, but jeez.

"Thinking drugs, myself." Ralph Woodward shrugged. "Who else kills like this?"

A review of their IDs pegged the victims from the Boston area. They all had sheets—petty crimes and B-class felonies. Break-ins, auto thefts. One of them had worked part-time at the bar at Bradley's, a hangout near the Intracoastal in West Palm. Another parked cars at one of the local country clubs. Another, Ellie winced when she read the report, was female.

She spotted Palm Beach's head of detectives, Vern Lawson, coming into the house. He chatted for a second with a few officers, then caught her eye. "A bit out of your field, Special Agent Shurtleff?"

He sidled up to Woodward as if they were old chums. "Got a minute, Ralphie?"

Ellie watched as the two men huddled near the kitchen. It occurred to her that maybe they were talking about her. *Fuck 'em, if they are.* This was her case. No one was bouncing her. Sixty million in stolen art, or whatever the hell it was, wasn't exactly petty theft.

Ellie went up to a series of crime photos. If staring at Tess McAuliffe in the tub had made her stomach turn, this almost brought up breakfast. One victim had been dropped right at the front door, shot through the head. The guy with the red hair was shot at the kitchen table. Shotgun. Two were killed in the bedroom, the heavyset one through the back, maybe trying to flee; and the girl, huddled in the corner, probably begging for her life, a straight-on blast. Bullet and shotgun marks were numbered all over the walls.

Drugs? Ellie took a breath. *Who else kills like this?*

Feeling a little useless, she started to make her way to the door. They were right. This wasn't her terrain. She also felt a need to get some air.

Then she saw something on the kitchen counter that made her stop.

Tools.

A hammer. A straight-edge file. A box cutter.

Not just tools. They wouldn't have meant a thing to someone else, but to Ellie, they were standard utensils for a task she'd seen performed a hundred times. For opening a frame.

Jesus, Ellie started thinking.

She headed back to the crime photos again. Something clicked. *Three* male victims. *Three* male thieves at Stratton's. She looked more closely at the photos. Something she was just seeing. If she hadn't been at both crime scenes, she wouldn't have noticed.

Each of the male victims had been wearing the same black laced shoes.

Ellie forced her mind back to the black-and-white security film at Casa Del Océano. Then she glanced around the room.

A dozen or so cops, guarding the scene. She looked more closely. Her heart started to race.

Police shoes.

Chapter 22

THE ROBBERS HAD BEEN dressed as cops, right? Score one for the fine-arts grad.

Ellie glanced around the crowded room. She saw Woodward over by the kitchen, still huddled with Lawson. She pushed her way through. "Ralph, I think I found something. . . ."

Ralph Woodward had that easygoing southern way of brushing you off with a smile. "Ellie, just give me a second. . . ." Ellie knew he didn't take her seriously.

All right, if they wanted her to go it alone, she would.

Ellie dropped a badge on one of the local homicide detectives who was identified as primary on the scene. "I was wondering if you guys found anything interesting? In the closets, or the car? Police uniforms, maybe a Maglite flashlight?"

"Crime lab took the car," the detective said. "Nothing out of the ordinary."

Of course, Ellie said to herself. *They weren't really looking. Or maybe the perps ditched them.* But this feeling she had was building.

There were chalk outlines and flags identifying each victim. And evidence bags containing whatever they had on them.

Ellie started in the bedroom. Victim number three: Robert O' Reilly. Shot in the back. She held up the evidence bag. Just a few dollars. A wallet. Nothing more. Next, the girl. Diane Lynch. The same wedding ring as Robert O'Reilly. She emptied out her purse. Just some keys, a receipt from Publix. Nothing much.

Shit.

Something urged her to go on, even though she had no idea what she was looking for. The male at the kitchen table. Michael Kelly. Blown back against the wall, but still sitting in his chair. She picked up the plastic evidence bag next to him. Car keys, money clip with about fifty bucks.

There was also a tiny piece of paper, folded up. She moved it in the bag. Looked like numbers.

She stretched on a pair of latex gloves and took the piece of paper out of the bag. She let the scrap unfold.

A surge of validation rushed through her.

10-02-85.

More than just numbers. Dennis Stratton's alarm code.

Chapter 23

I DROVE NORTH, straight through the night, pushing my old Bonneville at a steady seventy-five on I-95. I wanted to put as much distance as I could between me and Palm Beach. I'm not sure I even blinked until I hit the Georgia–South Carolina line.

I pulled off the highway at a place called Hardeeville, a truck stop with a huge billboard sign that advertised YOU'RE PASSING THE BEST SHORT STACK IN THE SOUTH.

Exhausted, I filled up the car and took an empty booth in the restaurant. I looked around, seeing only a few bleary-eyed truckers gulping coffee or reading the paper. A jolt of fear. I didn't know if I was a wanted man or not.

A red-haired waitress with DOLLY on her nametag came up and poured me a sorely needed cup of coffee. "Goin' far?" she asked in an amiable southern drawl.

"I sure hope so," I replied. I didn't know if my picture was on the news or if someone meeting my eye would recognize me. But the smell of maple and biscuits got to me. "Far enough that those pancakes sure sound good."

I ordered a juice to go with them and went into the men's room. A heavyset trucker squeezed past me on his way out. Alone, I stared in the mirror and was stunned by the face looking back at me: haggard, bloodshot eyes, scared. I realized I was still in the pitted-out T-shirt and jeans I'd been wearing when I tripped the alarms the night before. I splashed cold water over my face.

My stomach groaned, making an ugly noise. It dawned on me that I hadn't eaten since lunch with Tess the previous day.

Tess . . . Tears started in my eyes again. Mickey and Bobby and Barney and Dee. God, I wished I could just turn back the clock and have every one of them alive. In one horrifying night, everything had changed.

I grabbed a *USA Today* at the counter and sat back in the booth. As I spread the paper on the table, I noticed that my hands were shaking. Reality was starting to hit. The people I trusted most in my life were dead. I had relived the nightmare of the previous night a hundred times in the past six hours—and each time it got worse.

I started to leaf through the paper. I wasn't sure if I was hoping I would find something or not. Mostly, a lot of articles on the situation in Iraq and the economy. The new interest-rate cut.

I turned the page and my eyes nearly popped out of my head.

DARING ART THEFT AND
MURDER SPREE IN PALM BEACH

I folded back the page.

The posh and stately resort town of Palm Beach was shattered last night by a string of violent crimes, beginning with the drowning of an attractive woman in her hotel suite, followed by a brazen break-in and the theft of several priceless paintings from one of the town's most venerable mansions, and culminating hours later in the execution-style murder of four people in a nearby town.

Police say they have no direct leads in the brutal series of crimes, and at this point do not know if they are related.

I didn't understand. *Theft of priceless paintings . . .* Dee said the job had been a bust.

I read on. The names of the people killed. Normally, it's just abstract, names and faces. But this was so horribly real. Mickey, Bobby, Barney, Dee . . . and, of course, Tess.

This is no dream, Ned. This is really happening.

The article went on to describe how three valuable works of art were stolen from the forty-room mansion, Casa Del Océano, owned by businessman Dennis Stratton. *Valued at a possible $60* *million, the theft of the unnamed paintings was one of the largest art heists in U.S. history.*

I couldn't believe it.

Stolen? We *had* been set up. We'd been set up royally.

My pancakes came, and they did look great, as advertised. But I was no longer hungry.

The waitress refilled my glass and asked, "Everything all right, hon?"

I tried my best to smile and nod, but I couldn't answer. A new fear was invading my brain.

They'll make the connection to me.

Everything was going to come out. I wasn't reasoning very well, but one thing was clear: Once the police went to Sollie, they would make my car.

Chapter 24

FIRST THING, I had to get rid of my car.

I paid the check and drove the Bonneville down the road into a strip mall, where I tossed the plates into the woods and cleaned out anything that could be traced to me. I walked back into town and stood in front of a tiny Quonset hut that was the town's bus depot. Man, *paranoia* was now my middle name.

An hour later, I was on a bus to Fayetteville, North Carolina—headed north.

I guess I knew where I was going all along. At a lunch counter at the Fayetteville station, I chomped down a desperately needed burger and fries, avoiding the eyes of everyone I saw, as if people were taking a mental inventory of my face.

Then I hopped a late-night Greyhound heading to all points north: Washington, New York.

And Boston. Where the hell else would I go?

That's where the score started, right?

Mostly I just slept and tried to figure out what I was going to do when I got there. I hadn't been home in four years now. *Since my Big Fall from Grace.* I knew my father was sick now, and even before, when he wasn't, he wasn't exactly the Rock of Gibraltar. Not if you count convictions for everything from receiving stolen goods to bookmaking, and three stints up at the Souz in Shirley.

And Mom . . . Let's just say she was always there. My biggest fan. At least, after my older brother, John Michael, was killed robbing a liquor store. That left just me and my younger brother, Dave. *You won't be following in anybody's footsteps, Ned,* she made me promise early on. You don't have to be like your father—or your big brother. She bailed me out of trouble half a dozen times. She picked me up from the Catholic Youth Organization hockey practices at midnight.

That was the real problem now. I didn't look forward to seeing her face when I sneaked my way home. I was going to break her heart.

I changed buses twice. In Washington and New York. At every sudden stop my heart would clutch, freeze. *This is it,* I figured. There was a roadblock, and they were going to pull me off! But there never were any roadblocks. Towns and states passed by, and none too fast for me.

I found myself daydreaming a lot. I was the son of a small-time crook, and here I was returning—wanted, a big-time screwup. I'd even outdone my old man. I'd have surely been in the system growing up, just like Mickey and Bobby, if I didn't know how to skate. Hockey had opened doors for me. The Leo J. Fennerty Award as the best forward in the Boston CYO. A full ride to BU. More like a lottery ticket. Until I tore up my knee my sophomore year.

The scholarship went with it, but the university gave me a year to prove I could stay. And I did. They probably thought I was just some dumb jock who would drop out, but I started to see a larger world around me. I didn't have to go back to the old neighborhood and wait for Mickey and Bobby to get out of jail. I started to read, really read, for the first time in my life. To everyone's amazement, I actually graduated—with honors. In government. I got this job teaching eighth-grade social studies at Stoughton Academy, a place for troubled youths. My family couldn't believe it. *They actually pay a Kelly to be in the classroom?*

Anyway, that all ended. In a single day—just like this.

Past Providence, everything began to grow familiar. Sharon, Walpole, Canton. Places where I had played hockey as a kid. I was starting to get really nervous. Here I was, back home. Not the kid who'd gone off to BU. Or the one who'd been practically run out of town—and wound up in Florida.

But a hunted man, with a collar on a whole lot bigger than my old man ever managed to earn.

The apple doesn't fall far from the tree, I was thinking as the bus hissed to a stop at the Atlantic Avenue terminal in Boston. *Even when you throw it.*

Even when you throw it as far as you can.

Chapter 25

"SPECIAL AGENT SHURTLEFF put the whole thing together," Ellie's boss, George Moretti, said, and shrugged, like, *Can you believe it?* to Hank Cole, the assistant director in charge. The three of them were in his top-floor office in Miami.

"She recognized implements at the murder scene that could be used for prying open picture frames. Then she found numbers in the victims' personal effects that matched Stratton's alarm code. We located the stolen uniforms a short time later, stuffed in a bag in a car down the street."

"Seems you finally put that art degree to some real use, Special Agent Shurtleff," ADIC Cole said, beaming.

"It was just having access to both crime scenes," Ellie said, a little nervous. This was the first time she had been in front of the ADIC for any reason.

"The victims were all acquainted, from the

Boston area with minor rap sheets." Moretti slid a copy of the preliminary report across his boss's desk. "Nothing like a crime of this magnitude ever before. There's another member of this group who lived down here who's apparently missing." He pushed a photo over. "One *Ned Kelly.* He didn't show up for his shift at a local bar last night. Not surprising—since police up in South Carolina found an old Bonneville registered to him in some strip mall just off of I-95, four hundred miles north of here. . . ."

"Good. This Kelly have a record?" the ADIC inquired.

"Juvie," Moretti said, "expunged. But his father's a different story. Three stints on everything from bookmaking to receiving stolen goods. As a matter of routine, we're gonna flash the kid's photo around that hotel in Palm Beach, where that other incident took place. You never know."

"I actually took a look at that scene," Ellie volunteered. She told her bosses that the times of death didn't match up. Also, the Palm Beach police were treating the murder as a sex crime.

"Seems our agent here has designs on being a homicide detective as well," Hank Cole said with a grin.

Ellie caught herself and took the dig, her cheeks coloring. *They wouldn't be anywhere on this case without me.*

"Anyway, why don't we just leave something for the local authorities to clean up." Cole smiled at her. "So it seems this Ned Kelly may have ripped off his old buddies, huh? Well, he's sure graduated to the big time now. So whatya think, Special Agent," he said, turning to Ellie, "you ready to fly up North and put yourself on this guy?"

"Of course," Ellie said. Whether they were condescending or not, she loved the attention of being on the A team for once.

"Any ideas where he'd be headed?"

Moretti shrugged. He went over to a wall map. "He's got family, roots up there. Maybe a fence, too." He pushed in a red pin. "We figure Boston, sir."

"Actually," said Ellie, "Brockton."

Chapter 26

KELTY'S, ON THE CORNER of Temple and Main in south Brockton, usually closed around midnight. After the Bruins' postgame report or *Baseball Tonight,* or when Charlie, the owner, finally pushed the last jabbering regular away from his Budweiser.

Tonight, I was lucky. The lights dimmed at 11:35.

A few minutes afterward, a large guy with curly brown hair in a hooded Falmouth sweatshirt yelled, "Later, Charl," and closed the door behind him as he stepped onto the sidewalk. He started to head down Main, a knapsack over his shoulder, leaning into the early April chill.

I followed on the other side of the street, a safe distance behind. Everything had changed around there. The men's store and the Supreme B Donut Shop where we used to hang out were now a

grungy Laundromat and a low-end liquor store.
The guy I was following had changed, too.

He was one of those thick, strong-shouldered
dudes with a cocky smile who could break your
wrist arm wrestling if he wanted to. His picture
was up in the local high school. He'd once been
district champ at 180 pounds for Brockton High.

*You better plan how you're going to do this,
Ned.*

He made a left on Nilsson, crossing over the
tracks. I followed, maybe thirty yards behind.
Once, he looked back, maybe hearing footsteps,
and I huddled in the shadows. The same rows of
shabby, clapboard houses I'd passed a thousand
times as a kid, looking even shabbier and more
run-down now.

He turned the corner. On the left was the elementary school and Buckley Park, where we used
to play Rat Fuck on the basketball courts for
quarters. A block away on Perkins was the ruin
of the old Stepover shoe factory, boarded up for
years. I thought back to how we used to hide out
in there from the priests and cut classes, smoke a
little. When I turned at the corner, he wasn't
there!

Ah, shit, Neddie, I cursed myself. You never
were any good at getting the jump on somebody.

And then I was the one being jumped!

Suddenly, I felt a strong arm tighten around my
neck. I was jerked backward, a knee digging deep
into my spine. The sonuvabitch was stronger than
I remembered.

I flailed my arms to try and roll him over my

back. I couldn't breathe. I heard him grunting, applying more pressure, twisting me backward. My spine felt as if it were about to crack.

I started to panic. If I couldn't spin out quickly, he was going to break my back.

"Who caught it?" he suddenly hissed into my ear.

"Who caught *what*?" I gagged for air.

He twisted harder. "Flutie's Hail Mary. The Orange Bowl. 1984."

I tried to force him forward, using my hips as leverage, straining with all my might. His grip just tightened. I felt a searing pain in my lungs.

"Gerard . . . Phelan," I finally gasped.

Suddenly, the vise hold around my neck released. I fell to one knee, sucking in air.

I looked up into the smirking face of my younger brother, Dave.

"You're lucky," he said, grinning. Then he put out a hand to help me. "I was going to ask who caught Flutie's last college pass."

Chapter 27

WE HUGGED. Then Dave and I stood there and took a physical inventory of how we'd changed. He was much larger; he looked like a man now, not a kid. We slapped each other on the back. I hadn't seen my baby brother in almost four years.

"You're a sight for sore eyes," I said, and hugged him again.

"Yeah," he said, grinning, "well, you're making my eyes sore now."

We laughed, the way we did when we were growing up, and locked hands, ghetto-style. Then his face changed. I could tell that he'd heard. Surely everyone had by now.

Dave shook his head sort of helplessly. "Oh, Neddie, what the hell went on down there?"

I took him into the park and, sitting on a ledge, told him how I had gone to the Lake Worth house and saw Mickey and our other friends being wheeled out in body bags.

"Ah, Jesus, Neddie." Dave shook his head. His eyes grew moist, and he lay his head in his hands.

I put my arm around his shoulder. It was hard to see Dave cry. It was strange—he was younger by five years, but he was always so stable and centered, even when our older brother died. I was always all over the place; it was as though the roles were reversed. Dave was in his second year at BC Law School. The bright spot of the family.

"It gets worse." I squeezed his shoulder. "I think I'm wanted, Dave."

"*Wanted?*" He cocked his head. "You? Wanted for what?"

"I'm not sure. Maybe for murder." This version I told him everything. The whole tale. I told him about Tess, too.

"What're you saying?" Dave sat there looking at me. "That you're up here on the run? That you were *involved?* You were part of this madness, Ned?"

"Mickey set it up," I said, "but he didn't know the kind of people who could pull it off down there. It had to have been directed from up here. Whoever it was, Dave, that's the person who killed our friends. Until I prove otherwise, people are going to think it was me. But I think we both know"—I looked into his eyes, which were basically *my* eyes—"who Mickey was working with up here."

"*Pop?* You're thinking Pop had something to do with this?" He looked at me as if I were crazy. "No way. We're talking Mickey, Bobby, and Dee. It's Frank's own flesh and blood. Besides, you don't know—he's sick, Ned. He needs a kidney transplant. The guy's too sick to even be a hood anymore."

I guess it was then that Dave squinted at me. I didn't like the look in his eyes. "Neddie, I know you've been down on your luck a little. . . ."

"Listen to me"—I took him by the shoulders— "look into my eyes. Whatever you may hear, Dave, whatever the evidence might say, I had nothing to do with this. I loved them just like you. I tripped the alarms, that's all. It was stupid, I know. And I'm going to have to pay. But whatever you hear, whatever the news might say, all I did was set off a few alarms. I think Mickey was trying to make up for what happened at Stoughton."

My brother nodded. When he looked up, I could see a different look in his face. The guy I had shared a room with for fifteen years, who I had beaten at one-on-one until he was sixteen, my flesh and blood. "What do you want me to do?"

"Nothing. You're in law school." I rapped him on the chin. "I may need your help if this gets bad."

I stood up.

Dave did, too. "You're going to see Pop, aren't you?" I didn't answer. "That's stupid, Ned. If they're looking for you, they'll know."

I tapped him lightly on the fist, then threw my arms around him and gave him a hug. My big *little* brother.

I started to jog down the hill. I didn't want to turn, because I was afraid that if I did, I might cry.

But there was something I couldn't resist. I spun around when I was almost on Perkins. "It was Darren."

"Huh?" Dave shrugged.

"Darren Flutie." I grinned. "Doug's younger brother. He caught Doug's last pass in college."

Chapter 28

I SPENT THE NIGHT in the Beantown Motel on Route 27 in Stoughton, a few miles up the road from Kelty's bar.

The story was all over the late news. Brockton residents killed. The faces of my friends. A shot of the house in Lake Worth. Hard to get any sleep after that.

Eight o'clock the next morning I had a cab drop me off on Perkins, a couple of blocks from my parents' house. I had on jeans and my old torn BU sweatshirt. I tucked my head under a Red Sox cap. I was scared. I knew everyone there, and even after four years, everyone knew me. But it wasn't just that. It was seeing my mom again. After all these years. Coming home this way.

I was praying the cops weren't there, too.

I hurried past familiar old houses, with their tilting porches and small brown yards. Finally, I spotted our old mint green Victorian. It looked a

whole lot smaller than I remembered. And a
lot worse for wear. *How the hell did we all ever
fit in this place?* Mom's 4Runner was in the
drive. Frank's Lincoln was nowhere around. I
guess Thomas Wolfe was right about going home,
huh?

I leaned against a lamppost and stared at the
place for several minutes. Everything looked all
right to me, so I snuck around to the back.

Through a kitchen window I saw my mom. She
was already dressed, in a corduroy skirt and some
Fair Isle sweater, sipping a cup of coffee. She still
had a pretty face, but she looked so much older
now. Why wouldn't she? A lifetime of dealing
with Frank "Whitey" Kelly had worn her down
to this.

*Okay, Ned, time to be a big boy. . . . People you
loved are dead.*

I knocked on the glass pane of the back door.
Mom looked up from her coffee. Her face turned
white. She got up, nearly ran to the door, and let
me in. "Mother of God, what are you doing here,
Ned? Oh Neddie, Neddie, Neddie."

We hugged and Mom held me as tightly as if
I'd come back from the dead. "Poor kids . . ."
She pressed her face against me. I could feel tears.
Then she pulled back, wide-eyed. "Neddie, you
can't be here. The police have been around."

"I didn't do it, Mom," I said. "Whatever they
say, I swear to God. I swear on JM's soul, I had
nothing to do with what happened down there."

"You don't have to tell me." My mother put
her hand lightly on my cheek. She took off my

cap and smiled at my mess of blond hair, the Florida tan. "You look fine. It's so good to see you, Neddie. Even now."

"It's good to see you, too, Mom."

And it was—to be back in the old kitchen. I felt free for a moment or two. I picked up an old Kodak print taped to the fridge. The Kelly boys. Dave, JM, me on the field behind Brockton High. JM in his red and black football jersey. Number 23. All-Section safety his junior year . . .

When I looked up, my mother was staring at me. "Neddie, you've got to turn yourself in."

"I can't." I shook my head. "I will, eventually. But not yet. I have to see Pop. Where is he, Mom?"

"Your father?" She shook her head. "You think I know?" She sat down. "Sometimes I think he even sleeps at Kelty's now. Things have gotten worse for him, Neddie. He needs a kidney transplant, but he's past the age when our coverage is gonna pay for it. He's sick, Neddie. Sometimes I think he just wants to die. . . ."

"Trust me, he'll be around long enough to bring you more misery," I snorted.

Suddenly we heard the sound of a vehicle pulling up to the curb outside. A car door slamming shut. I was hoping it was Frank.

I went over to a window and pulled back the blinds.

It wasn't my father.

Two men and a woman were coming up the driveway toward the house.

My mother rushed to the window. There was worry in her eyes.

We'd seen my father taken off to jail too many times not to recognize the law.

Chapter 29

BOTH OF US STARED wide-eyed at "twenty to life" in prison coming toward the house.

One of the agents, a black guy in a tan suit, peeled away from the other two and headed around back.

Shit, Neddie, think! What the hell do we do now . . . ?

I've never felt my heart pounding the way it did for those seconds it took the agents to make their way up the stairs. It was useless to run.

"Neddie, turn yourself in," my mother said again.

I shook my head. "No, I've got to find Frank." I took my mother by the shoulders, a pleading glimmer in my eye. "I'm sorry. . . ."

I pressed up against the wall next to the front door, not knowing what the hell I would do next. I didn't have a weapon. Or a plan.

There was a knock at the door. "Frank Kelly?" a voice called. "Mrs. Kelly? FBI!"

My imagination was running wild but coming up with nothing that could help me. Three agents, one a woman. The female was tanned, which probably meant she'd come from Florida.

"Mrs. Kelly?" They knocked again. Through the blinds I could see a husky guy in front. My mother finally answered. She looked at me sort of helplessly. I nodded for her to open the door.

I closed my eyes for half a second. *Please, don't do the stupidest thing of your entire life.*

But I went and did it anyway.

I barreled into the agent as soon as he walked through the door. We rolled onto the floor. I heard the guy grunt, and when I looked up, his handgun had slid out of his hand and was about four feet away. We both fixed on it. *He,* not knowing if a vicious killer had just gotten the jump on him. *I,* knowing once I made a move for that gun, my life as I knew it was over. I didn't care about the woman, or the guy sneaking around to the back. I just went for the gun. There was no other way.

I rolled off him and wrapped both hands around the gun. *"Nobody moves!"*

The agent was still on the floor. The woman—who was small and cute, actually—fumbled under her suit jacket for her own weapon. The third agent had just made it through the back door.

"No!" I shouted, and extended the gun. The woman looked at me, her hand on her holster.

"*Please* . . . Please, don't pull that out, now," I told her.

"Please, Neddie," my mother was begging me, "put the gun down. He's innocent." She looked at the agents. "Ned wouldn't hurt anyone."

"I don't *want* to hurt anybody," I told them. "Now put your guns on the floor. Do it."

They did what I asked, and then I scurried around, picking up the guns. I backed over to the sliding door and hurled them into the woods behind my house. *Now, what the hell to do?* I looked at my mom and gave her a half-hearted smile. "Guess I need to borrow the car."

"Neddie, please . . ." My mother was begging again. She had already lost one son in a shoot-out. Poor John Michael.

I was dying inside, knowing how much I was hurting her. I went over to the pretty FBI agent. I could almost pick her up with one arm. As much as she was trying to look brave, I could see she was scared. "What's your name?"

"Shurtleff." The agent hesitated. "Ellie."

"I'm sorry, Ellie Shurtleff, but you're coming with me."

The agent on the floor rose up. "No way. You're not leaving with her. You take anyone, take me."

"No," I backed him down with the gun. "It's her. She's coming."

I took her by the arm. "I'm not going to hurt you, Ellie, if this goes right." Even in that crazy moment, I gave her the edge of a smile.

"I know this doesn't mean much," I said, turn-

ing back to the guy on the floor, "but I didn't do
what you came here to get me for."

"There's only one way to prove that," the FBI
man said.

"I know," I said, nodding, "that's why I'm
doing this. I've got something to prove—I'm innocent."

I took Agent Shurtleff by the arm and shoved
open the door. The two other agents hung back as
if they were suspended in midair. "I just want five
minutes," I said. "That's all I ask. You'll have her
back as good as new. Her clothes won't even be
wrinkled. I didn't kill those people down there.
What happens next is up to you."

I turned to my mom. "Guess it's fair to say I
won't be around for dinner anytime soon." I
winked a good-bye. "Love you, Mom."

Then we backed out the door, my arm locked
on Agent Shurtleff's. I took her down the steps.
The FBI guys were already at the windows, one of
them pulling out his phone. I opened the door to
the 4Runner and pushed her in. "I'm just praying
the keys are there." I actually smiled. "Usually,
they are."

They were, thank God! I backed out the driveway. A few seconds later we were careening down
Perkins, across the tracks, onto Main.

No lights yet. No sirens. There were a few
ways out of town, and I figured the best way was
north on Route 24.

I glanced behind and breathed a sigh of relief.

*Nice work. You've just added kidnapping a
federal agent to your résumé.*

Chapter 30

"YOU SCARED?" this thug Ned Kelly turned and asked her, gunning the 4Runner north on Route 24. He held the gun loosely in his lap, pointed her way.

Scared? Ellie hesitated. *The guy is wanted for questioning in a quadruple homicide!*

Her mind ran through the hostage scenarios. There was probably some textbook thing she should say. Stay calm. Start a dialogue. She was sure there was an APB out on the car already. Every cop within fifty miles of Boston would be on the lookout. Finally, she just went with what she felt.

"Yeah, I'm scared," Ellie said with a nod.

"Good," he said, nodding back, " 'cause I'm scared, too. Never done anything like this before. But you can relax. Honest. I'm not going to hurt you. I just needed to get out of there. I'll even unlock the car. You can jump out the next time we stop. . . . I'm not kidding. Good as my word."

To Ellie's amazement, she heard the automatic locks lift. There was an exit approaching, and he slowed at the upcoming ramp.

"Or"—he looked sort of helpless—"you can stick around for a while longer. Help me figure out how I'm going to get out of this mess."

Kelly brought the car to a stop and waited for her to move.

"Go on. I figure I've got, what, about three minutes before every exit on this highway is covered with cops?"

Ellie looked at him, a little stunned. She placed her hand on the door latch. *You're being handed a gift,* said a voice inside her. *Take it!* She'd been to the house in Lake Worth. She'd seen the blood and the slaughtered bodies. This guy was connected to the victims. He'd fled.

But something held her back. The guy had this scared, fatalistic smile.

"I wasn't lying, what I said back there. I'm no killer. I had nothing to do with whatever went on down in Florida."

"Taking a federal agent hostage doesn't exactly strengthen your case," Ellie said.

"They were my friends, my family. I've known all of them my whole life. I didn't steal any paintings and I didn't kill anyone. All I did was set off some alarms. *Look*"—he waved the gun—"I don't even know how to use this fucking thing."

It did look that way, Ellie thought. And she

did recall a series of house alarms being triggered at mansions around town just prior to the theft. They assumed it was a diversion.

"Go on, get out." Kelly took a look back. "I'm expecting company."

But Ellie didn't get out. She just sort of held there, looking at him. He didn't seem so crazy all of a sudden. Just confused, scared. In way, way over his head. And somehow she didn't feel so threatened. Cops were on their way. Maybe she could talk him in. *Jesus, Ellie . . . This is a long way from the Rare Prints Department at Sotheby's!*

"Two," Ellie looked at him, slowly releasing the door handle. "You've got about *two* minutes. Before every cop car south of Boston is here."

Ned Kelly's face seemed to brighten. "Okay," he said.

"You tell me everything that happened down there," Ellie said. "*Maybe* I can do something. Names, contacts. Everything you know about the robbery. You want to get out of this mess? That's the only way."

A halting smile crossed Ned Kelly's face. In it, Ellie didn't see some cold-blooded killer, just a guy who was as nervous as she was, who had dug himself a very deep hole he might never pull himself out of. She thought maybe she could gain his trust. Talk the guy in, with no one getting hurt. If the cops caught up to him now, she wasn't sure what would happen.

"Okay," he said.

"And if I were you, I'd keep that gun pointed at me every once in a while," Ellie said. She couldn't believe she was doing this. "They do teach us ways to disarm someone, you know."

"Right." Ned Kelly grinned nervously. He gunned the 4Runner up the ramp. "First thing we'd better do is ditch my mom's car."

Chapter 31

WE SWITCHED THE 4RUNNER for a Voyager minivan left running in a supermarket parking lot.

An old maneuver. Growing up, I'd watched Bobby pull it off a dozen times. The owner was just wheeling her shopping cart back to the market. With everything that was going on, I figured I had at least an hour before anyone would respond to the call.

"I can't believe I just did that." Ellie Shurtleff blinked, amazed, as a minute later we were cruising back on Route 24. The look on her face read, *It's one thing to stay with this guy, another thing entirely to be part of stealing someone's car.*

An evergreen car freshener was dangling from the rearview mirror. A yellow notepad fastened to the dash. On it was scribbled, *Groceries. Manicure. Pick up the kids at 3:00.* A bag of groceries bounced up in the back. Pizza puffs. And Count Chocula.

We looked at each other and almost laughed as the thought hit us at the same time: a wanted killer driving a minivan.

"Some getaway car," she said, shaking her head. "A real Steve McQueen!"

I had no idea where to go next. But I figured the safest place was my little motel room back in Stoughton. Fortunately, it was a motor lodge, so I could get around to the room without going through the lobby.

I locked the door to the room behind us and shrugged. "Look, I have to pat you down."

She rolled her eyes at me, like, *What, are you kidding? Now?*

"Don't worry," I said. "I never take advantage of an FBI agent on the first date."

"You think if I was trying to apprehend you, I wouldn't have done it by now?" Ellie Shurtleff said.

"Sorry," I said, a little embarrassed. "Just a formality, I guess."

I was lucky that if I had to abduct an FBI agent, I had stumbled onto Ellie Shurtleff and not some Lara Croft type who would've had my arm twisted out of its socket by now. Truth was, I would never have pinned her for a fed. An elementary-school teacher, maybe. Or some MBA. With wavy, short brown hair and a couple of freckles on her cheek, a button nose. And nice blue eyes, too, behind the glasses.

"Arms up"—I waved the gun—"or out to the side, whatever it is."

"It's up against the wall," she said turning, "but what the hell. . . ."

She extended her arms. I knelt, patting her pants pockets and thighs. She was wearing a tan pantsuit with a white cotton T-shirt underneath, which she filled out pretty nicely. Some kind of green, semiprecious stone hanging from her neck.

"You know, it wouldn't exactly take much to drive an elbow into your face right now." I could see she was losing patience. "They do teach us stuff like that, you know."

"I'm not exactly a pro at this." I edged away from her. I didn't like that "elbow to the face" comment.

"You might as well check the ankles while you're down there. Most of us keep something strapped there when we're in the field."

"Thanks." I nodded.

"Just a formality," Ellie Shurtleff said.

I didn't find anything, except some keys and breath mints in her purse. I sat down on the bed. All of a sudden I realized what I'd just done. This wasn't a movie. I wasn't Hugh Jackman and this wasn't Jennifer Aniston, and this scene wasn't exactly moving toward a happy ending.

I placed my forehead in my hands.

Ellie sat on a chair, facing me.

"What do we do now?" I asked. I flicked on the tinny TV, just to hear the news. I tried to moisten my mouth, but it stayed as dry as the Sahara Desert.

"Now," Ellie Shurtleff said with a shrug, "now we talk."

Chapter 32

I TOLD ELLIE SHURTLEFF everything.

Everything I knew about the art heist down in Florida. I left out nothing.

Except the part about meeting Tess. I didn't know how to tell her about that, and have her believe me about everything else. Besides, I found it really hard to even think about what had happened to Tess.

"I know I've done some stupid things in the past few days," I said looking at Ellie, earnestly. "I know I shouldn't have run back in Florida. I know I shouldn't have done what I did today. But you have to believe me, Ellie . . . killing my friends, my cousin . . ." I shook my head. "No way. We didn't even take that art. Someone set us up."

"Gachet?" Ellie asked, making a few notes.

"I guess," I said, frustrated. "I don't know."

She looked at me closely. I was praying she believed me. I needed her to believe me. She switched gears. "So why did you come up here?"

"To Boston?" I put the gun down on the bed. "Mickey didn't have connections down there. At least, not the kind who could set up that kind of heist. Everyone he knew was from up here."

"Not to locate a fence for the art, Ned? You know people up here, too."

"Look around, Agent Shurtleff. You see any art here? I didn't do those things."

"You're going to have to come in," she said. "You're going to have to talk about whoever your cousin knew and worked for. Names, contacts, everything, if you want my help. I can soften the blow on the abduction thing, but that's your only way out. You understand that, Ned?"

I nodded resignedly. I had a sour taste in my mouth. Truth was, I didn't know Mickey's contacts. Who was I going to give up, my father?

"So how'd you know where I was headed, anyway?" I asked. I figured Sollie Roth had called the police when I ran.

"There aren't that many old Bonnevilles out there," Ellie said. "When we found it in South Carolina, we had a pretty good idea where you were headed."

No shit, I said to myself. *Sollie never turned me in.*

We ended up talking for hours. It started out about the crimes, but Ellie Shurtleff seemed to want to go through every detail of my whole life. I told her what it was like growing up in Brockton. The neighborhood and the old gang. How my ticket out had been the hockey scholarship to BU.

That seemed to surprise her. "You went to BU?"

"You didn't know you were talking to the 1995 Leo. J. Fennerty Award winner. Top forward in the Boston CYO," I grinned with a self-deprecating shrug. "Graduated," I said. "Four years. A BA in government. You probably didn't figure me for the academic type."

"Somehow when you were trolling around the supermarket parking lot, searching for a car to steal, I just never went there." Ellie smiled.

"I said I didn't kill anyone, Agent Shurtleff." I smiled back. "I never said I was a saint!"

That actually made Ellie Shurtleff laugh.

"Want another surprise," I said, leaning back on the bed, "as long as I'm doing the résumé? I actually used to teach for a couple of years. Eighth-grade social studies, at this middle school for troubled kids, here in Stoughton. I was pretty good. I may not have been able to give you chapter and verse on every constitutional amendment, but my kids could relate to me. I mean, I'd been there. I'd faced the same choices."

"So, what went wrong?" Ellie asked, putting down her notepad.

"You mean, how does a hotshot like me end up as a lifeguard down in Palm Beach? That's the million-dollar question, right?"

She shrugged. "Go on."

"My second year, I took an interest in one of my students. A girl. She was from south Brockton, same as me. Dominican kid. She was running with a rough crowd. But she was smart as a whip. She tested well. I wanted her to do well."

"What happened?" Ellie leaned forward. I could see this wasn't about Florida anymore.

"Maybe I scared her, I don't know. You have to understand, teaching that class meant everything to me. She accused me of something. A grade for a favor, that sort of thing."

"Oh, no." Ellie pulled back. She looked at me warily now.

"There was nothing to it, Ellie. Maybe I did a few stupid things. Like drive her home a couple of times. Maybe she got trapped in a lie about me, and it just snowballed. All of a sudden her story grew. Suddenly I had accosted her. In my classroom after school, right on school grounds. They gave me a hearing. But that kind of thing—it doesn't go away. They gave me a chance to stay, in some sort of lesser capacity, an admin job. I quit, walked away.

"A lot of people gave up on me. My dad . . ."

"Your father's got a record, right?" Ellie injected.

"A record? More like his own cell up at the Souza Correctional Center in Shirley permanently on reserve. *The apple doesn't fall far from the tree,* I remember him saying, like I proved him right. Imagine, he was the one who gave up on me. A few years before, he got his own goddamn son killed. My older brother. You know what the real joke was, though?"

Ellie shook her head.

"About a month after I left, the girl recanted. I got a nice letter of apology from the school. But by then, the damage was done. I couldn't be a teacher."

"I'm sorry," Ellie said.

"But you know who didn't give up on me, Agent Shurtleff? My cousin Mickey didn't. And Bobby O'Reilly. Or Barney or Dee. For a bunch of Brockton losers, they understood how that teaching job meant everything to me. And you think I'd kill those guys. . . ." I tapped my chest, close to my heart. "I'd kill myself if it would bring them back. Anyway"—I smiled, feeling that I'd gotten a little emotional—"you think if I had sixty million in stolen art, I'd be talking to you in a fleabag motel like this?"

Ellie smiled, too. "Maybe you're more clever than you look."

Suddenly a news bulletin interrupted the TV show. *Breaking news* . . . A report of today's abduction. My eyes got wide. Here we go again. My face was on the screen. Jesus Christ . . . My name!

"Ned," Ellie Shurtleff said, seeing the panic on my face, "you've got to come in with me. It's the only way we can work this out. *The only way.*"

"I don't think so." I took the gun and grabbed her by the arm. "C'mon, we're getting out of here."

Chapter 33

I TOSSED MY FEW BELONGINGS into the back of the minivan. I'd managed to locate a screwdriver in a tool kit and switched the Massachusetts plates with Connecticut ones off another car in the lot.

And I had to get rid of the van now, too. They would've found the 4Runner by now. And I had to ditch Ellie Shurtleff. But what I *couldn't* do was turn myself in. Not until I found out who'd set us up and murdered my friends. Not until I found fucking Gachet.

I hopped in the van, nervously driving around. "Where we going?" Ellie asked, sensing that everything had changed.

"I don't know," I said.

"You want me to help you, Ned," Ellie said, "you have to let me take you in. Don't do something even more stupid than you've already done."

"I think it's too late for that," I said. I was searching for a place I could drop her.

I found a quiet section on Route 138, between a granite yard and a used-car dealership. I turned off the main road and pulled up to a quiet spot hidden from view.

Ellie was getting alarmed. I could see it in her eyes. It was clear we weren't headed where she thought we were. What was I going to do?

"Please, Ned," she said. "Don't do something stupid. There's no other way."

"There's *one* other way." I put the van in park. I nodded—like *Go on, out the door.*

"They're going to find you . . . ," she said. "Today. Tomorrow. You're going to get yourself killed. I'm serious, Ned."

"Everything I told you is true, Ellie." I looked into her eyes. "I didn't do these things. And I didn't do some other stuff you may eventually hear about. Now, go on, get out."

I popped the locks. I reached across her body and flung open the door.

"You're making a mistake," Ellie said. "Don't do this, Ned."

"Well, you heard my story. I've been making them for years."

Call it the Stockholm syndrome in reverse, but I had grown a little attached to Special Agent Ellie Shurtleff. I knew she truly wanted to help me. She was probably the last, best chance I had. So I was sorry to see her go.

"Not a wrinkle in your clothes, just like I

promised." I smiled. "Be sure and tell your partner that."

Ellie looked at me, with a combination of disappointment and frustration. She slid out of the
van.

"Answer me one question," I said.

"What's that?" She stood, looking at me.

"How come you weren't wearing an ankle
weapon, if you were in the field?"

"My department," she said, "it doesn't call for
it."

"What department is that?" I looked at her,
confused.

"Art Theft," Agent Shurtleff answered. "I was
following up on the paintings, Ned."

I blinked. It was sort of like Marvelous Marvin
Hagler had stunned me with a short right to the
chin. "I'm about to hand my life over to an FBI
agent and she's in Art Theft? Jesus, Ned, can you
ever get it right?"

"You still could," Ellie said, standing there,
looking incredibly sad.

"Good-bye, Ellie Shurtleff," I told her. "I have
to admit, you were pretty damn brave. You never
thought I was going to shoot you, did you?"

"No." Ellie shook her head. I caught her smile.
"Your gun. It's been on safety the whole time."

Part Three

GACHET

Chapter 34

"I DON'T THINK he did it, George!" Ellie said into the speakerphone. "Not the murders, anyway."

The FBI Crisis Team in Boston had just debriefed her about her ordeal. Maybe she was a little out of her league, but she told them what she saw. That this Kelly was no killer. Just someone in way over his head who panicked. That until his picture flashed unexpectedly on the TV, she was sure she was about to get him to come in.

Now, in the regional director's conference room in Boston, she was able to report back to her boss in the Florida office. "You remember how the local police said alarms were going off all over town at the time of the theft, George? That's what he did. He didn't kill those people or take the art. He set off the alarms."

"Sounds like you two got pretty cozy in your time together," Moretti said.

"What's that supposed to mean?" Ellie asked.

"I don't know, just that it seems you were able to pick up so much about the guy. Heisted a car together, exchanged life stories."

Ellie stared at the speaker box. She had just spent eight hours with a gun pointed at her, the most nerve-racking day of her life. "I did mention he had a gun, didn't I, George?"

"You did—and not a single opportunity presented itself in all the time you were together, including two venue changes, to take it away from him? Or to get out of there, Ellie? I was only thinking, maybe another agent . . ."

"I guess I thought I could bring him in without anyone getting hurt. My read was that it didn't seem like murder was in the guy's makeup."

Moretti sniffed. "You'll pardon me if I just don't buy into that, Ellie."

"Into *what*?" she asked, hesitating.

"Your read. With all due respect, of course."

"On the basis of what?" she shot back. *The asshole was holding back something from her.*

"On the basis that innocent guys don't abduct federal agents," Moretti replied.

"I did say he panicked, George."

"And that we ran the guy's picture around the Brazilian Court in Palm Beach. He was seen with Tess McAuliffe, Ellie. He had lunch with her. The same afternoon she was killed."

Chapter 35

I'M PRETTY SURE that night was the longest and loneliest of my life.

It was my third night on the run. I didn't know whom I could trust, except Dave, and I was determined not to get him involved. Everyone else I would've gone to, who would've helped me out, was dead.

The worst thing was, some of those people I couldn't trust had the same last name as I did.

I ditched the minivan and spent the night curled up in an all-night movie theater in Cambridge, watching *Lord of the Rings* over and over with a bunch of overenthused college students. I was bundled up in my hooded sweatshirt, too scared to let anybody see my face. When the final showing was over, I actually felt as though I'd been reprieved.

About eight the next morning I took a cab out to Watertown, fifteen minutes away. I caught a glimpse of the morning *Globe* on the cabbie's front seat. LOCAL MAN HUNTED IN FBI HOSTAGE AB-DUCTION. SOUGHT IN CONNECTION WITH FLORIDA MURDERS. I sank back in the seat and pulled down my cap.

Watertown is one of those working-class suburbs of Boston, except instead of just the Irish and the Italians and the blacks, it was home to a lot of Armenians. I had the cab let me off on Palfrey, and walked back a couple of blocks to Mount Auburn. I stopped in front of an ordinary white Victorian just off the corner.

A sign hung over the front steps: WATCHES RE-PAIRED. JEWELRY BOUGHT AND SOLD. A wooden arrow pointed up to the second floor. I climbed the steps and made my way around to the porch. A bell tinkled as I opened the door.

A heavyset man with bushy gray hair in a jeweler's apron looked up from behind the counter. His jowly face broke into a thin smile. "You're taking a helluva chance coming here like this, Neddie-boy. But how the hell are you?"

Chapter 36

I FLIPPED a hand-scrawled sign to closed. "I need to talk to you, Uncle George."

George Harotunian wasn't my real uncle. It was just that I had known him my whole life. He was my father's trusted friend, his business partner. His fence.

When we were growing up, George was as close to a real uncle to Dave and me as we ever had. He always gave my mother money when my father was in jail. He had connections for choice Celtics seats at the Garden. Somehow he managed to steer clear of the law himself. Everyone seemed to find a way to like Uncle George. The good guys and the bad. So I was thinking, *Is he Gachet?*

"Congratulations, Neddie." George shook his head. "Always thought it would be for hockey, but you certainly made the big leagues now."

"I need to find Frank, Uncle George."

He took out his eyepiece and wheeled his chair back from the counter. "I don't think that would be wise right now, son. You want some advice? You need a lawyer. Let me hook you up with somebody good. Turn yourself in."

"C'mon, Uncle George, you know I didn't do anything down there."

"*I* know you didn't do anything," George said, tossing a copy of the morning paper on the counter, "but you got a helluva novel way of showing that to everyone else. You think your father was involved? Jesus, Neddie, you don't know him now. Whitey's too sick to do anything these days. Except cough and complain."

"He needs a kidney, right?"

"He needs a lot of things, kid. You think your father would trade his brother's son, and the rest of those kids, just to pee in a tube for a couple more years? You're judging him a bit too hard, son."

"You know better than anyone that Mickey wouldn't make a move without Frank," I said. "I'm not saying he had anybody killed, but I damn well think he knows who set them up. He knows something, and I need to know it, too. My best friends are dead."

"Christ, Ned," George wheezed, "you think your father knows the difference between a Jackson Pollock and a fucking Etch-A-Sketch? The man's no saint, I know, but he loves you more than you think."

"I guess I figure he loves his life more. I need to find him, Uncle George, please. . . ."

George came around the counter and stared at me, shaking his large, bushy head. "You must need money, kid."

He reached under his apron and peeled off five fresh hundred-dollar bills from a large roll. I took them and stuffed them in my jeans. Accessing my ATM account would have been like a homing signal now. "I know people you could stay with, but your best bet is to come clean."

"Tell my father I need to see him, George. Somewhere safe, if he doesn't trust me. He should be pleased. I finally landed in the family business."

George's hooded eyes grew soft. He stared at me for a long time, then shook his head. "Try calling me Thursday, Neddie. I may run into him by then."

"Thanks, Uncle George." I smiled.

He stuck out his fleshy palm, and when I took it, he pulled me close in a hard embrace. "Everyone knows you had nothing to do with what happened down there, son. I'm sorry about Mickey and your friends. But you're in trouble, Ned, and I don't think Frank can get you out. My offer stands. You think it over. Most of all, you take care."

I nodded and patted him on the back. I made my way toward the door.

"No offense, kid," he said, stopping me, "but you mind leaving through the back?"

The stairs led to a small parking lot that hooked around to an alley. I waved back at Uncle

George as he watched me go. I knew he loved me like a real nephew.

But he had made a mistake, and I caught it.

In no report I had read or seen on TV had anyone mentioned a Jackson Pollock being stolen.

Chapter 37

ELLIE WAS FUMING and, actually, she liked herself best when she got like this—feisty, combative, standing up for herself.

She'd been conned. She'd gone to bat for Ned and he'd let her down. *The sonuvabitch knew,* she kept telling herself over and over. He knew Tess McAuliffe. He was with her the day she was killed. She felt like a complete fool.

Ellie was still in the Boston office, but was headed back home that night. She spent the day fielding calls—a frantic one from her parents in New Jersey, one from the regional director of the FBI, going over her ordeal with the Crisis Team one more time. And then trying to dig up someone in the business who had gone by the name Gachet.

She knew the name, of course. Anyone with an art degree did.

Gachet was the subject of one of van Gogh's

last paintings. It was finished in Auvers, in June of 1890, only a few weeks before he died. The famous doctor with the achingly sad blue eyes. It was first sold from van Gogh's estate for 300 francs, $58. In 1990 a Japanese businessman paid $82 million for it, the most ever paid for a piece of art at the time. But what the hell did any of that have to do with the theft in Florida?

She also spent some time pulling up whatever she could find on Ned Kelly. His friends' police records. His father's. The older brother, who'd been shot in 1997 by the police in the middle of a robbery, possibly set up by the father.

That stuff was all true.

Then she found Ned in a team picture of the 1998 BU hockey team on the university's Web site. She checked with Stoughton Academy. He *had* been accused, unjustly, by a female student. And cleared a few weeks later. Just as Ned told her. He hadn't been lying about that.

Just about the past four days?

The guy had never been in any real trouble in his life; now he was wanted for two sets of grisly murders? No matter what the evidence said, Ellie still felt sure: he was no killer. A liar, maybe. Someone in totally over his head. A womanizer, possibly. But a cold-blooded killer? Shit, he didn't even know how to use a gun.

She pushed herself away from the desk. Maybe Moretti was right. Stick to the art. Sure, it was fun playing with the A team for a while, but her days of chasing murderers were through.

"Shurtleff?" One of the Boston agents stuck his head in her cubicle.

Ellie nodded.

"Someone for you on line two."

"Who is it?" she asked. The story was all over the media. She'd been dodging calls from the press all day.

"Celebrity call," the agent said with a shrug. "Someone named Steve McQueen."

Chapter 38

THIS TIME she was determined to handle it right. By the book. Not like the day before. Though the crack about Steve McQueen was making her suppress a smile. Ellie pressed a button to record the call. She cupped her hand over the receiver and whispered to the agent, *Trace this call.*

"You miss me, Ellie?" Ned Kelly said when she came on the line.

"This isn't a game, Ned," Ellie said. "People here think you're guilty as shit. I told you we had one chance to help you, but that chance is fading fast. Tell me where you are. Let me come get you. Give yourself up."

"Guess that's a no," Ned sighed, as if disappointed.

"You want to know what I miss?" Ellie said, feeling herself getting angry. "I miss not taking that gun from you and putting you in cuffs when

I had the chance. I trusted you, Ned. I went way out on a limb for you. And you didn't tell me the truth."

"What are you talking about?" he said, caught by surprise.

"About the Brazilian Court, Ned. About Tess McAuliffe. About the part that puts you with her that very afternoon. Or was that just something you forgot to slip in when you were going through your life story?"

"Oh." Ned cleared his throat. There was silence on the line. He was probably running through what he could say to save his charade. "If I told you about that, Ellie, would you have believed anything else I said?"

"Whatever would give you that idea? At two murder scenes within just a few hours. Busy day, huh, Ned?"

"I didn't do it, Ellie."

"Is that your answer to everything, Ned? Or only for homicides and interstate trafficking of stolen goods? Oh, yeah, the sexual harassment of minors, too." *A low blow,* Ellie told herself as soon as it left her mouth. She wished she could take it back. She knew it wasn't true.

"I guess I deserved that," Ned said, "but I figure by now you already checked with Stoughton, so you know I was telling you the truth. Are you tracing this, Ellie?"

"No," she quickly replied, though she knew it sounded more like *Of course I'm tracing this, you dope. I'm with the FBI.*

"Great." Ned blew out an exasperated breath.

"Guess there's not a whole lot more I have to lose. Okay, I was with her, Ellie. But I didn't kill Tess. You don't understand. . . ."

"Here's one thing I understand perfectly, Ned. You say you're innocent—then prove it. *Turn yourself in!* I give you my word I'll make sure every part of your story gets fully checked out. You never threatened me yesterday. That was good. That can work for you. But, please, I'm trying to help you, Ned. This is the only way."

There was a deep, extended pause. For a while she wasn't sure if she had lost him. Finally Ned sighed. "I think I should go."

"What are you going to do?" Ellie heard the emotion in her own voice. "Get yourself killed?"

He hesitated a moment. "You find Gachet?"

She glanced at her watch. She was sure they had had enough time to establish some kind of whereabouts for him. He was probably in a phone booth anyway, and in a minute he'd be gone. "No," she replied, "we haven't found him yet."

"Then keep looking, Ellie, please. But you're wrong. You're wrong about Tess. I would never have killed her, Ellie."

"Another lifelong friend?" Ellie said, angry, blowing out a frustrated breath.

"No," Ned said softly. "Nothing like that. You ever felt yourself falling in love, Ellie?"

Chapter 39

DENNIS STRATTON was fuming.

He had a copy of *USA Today* on the desk in front of him—and a *Boston Globe*.

This total fucking amateur was screwing up everything in a major way.

As Stratton read about the botched FBI arrest up in Boston, the lining in his stomach began to tighten. He had told them to get professionals, and who had they sent? That bitch from the Art Theft Department down here. Now they had blown it. This Ned Kelly character could be anywhere.

And the son of a bitch had something very precious that belonged to him.

The FBI had bungled things. Damn it, he had warned them. Now he couldn't take any more chances. Kelly needed to be found. He didn't give a shit what happened to him. As far as he was concerned, Kelly should have ended up in that house in Lake Worth with the rest of them. Stratton straightened the newspaper and read. FBI sources said they had no direct leads on the suspect's whereabouts. This was becoming a very public nightmare for him.

Stratton took out a cell phone and punched in a private number. After three beeps, a familiar voice answered. "Gimme a minute, okay?"

Stratton waited impatiently, checking the morning faxes. He had nurtured this particular relationship for a long time. Now it was time to call in the chits. He'd been paying for the guy's godforsaken kids in private school. For bonefishing trips to his house in the Keys. And right now, Stratton needed to collect on his investment.

The voice came back a few seconds later. "You've seen the morning papers, huh?"

"I've seen them," Stratton spat into the phone, "and I'm not liking what I read. The FBI has made a mess of things. Kelly has something very important that belongs to me. Don't be fooled—*he has the goods*. You said you were handling things. So far, I don't see any evidence that the situation is 'handled.' It's only getting worse."

"It'll be taken care of," the man said, trying to sound calm. "I have a man in the area already. He assures me we have a lead on Mr. Kelly."

"I want what's mine. I don't have to make that any clearer, do I? Whatever else happens is of no concern to me. This is just business."

"I think I get the picture, Mr. Stratton. Relax," the man said. "I know you're a busy man. Play some golf. Get yourself a massage. I should be hearing from my man anytime. You can count on him. Like I told you a hundred times, Mr. Stratton"—the man laughed—"what's the point of having friends—"

Stratton punched off the line. He placed the cell in his jacket and stood up and straightened his Thomas Pink shirt. This is the way he should've handled it from the start, with a *real* professional.

His wife came into the room. She was wearing black running tights with an orange cashmere sweatshirt wrapped around her waist. "Going out for a run, dear?"

"I should be back in half an hour," Liz Stratton said, going over to the desk. "I was just looking for my keys. I thought I left them here."

"I'll alert the boys." Stratton reached for the phone.

"Don't bother, Dennis." She picked up her keys on the desk. "I'm only going down along the lake."

Stratton grabbed Liz by the wrist and jerked her to a stop as she went by. "No bother at all," he said, squeezing.

"Get your hands off me, Dennis. Please."

"I'm surprised at you, darling. You know the rules." He had that look of pretend caring in his eyes that was nothing but ego, control. They stood for a second, eye to eye. She tried to pull away from him. Then she backed down. "Call your goons."

"That's better," Stratton said, relaxing his grip

and revealing a large red mark on her wrist. "I'm sorry, darling. But we can never be too safe, can we?"

"Don't be sorry, Dennis." Liz tried to rub the pain out of her wrist. "You squeeze everybody, dear. That's your style. It's what's so charming about you."

Chapter 40

I PUSHED THROUGH the metal turnstiles, blending in with the crowd, and headed up the ramp to the sign that said FIELD LEVEL BOXES down the left-field line.

That familiar rush of adrenaline raced through me as soon as I saw the field: the old-time placard scoreboard. The closeness of the Green Monster, where in 1978 Bucky Dent had ended our dreams yet again.

Fenway Park.

It was a gorgeous spring afternoon. The Yankees were in town. I only wished for a goddamn minute that they were why I was there.

I walked down toward the field to Box 60C. Then I stood for a second behind the thin, narrow-shouldered man in a white open-collar shirt facing the field.

Finally, I sat down next to him. He barely turned. "Hello, Neddie."

I was shocked at how frail and weak my father looked. His cheeks were sharp-boned and sunken; his hair, which had always been white, had thinned to a few feathery wisps. His skin was parchment gray. My father's hands, which had always been tough, workmanlike hands, looked more like skin-covered bones. He had a scorecard rolled up in them.

"I heard you wanted to see me."

"Gee, Pop, I'm all choked up," I said, staring at him for a second. "They actually the Yankees down there, or some more undercover guys from the FBI?"

"You think I had something to do with what went on at the house?" My father shook his head. "You think, Ned, if I wanted to sell you out, I'd do it in front of your mother? But to your question," he said, grinning, "see number thirty-eight, I'm not so sure he could hit *my* fastball."

I couldn't help smiling. Frank lit up, too. For a second I saw the old, familiar sparkle in his eyes, the Boston Irish con heating up.

"You're looking good, Ned. You're quite the celebrity now, too."

"You look . . ." I wasn't sure what to say. It wasn't so easy to see my father looking like that.

"You don't have to say it." He tapped the program on my knee. "I look like a ghost who doesn't know he's fucking dead."

"I was gonna say, better than I'd heard." I smiled.

The game was already in the third inning. The Sox were at bat, down 3–1. A chant rippled through the crowd, pushing for a rally. My father shook his head. "In a million years, I never thought I'd have to tip my hat to you, Neddie-boy. I spent my whole life slowly sliding down the pole of life's opportunities. And look at you! You knock it out of the park on your very first try."

"Guess I was always holding back a bit." I shrugged. "Always knew I had greatness in me."

"Well, it breaks my heart, Neddie." Frank curled a wistful smile. "Wasn't it that Senator Moynihan who called it the plight of the Irish to have our hearts continually broken by life?"

"I think he was talking about the Kennedys, Pop. Or the Sox."

"Well, it breaks an old man's heart anyway," my old man said. "Whatever's left of it."

I looked into his light blue, almost transparent eyes. Not at the wasting old man I hadn't seen for four years. But at the lifelong con man, who I knew was conning me again. "It breaks mine, too, Pop. Who's Gachet?"

My father kept his gaze trained on the field. "Who's *who?*"

"Come off it, Pop. You lived your life how you wanted, but now I'm caught up in it. I need you to get me out. Who's Gachet?"

"I have no idea who or what you're talking about, son. I swear to God, Ned."

It always amazed me how my father could take a bald-faced lie and feed it back just like the truth. "Georgie slipped up," I said.

"Yeah?" My father shrugged. "How is that?"

"He mentioned a Jackson Pollock that was stolen. I don't think that's ever come out."

Frank smiled. He tapped me on the shoulder with the program. "You missed your calling, Ned. You should've been a detective, not a lifeguard."

I ignored the dig. "Please, Pop, who's Gachet? Don't play me. We both know Mickey would never have made a move without running it by you."

I heard the crack of the bat. The crowd rose and gasped with expectation. A line-drive double off the wall by Nomar, two runs home. Neither of us was really paying attention.

"I'm gonna die, Ned," my father said. "I don't have the strength, or the time."

"Not if you get yourself a kidney."

"Kidney?" For the first time he turned to me, anger flaring in his pupils. "You think I could *live* with setting up those kids, Neddie?"

"I don't know. I wouldn't think you'd set up your own son to take a murder rap, and you manage to live with that. You already lost one son, Pop. He was doing a job for you, right? Right?"

Frank took a short breath, then coughed. I couldn't tell what was going on inside his head. Remorse; more likely, denial. He just sat there, his eyes following the game. He pointed to the Wall. "You know, they got seats up there now."

"Pop," I said, turning to him. "Please . . . cut the shit! I'm wanted for *murder.*"

Frank gritted his teeth, as though he were the one suffering. He squeezed the program firmly in his spidery hands. "Nobody was supposed to get hurt," he finally said. "That's all I have to say."

"But people did, Pop. Mickey. Bobby. Barney. Dee. They're all dead. You know how it makes me feel, that the only person I can come to for help is you. Help me find their killers, Pop. Help me avenge my friends."

He turned to me. For a second I thought he was going to break down. "Georgie gave you good advice, Ned. Get yourself a good lawyer. Then turn yourself in. Anyone with a head on their shoulders knows you didn't kill those kids. I don't know any more."

"You don't know any more?" I said, my eyes growing hot with tears.

"Get yourself out of this, Neddie." Frank turned and glared at me.

I don't think I ever felt any lower than at that moment, knowing my old man was going to let me get up and walk out, without doing a thing to help. My blood was boiling. I stood up and stared him down.

"I'm gonna find him, Pop. And when I do, I'm gonna find out about you, too. Isn't that right?"

A couple of Yanks had reached base. The Sox had made a pitching change. Suddenly, A-Rod unloaded a shot over the left-field wall.

"You believe that?" my father spat. "Just like I said, a goddamn curse."

"I believe it, Pop." I gave him just long enough to change his mind, but he never even looked at me.

I pulled my cap down over my eyes and left the ballpark.

And my father.

Chapter 41

IT DIDN'T TAKE me much farther than the lower ramp of the stadium to realize I was kidding myself. All that big bravado talk about finding Gachet . . . All I had was the few hundred bucks Uncle George had stuffed in my hand. My face was all over the news. Any second the police could rush out and surround me.

I didn't even know what my next move was.

I stood outside the park on Yawkey Way, and for the first time I had no idea where to turn. I knew the Tess McAuliffe thing looked bad. I knew my DNA was probably all over the room, my fingerprints. But the truth was, I hadn't done anything other than set off a few crummy alarms. Maybe Ellie was right. Maybe there was only one choice. Turn myself in. And I was blowing it every second I stayed out there.

I found a pay phone a few blocks over in Kenmore Square. I needed someone to talk to, and only one name came to mind: Dave. Just dialing his cell, I felt as if the weight of the world had been eased off my shoulders.

"Ned!" Dave exclaimed in a hushed tone when he heard my voice. "Jesus, Neddie, I've been waiting to hear from you. Where are you? Are you all right?"

"I'm okay. I'm thinking about a lot of stuff. I didn't resolve the situation quite as I planned."

He lowered his voice. "You saw Pop."

"Yeah, I saw him. He basically wished me luck and told me to drop him a line from jail. Got to see the Sox play, though. That was a plus. Listen, I've been doing some thinking. About what you said. I have to talk to you, Dave."

"I need to talk to you too, Neddie." He sounded excited. "I've got something to show you, too. About this Gachet . . . But, Ned, the police have been to see me. They're all over this, guy. I talked to a few people. . . . Everyone knows you didn't kill Mickey and the guys down there. It turns out there's something called agitated capacity. Basically, it means when you resisted arrest, you weren't in your right mind."

"That's my defense? That I'm a whack job?"

"Not wacko, Ned. That you were pressured into doing something you wouldn't have if you were clearheaded. If it helps you to get a pass on some of this, why not? But you've got to stop digging yourself deeper. You need a lawyer."

"You putting up a shingle, Counselor?"

"What I'm trying to do, you jerk, is save your life."

I closed my eyes. *It's over now, isn't it?* I had to do the right thing. "Where can we meet, bro? I can't risk coming by the bar."

Dave thought it over for a few seconds. "You remember X-man?"

Philly Morisani. We used to watch the tube in his basement, on Hillside, in the same neighborhood where we grew up. It was like our private club. He was so into the *X-Files*, we called him X-man. I heard he was working for Verizon now. "Sure, I remember."

"He's away on business, and I've sort of been watching his place. The basement key's where it's always been. I'm at school right now. I need to finish up a few things here. How's six? If I get there first, I'll leave the door open for you."

"I'll use the time to practice putting my hands behind my back. For the cuffs."

"We're gonna get you out of this, Ned. I never told you, guy, I got an A in writs and statutes."

"Jeez, everything's coming up roses now! More to the point, how'd you do in litigation?"

"Litigation?" Dave groaned. "Nah, flunked that."

We started to laugh. Just hearing the sound of my own laughter, feeling that someone was on my side, sent a little bolstering warmth through my blood.

"We're gonna get you out of this," Dave said again. "Stay out of sight. I'll see you at six."

Chapter 42

I HAD A COUPLE of hours to kill, so I walked around Kenmore Square. I had a beer in an empty Irish bar and sort of watched the end of the game. The Sox actually came back with three in the ninth off Rivera to win. Maybe I should believe in miracles after all.

I sucked down the last of my beer—I figured it would be my last for a long, long time. Life as I knew it was about to end. I was definitely going to prison. I flipped down a ten for the bartender. *Agitated capacity . . . Swell, Ned, your life's been reduced to the hope that you were acting while completely out of your mind.*

It was a little after five, and I found a cabbie who for forty bucks took me down to Brockton. I had him let me off on Edson and I cut over behind the elementary school to Hillside, where Dave was going to meet me.

The house was the third one down the block, a

weather-beaten gray Cape with a short, steep driveway. I felt a wave of relief. My brother's black WRX was parked on the street.

I waited a few minutes by a lamppost, watching the street. No cops. No one had followed. *Time to get this done . . .*

I jogged around to the side of the house. As Dave had said, the storm door to the basement was open. Just like old times. We used to hang out there, watch some ball games, occasionally smoke a little weed.

I rapped on the glass. "Dave!"

No one answered.

I pushed open the door, and the musty mothball smell brought back a lot of good memories. Philly hadn't exactly redecorated the place since I left. The same plaid, basket-weave couch and chewed-up recliner. A pool table with a couple of Miller Lite lanterns over it, a cheap barnwood bar.

"Hey, Dave!" I yelled.

I noticed a book opened on the couch. An art book. I turned it over: *The Paintings of van Gogh.* Unless Philly had somehow elevated his reading material since I'd been away, I figured Dave had brought it. There was a stamp on the inside flap from the Boston College library. He had said he had something to show me on Gachet.

"Davey, where the hell are you, man?"

I plopped down on the couch and flipped the book open to a page that had been marked by a yellow Post-it sticker.

There was a portrait of an old man leaning on his fist, wearing a white cap, with a melancholy look, piercing blue eyes. Those identifiable van Gogh swirls brilliant in the background.

My eyes focused on the text.

Portrait of Dr. Gachet.

I stared closer, my eyes magnetized to the small print. *Portrait of Dr. Gachet. 1890.*

I felt a surge of excitement. The painting was done over a hundred years ago. Anyone could be using the name. But suddenly I had hope. Gachet was real! Maybe Ellie Shurtleff would know.

"Dave!" I called, louder. I looked up the stairs to the main floor.

Then I noticed the light in the bathroom, the door slightly ajar.

"Jesus, Dave, you in there?" I went over and rapped on the door. The force of my knock edged it open.

All I remember for the next sixty seconds or so was standing there as if I'd been slammed in the midsection by a sledgehammer.

Oh, Dave . . . oh Dave.

My brother was propped up on the toilet seat in his hooded BC sweatshirt. His head was cocked slightly to the side. Blood was everywhere, leaking out of his abdomen, onto his jeans, the floor. He wasn't moving. Dave was just staring at me with this placid expression, like, *Where the hell were you, Ned?*

"Oh my God, Dave, no!"

I rushed over to him, feeling for a pulse I knew wasn't there, trying to shake Dave back to life somehow. There was a large puncture wound through the sweatshirt on the left side over his ribs. I pulled the sweatshirt up, and it was as if the left side of Dave's abdomen fell into my hands.

I stumbled backward, my legs buckling. I punched the bathroom wall and sort of slid, helpless, to the linoleum floor.

Suddenly, the sweats started to rush over my body again. I couldn't just sit there, staring at Dave any longer. I had to get out. I staggered to my feet, leaving the bathroom. I needed some air.

That was when I felt the arm wrap around my neck. Tight, incredibly tight. A voice hissed in my ear, "You've got a few things that belong to us, Mr. Kelly."

Chapter 43

I COULDN'T BREATHE. My neck and head were jerked back by a very strong man. The edge of a sharp blade dug into my rib cage.

"The art, Mr. Kelly," the voice said again, "and unless I start hearing about the paintings in the next five seconds, that's about all the time you have left in this world."

Just to make his point, the guy let me feel the edge of the blade again.

"Last chance, Mr. Kelly. See your brother over there? Sorry about the mess, but he just didn't know *anything* about you coming here. It's just not gonna go so easy for you." He stretched my head farther back and pressed the tip of the blade under my chin. "No one fucks the people I work for."

"I don't have any paintings! You think I'd lie about it—now?"

He scraped the serrated edge of the blade

against my neck. "You think I'm a complete imbecile, Mr. Kelly? You have something that belongs to us. About sixty million dollars' worth. I want to start hearing about the art. Now."

What was I supposed to tell him? What could I tell him? I didn't know a thing about the missing art.

"Gachet!" I shouted, twisting my head. "Gachet has it. Find Gachet!"

"Sorry, Mr. Kelly, I'm afraid I don't know any Gachet. I gave you to five and now it's one." He squeezed tighter. "Say hi to your brother, asshole. . . ."

"No!"

I yelled, expecting to feel the blade dig into my neck, and then my legs lifted off the ground. Maybe he was giving me a last chance to talk. I knew whatever I told him, I wasn't leaving there alive.

I slammed my elbow with everything I had into the guy's rib cage, heard a deep exhalation of air. His grip loosened enough for my feet to hit the ground, and his other arm dropped for just a second. Then I rolled forward, lifting him across my back. He flailed with the blade and I felt a slash against my arm. I slammed him as hard as I could against the wall.

Suddenly the guy was on the floor.

He looked about forty, bushy dark hair, wearing a nylon jacket, built like a brick, a bodybuilder. No way I could take him. He still had the knife and spun quickly into a crouch. I had about one second to find a way to save my life.

I reached around for whatever I could find. There was an aluminum baseball bat against the wall. I swung it with all my might. The goddamn bat shattered the beer lights over the pool table.

The guy stepped back in a shower of splintering glass. He was laughing at me.

"I don't have the art!" I screamed.

"Sorry, Mr. Kelly." He started to wave the knife again. "I don't fucking care."

He came at me, and the blade slashed against my forearm. Incredible pain shot up my arm, probably because I saw the cut happen. "That's only the beginning," he said, smiling.

I swung the bat across his arm and managed to nail him. He grunted. The knife dropped and clattered to the floor.

He barreled into me. I hit the wall and saw stars and bright colors. I tried to ward him off with the bat, but he was in too close. And too strong.

He started to press the bat into my chest, increasing the pressure against my ribs, my lungs. Slowly he elevated it higher. Until it was on my windpipe.

I started to gasp. I mean I was strong, but I couldn't budge him. I had no air.

I felt the veins in my face bulge. With the last of my strength, I jerked my knee upward and caught him in the groin. I threw myself into him. We rolled across the room, crashing into shelves behind the pool table—toppling games, pool sticks, the VCR.

I heard the guy groan. *Jesus, maybe he hit his*

head. I spotted his knife across the floor. I scurried over and was back before his eyes cleared.

I wrenched the guy's head back and jammed his own knife under his chin. "Who sent you?" This bastard had killed my brother. It wouldn't have taken much for me to drive the blade into his throat.

"Who sent you? *Who?*"

His eyes rolled back, all the way to the whites. "What the hell?"

I grabbed him by the collar of his jacket as if I were trying to lift him into a boat, and the guy just toppled forward into my arms.

The blade of a hockey skate was wedged in his back. I pushed him forward and he rolled over, dead.

I was drained and exhausted. I could barely move. I just sat there, breathing hard, looking at him. Then reality hit me. *You just killed a man.*

I couldn't think about it—not now. I went back to my brother and knelt next to him a last time. Tears stung my eyes. I ran my hand across Davey's cheek. "Oh, Dave, what did I do?"

I pulled myself up and stumbled back to the art book on the couch. I ripped out the page with *Portrait of Dr. Gachet.*

Then I slipped out of the basement, back into the night. My arm was bleeding, so I wrapped my sweatshirt around it like a bandage. Then I did something I was becoming very good at lately.

I ran.

Chapter 44

THE CELL PHONE jolted him out of bed. Dennis Stratton hadn't been sleeping anyway. He'd been waiting up, watching the overseas news on CNBC. He jumped up in his shorts and caught the phone on the second ring. Liz was curled up, sleeping. He checked the lit-up number. *Private caller.*

He felt excited. The situation had been resolved.

"Do we have it?" Stratton said under his breath. He wanted to wrap up this thing now. It was making him nervous. And he didn't like feeling nervous. Dennis Stratton was a man who liked feeling in control.

"Almost," the caller said, hesitating. Stratton felt something change between them. "We're going to need a little more time."

"More time . . ." Stratton's lips were dry. He wrapped his robe around him and headed out to the balcony. He looked back at Liz. He thought he heard her stir in their black-lacquer chinoiserie bed.

"There is no 'little more time' on this one. You said we had him. You assured me we had professionals."

"We do," the caller said. "It's just that . . ."

"Just that *what?*" Stratton snapped. He stood there in his robe, staring out at the ocean, the breeze brushing back the little hairs on the side of his balding head. He was used to results. Not excuses. That's why he paid people.

"There's been a glitch."

Part Four

BOX!

Chapter 45

BACK IN THE FLORIDA OFFICE, Ellie scanned the Boston office report on the murder of David Kelly and another man two days earlier in Brockton. She felt just awful—the murders could have been her fault.

It had been a bloody, professional job. A knife wound under the fifth, left rib, the blade viciously jerked up into the heart. Whoever did that meant for the victim to suffer. And the other guy—the one with the skate blade in his back, a career criminal named Earl Anson with roots in Boston and south Florida.

And something that disturbed her even more: Ned's fingerprints were all over the crime scene.

How could she have totally misjudged him? Either he was the most cold-blooded killer she had ever heard of or an incredibly cold-blooded killer was after him. Someone who knew whom he would contact in Boston. Someone who wanted something Ned had.

Like stolen paintings, maybe.

Ned was tied to *seven* murders now. He was more than the prime suspect. His face was on every police department fax machine. He was the subject of the largest manhunt in Boston since—what?—the Boston Strangler.

No, Ellie thought as she closed the file, picturing the scene. No way it could have gone down that way. Not after how Ned had talked about his brother. No way she could see him killing Dave. *No! Not possible!* She pulled out the scribbled notes she'd made after her abduction:

BC Law School. The hope of the family now . . .

The police had found an art book at the scene with a page ripped out. Van Gogh's famous portrait. So now Ned knew, too.

Keep looking, Ned had begged her. *Find Gachet.*

Then there was Tess. How was she connected to all of this? Because she *had* to be connected. The police reports had come up sketchy on her. To the point of zero. Her IDs led nowhere. Her hotel bills had always been paid in cash.

A strange sensation tickled her brain. *You ever felt yourself falling in love, Ellie?*

Get real, she told herself. *Be sane!* The guy had kidnapped her and held a gun on her for eight hours. He was wrapped up in seven murders. There were as many law enforcement agents out looking for him as there were for bin Laden. Could she actually be feeling jealous?

And why was it that in spite of all the evidence, she actually believed this guy?

Go back to the art, Ellie told herself. The key was in the heist. That was the feeling she'd had from the beginning.

The cable was cut—the thieves knew the alarm code. Could it be that the person behind the heist had panicked that the police would put two and two together when they realized the thieves had used the alarm code? Cut the wires in the hope of hiding the fact the code had been revealed? If Ned's buddies never stole the art, someone else did. Who?

The same two words. *Inside job.*

Chapter 46

ELLIE WAITED PATIENTLY as a champagne-colored Bentley convertible pulled through the opening gates and crunched toward her on a long white-pebbled driveway.

"Agent Shurtleff." Stratton stopped in the circular drive, acting surprised. He was wearing golf clothes, and the expression on his face showed that he was about as pleased to see her as a heavily sliced drive into the woods.

"Nice job on the arrest up in Boston," Stratton said, getting out of the car. "Don't suppose, in all that time you and Kelly got to spend together, you managed to come up with anything on my art?"

"We have lines out to dealers and police agencies all over the world," Ellie said, trying not to scowl. "Nothing's turned up on the radar so far."

"Nothing on the radar, huh?" Stratton smiled behind Oakley sunglasses. "Well, let me let you in on a little secret. . . ." He leaned close and whispered sharply in Ellie's ear, *"They're not here!"*

Stratton headed into the house and Ellie followed. A housemaid came up and handed him a few messages. "And what about that little friend of yours? The lifeguard who managed to break through my security? Is he under the radar, too?"

"I guess that's why I'm here," Ellie said, her voice echoing in the huge alcove. "Truth is, we're not certain anyone actually *broke* through your security."

Stratton turned around, exasperated. He raised his shades up on his bald brow. "I would've thought that having a gun held to your head by this man would have rid you of that 'inside job' theory. How many has he killed now? Five, six? I admit I didn't go to detective school, but it's not exactly a stretch to think maybe he might have my paintings too."

Ellie felt her face muscles twitch. "I'll only take a minute of your time."

Stratton glanced at his watch. "I have a lunch meeting at Club Collette in about twenty minutes. I guess that leaves me about one minute to hear your latest brainstorm."

Ellie followed him, uninvited, into his study and Stratton threw himself behind the desk into a tufted leather chair.

"You remember I was questioning why the alarm cable was cut, even after the maid recalled that the intruders had the interior code?" Ellie took a seat across from him and opened her satchel.

He circled his hand impatiently. "Surely we've gone beyond that one?"

"We will," Ellie said, producing a manila envelope. "Once we can figure out what to do with *this*."

She pulled out a plastic evidence bag and placed it on the desk in front of him. Inside was a flattened-out piece of paper. Stratton looked at it, and the cocky smirk on his face melted away.

10-02-85. His alarm code.

"It's not exactly a stretch, is it," Ellie said, biting her lip, "for us to be puzzled why your thieves had such an avid interest in the date of your first IPO?"

"Where did you find this?" Stratton's face grew taut.

"On one of the bodies of the people murdered in Lake Worth," Ellie replied. "I think I asked you before if you could provide a list of everyone who had access to your alarm code. I believe you mentioned a caretaker, the housekeeper, your daughter, Mrs. Stratton, of course. . . ."

Stratton shook his head, as if amused. "You really fancy yourself a hotshot detective, don't you, Agent Shurtleff?"

Ellie felt her spine tighten. "Sorry?"

"You have a degree in art," Stratton said. "Your job is to assist other agents in matters of provenance, I believe, and authenticity. I imagine it must be very difficult for you to have such an admiration for beauty and have to spend your life chasing down the wonderful objects that other people own?"

"My job is to uncover fakes," Ellie said, shrugging. "Whether they're on canvas or not."

There was a knock on the door. Liz Stratton stuck her head in. "Excuse me." She smiled at Ellie, then a little dully to Stratton. "Dennis, the tent people are here."

"I'll be right there. . . ." He looked up at her and smiled. Then back to Ellie: "I'm afraid our money-wasting moment is over now, Agent Shurtleff." He stood up. "We're getting the house ready for a little gathering Saturday night. The Shoreline Preservation League, wonderful cause. You should come. We just got our settlement from the insurance company. There'll be all sorts of new art on the walls. I'd like your opinion."

"Sure," Ellie said. "You overpaid."

Stratton kept looking at her with a smug smile. He put his hand in his trouser pocket and came out with a wad of bills, credit cards, some change and left it on the desk. "As long as we understand: one of my jobs, Agent Shurtleff, is to protect my family from people making accusations about our private affairs."

Ellie scooped up the evidence bag and was about to put it back in the envelope. Something made her stop and stare.

"You a golfer, Mr. Stratton?"

"Play at it, Agent Shurtleff." Stratton smiled. "Now if you'll excuse me . . ."

Among the wad of bills and loose change Stratton had dumped on his English leather desk was a black golf tee.

Chapter 47

WHEN I LEFT PHILLY'S, I jumped in Dave's Subaru. I figured I had some time before the bodies were detected—a day, at most—and by then I had to be miles away. But miles where?

I drove wildly, seeing over and over again the horrible image of my brother sitting there like some kind of gutted animal. Knowing I had dragged him into this. Seeing his stuff all over the car—schoolbooks, a pair of beat-up Nikes, CDs, *Dave's Muzak*.

I ditched the car in some podunk town in North Carolina and found some salesman in a used-car lot who sold me a twelve-year-old Impala for $350, no questions asked. I went into the men's room of a roadside diner and dyed my hair. Then I carefully sheared most of it off.

When I looked in the mirror, I was a different person. My thick blond hair was gone. Along with a lot of other things.

I thought about ending my life on that trip. Just making a turn off some remote stop on the highway, driving this old ruin of a car off a cliff, if I could find a cliff. Or a gun. That actually made me laugh. There I was, wanted for seven murders and I didn't have a gun!

And I might have—ended it on that trip. But if I did, everyone would think I was guilty and had killed the people I loved. And if I did, who would look for their murderer? So I thought maybe I'd just go back to Florida, where it all had started.

In a twisted way it made sense. I'd show them. The cops, the FBI, the whole world. I didn't do it, didn't kill anyone—well, except that one murderer up North.

So about a day later I rumbled my clunker over the Okeechobee Bridge into Palm Beach. I parked across from the Brazilian Court. I sat staring at the yellow-hued building, smelling the breeze off the gardens, realizing I'd come to the end of my journey—right where it all had started.

I closed my eyes, hoping some karmic wisdom would hit me about exactly what to do next.

And when I opened my eyes, I saw my sign.

There was Ellie Shurtleff coming out the front door.

Chapter 48

THERE WERE A couple of ways she could play it, Ellie decided.

Turn what she had found over to Moretti and let him handle it. After all, the Tess McAuliffe homicide wasn't even their case. Or toss it in the lap of the Palm Beach PD. But Ellie had already seen the star treatment Stratton seemed to get from them.

Or she could do what every cell in her body was crying out to do.

Take it a step forward. Just one or two more steps . . . What could that hurt?

She had the assistant she shared at the office print a photo of Stratton from the Internet and jammed it in her purse. She left word for Moretti that she was headed out for a few hours. Then Ellie climbed in her office Crown Vic and headed up the highway, back to Palm Beach.

She knew Moretti would have a coronary, and
a smile crossed Ellie's lips: *Fuck the art!*

Crossing over the bridge on Okeechobee, she
headed for the Brazilian Court. It was a whole lot
quieter now than a few days before.

Ellie went into the lobby. An attractive blond
guy was behind the reception desk. Ellie flashed
the FBI badge hanging loosely around her neck.
She showed the man Dennis Stratton's picture.
"Any chance you've seen this person around
here?"

The desk clerk studied it for a second and then
shrugged no. He showed it to a colleague. She
shook her head. "Maybe you want to show it to
Simon. He works nights."

Ellie flashed the photo around to the door
staff and then the restaurant manager. She
showed it to a couple of waiters. Everybody
shook his head, no. It was a long shot, Ellie reminded herself. Maybe she'd come back at night
and try Simon.

"Hey, I know that dude," one of the room-
service waiters said. She'd found him in the
kitchen. His eyes lit up as soon as he saw the
face. "That's Ms. McAuliffe's friend."

Ellie blinked. "You're sure?"

"Sure I'm sure," the waiter, Jorge, exclaimed.
"He comes around here every once in a while.
Good tipper. Gave me twenty bucks to pop a bot-
tle of champagne."

"You're saying they were friends?" Ellie asked,
feeling her pulse come alive.

"You could call them *friends*." Jorge tossed a

smile. "Like, I gotta learn how to get me some *friends* like that, too. Hard to figure, short bald dude with someone who looked like that. Gotta figure he had bucks, right?"

"Yeah." Ellie nodded. "Lotta bucks, Jorge."

Chapter 49

I TURNED THE IMPALA into a half-full lot on Military Trail south of Okeechobee. Next to Vern's Tank and Tummy and Seminole Pawn, a long way from the mansions on the beach.

The place looked more like some run-down shipping office or one of those whitewashed stucco huts that housed seedy, ambulance-chasing lawyers. Only the handful of retuned Vespas on the sidewalk and the cracked Yamaha sign in the window gave it away.

Geoff's Cycles. NATIONAL MINI RACING CHAMPION. 1998.

I parked the car and stepped inside. No one at the counter. I heard the sound of an engine being revved in the back. I wedged through shelves of helmet boxes into the garage. I saw a half-finished bottle of Pete's Wicked Ale on the floor and a pair of beat-up Addidases sticking out from under a gleaming Ducati 999. The engine revved again.

I kicked the sneakers. "That thing run like an old lady having a coughing fit, or does it just sound like one?"

An oily face wheeled out from under the blocks. Close-cropped orange hair and a fuzzy smile. "Dunno, mate. Guess that depends on how fast the old bag can run."

Then his eyes bulged as wide as if I'd crawled out of a crypt in *Dawn of the Dead*. "Holy shit, Ned!"

Geoff Hunter dropped the wrench and hopped to his feet. "It *is* you, Ned. Not some body double for Andrew Cunanan?"

"It's me," I said, taking a step forward. "Whatever's left."

"Mate, I'd like to say you're a sight for sore eyes," Geoff said, shaking his head, "but, frankly, I was hoping you were a whole lot farther away from this sorry-assed place than *here*." He wrapped his greasy, oil-stained arms around my back.

Champ was a Kiwi, who'd been on the world minicycle racing tour for several years. Once, he even held the tour speed record. After a bout or two with Jack—Daniel's—and a sticky divorce, he ended up performing motorcycle stunts in cycle shows, like jumping over cars and through hoops of fire. I'd met him working the bar at Bradley's. You put anything crazy enough in front of him and chased it with a beer, Champ was in!

He went over to a minifridge and opened a Pete's for me. Then he sat on the fridge. "I figure you're not here for the brew, now, are you, mate?"

I shook my head. "I'm in deep shit, Geoff."

He snorted. "You think just 'cause my brain's half fried and I'm drunk the other half of the time, I can't read the papers, Ned? Well, that might be true—but I can turn on the TV."

"You know I didn't do any of that stuff, Champ." I looked him in the eye.

"You're preaching to the choir, mate. You think anyone who actually knows you believes you're going around the country, killing every bloke you meet? It's the *rest* of the world I'd be worried about. I was sorry about those friends of yours, Ned, and your brother. Just what kind of mess are you in?"

"The kind that needs help, Geoff. Lots of it."

He shrugged. "You can't be aiming very high if you're coming to me."

"I guess I'm coming"—I swallowed—"to the only place I can."

Geoff winked, and tipped his beer toward me. "Been *there,*" he said, nodding. "It's a long straight shot down from number one, 'specially when you can't see straight in the morning, not to mention trying to drive it, taking spoon curves at one hundred eighty miles an hour. I don't have much cash, mate, sorry. But I know how to get you out of here, if that's what you need. Know these boats that sneak in past the Coast Guard down the coast a bit, whatever the hell they're carrying. Guess they go back out as well. I bet Costa Rica sounds good about now, right?"

I shook my head. "I'm not trying to leave, Geoff. I want to prove I didn't do these things. I want to find out who did."

"I see. . . . You and which army, mate?"

"I figure it's that, or kill myself," I said.

"Been there, too." Geoff rubbed an oily hand over his orange hair. "Shit, seems I'm perfectly qualified to lend a hand after all. That, and I'm a sucker for a lost cause. But you know that, don't you, Neddie-boy? That's why you're here."

"That," I said, "and no other place to go."

"Flattered." Champ took another swig of beer. "You know, of course, I get caught just in the general zip code with you, I could risk everything here. My business, the comeback."

He got up and limped over to a sink, looking as if he had crawled out of a scrum after two hours of rugby. He washed the grease off his hands and face. "Oh, screw the comeback, mate. . . . But we oughta get one thing straight before I commit."

"I won't put your ass in any danger, Champ, if that's what you mean."

"*Danger?*" He looked at me as if I were crazy. "You must be joking, mate. I fly through gasoline fires for three hundred bucks a shot. I was only thinking . . . You are fucking innocent, aren't you, Ned?"

"Of course I'm innocent, Geoff."

He chewed on the beer bottle for a few seconds. "Okay, that makes things easier. . . . Anyone ever tell you, you're a hard fucking bargainer, Ned?" Champ's eyes crinkled into a smile.

I went over and extended a hand, then pulled him toward me. "I didn't have anyone else to turn to, Geoff."

"Don't get all maudlin on me, Neddie. Whatever you got in store is a whole lot safer than the usual line of work. But before we crack a beer on it, you must have some kind of plan. Who else do we have in the pit?"

"Some girl," I said. "I hope."

"Some girl?" Geoff squinted.

"Good news is, I think she believes me, too."

"Good to know, mate. We'll overwhelm 'em with numbers. So what's the bad news, then?"

I frowned. "Bad news is, she's with the FBI."

Chapter 50

"LET ME GET THIS STRAIGHT." Special Agent in Charge Moretti stood up at his desk, staring at Ellie. His jaw had dropped in something between shock and disbelief. "You want me to bring in Dennis Stratton for questioning for murder?"

"Look," Ellie said, taking out the evidence bag containing the black golf tee from Tess McAuliffe's room. "You see this, George? When I questioned Stratton at his home, he took the same black golf tee out of his pocket. They're from the Trump International Golf Club. Stratton's a member there. It ties him to the scene."

"It ties in a couple of hundred other people," Moretti said, blinking. "I hear Rudy Giuliani's a member. You want to bring him in too?"

Ellie nodded. "If he was having a relationship with Tess McAuliffe, George, *yes.*"

Ellie opened her file, placing Dennis Stratton's

photo on his desk. "I went back to the Brazilian Court and showed this around. He knew her, George. He more than knew her. They were having an affair."

Moretti stared right through her. "You went around to a crime scene that's not even our jurisdiction with a picture of one of the most prominent men in Palm Beach? I thought we had an understanding, Ellie. You don't get to look into the dead people. You get to trace the art."

"They're tied together, George. The art, Stratton, Tess McAuliffe too. A waiter recognized him. They were having an affair."

"And what would you like me to charge him with, Special Agent? Cheating on his wife?"

Moretti came around the desk and shut his door. Then he leaned on the edge of his desk, towering over her, like a reproving school principal.

"Dennis Stratton isn't some punk you slap up against the wall without real evidence, Ellie. You went back to the Brazilian Court, overriding my orders, on a case that's not even ours? You've been baiting this guy from the beginning. Now you want to bring him in. For murder?"

"He had a relationship with the victim. How do we *not* look into it?"

"I don't quite get you, Ellie. We've got a suspect who put a goddamn gun to your head in Boston, whose prints are all over two murder scenes. Whose brother turns up dead and who turns out to have been with this McAuliffe gal the day she was killed. And it's *Dennis Stratton* you want me to bring in?"

"Why would Kelly kill the girl? He was falling for her, George. Stratton's lying, George. He didn't come clean about knowing the victim. He didn't mention it when the Palm Beach police were there."

"How do you know he didn't mention it to the Palm Beach PD?" Moretti asked. "Have you checked their depositions on the case?" Moretti blew out a frustrated breath. "I'll run it by the PBPD. I give you my word. How's that, okay? You're just going to have to learn to trust that the agencies assigned to see these cases through are doing their job. Just like you have to do, right? *Your job.*"

"Yeah." Ellie nodded. She had taken it as far as she could.

"Just one more thing . . . ," Moretti added, putting his arm around Ellie's shoulder as he ushered her to the office door. "You ever go around me again on something like this, your next job'll be investigating 'going out of business' sales for fraud in the stores down on Collins Avenue.

"Now that sure would be a waste of that fancy degree of yours, wouldn't it, Special Agent Shurtleff?"

Ellie tucked the evidence folder under her arm. "Yes, sir," she said, nodding, "it would be a waste."

Chapter 51

ELLIE ROLLED HER KAYAK through a cresting wave, righting the craft as the next wave started to swell.

It was a beauty, and she held the kayak in a tight draw, climbing, anticipating the moment, as the wave peaked.

Then she hit the sucker hard. For a second Ellie hung there in stationary bliss, then released into the curl as though she were shot out of a rocket, cold spray slapping her face.

She was inside it, almost as if there were a tube. *This is a ten.* In the stillness, waiting for the wave to crash, she felt a hundred percent alive.

Finally the wave collapsed over her. She shot up, the kayak bucking in the air. She rode it for a few strokes, gliding in toward shore. Another wave bumped her from behind. Then Ellie slid up onto the beach. She shook the salt spray off her face.

A ten!

She thought about one more ride, then dragged the fiberglass craft out of the surf. She tucked it under her arm and headed back to the pink two-bedroom bungalow in Delray she rented, a block away.

These late-afternoon rides, after work, when the tide was high, were the only time Ellie could feel alone and free enough from the rest of the world to think. Really think. It was a bonus to moving down there: her own little world when something was troubling her. And it seemed as if everything were troubling her right now.

She knew Moretti wasn't going to do crap about Stratton's connection to Tess. They already had Ned wrapped up with a yellow ribbon. Fingerprints, a connection to the victims, kidnapping a federal officer.

Be a good little agent, Ellie said to herself. As Moretti said, this Tess McAuliffe thing, it wasn't even their case.

Something drifted into her mind, something her grandfather used to say. He was one of those self-made men who had battled mobsters in the thirties. He called the bad guys "crumb-bums." And he had built a small blouse factory into a large sportswear firm.

When life boxes you in a corner, he would always say, *box back!*

Ellie was sure that bastard Stratton was involved somehow. In the theft of his own art, maybe in Tess's murder. The way he laughed at her, it was almost as if he were egging her on. *Find something on me. I dare you.*

So find something, Ellie. She dragged the fiberglass kayak up to her porch.

Box back!

Like that's so easy, right? Still in her tight-fitting neoprene suit, Ellie rinsed the salt off the craft's hull.

She was in the FBI, not the blouse business. There was a chain of command. She had this well-defined job. Someone she reported to. This wasn't just some hunch she was following up on. This was going over people's heads.

It was her career.

Ellie leaned the kayak against the wall and peeled off her rubber river shoes, shaking the spray out of her hair. *That sure would be a waste of that fancy degree of yours, wouldn't it?* Moretti had sniffed. She was losing ground with him every day. And Ned? Why was she doing this?

"What're you trying to do," she muttered, shaking her head, exasperated, "let this guy destroy your career?"

She heard a voice from behind, scaring the wits out of her. Ellie spun around.

"Be careful what you wish for, Ellie. . . . You never know what the tide will roll in."

Chapter 52

"JESUS, NED!" Ellie's eyes grew wide.

Or at least it looked like Ned, with his hair short and darker, and a four-day growth on his chin.

"Don't be scared." Ned put up his hand. "No abductions this time, Ellie. I swear."

Ellie *wasn't* scared. Just angry and aware this time. Her training kicked in. Her eyes darted to her holster on the coatrack just inside the kitchen. This time, she was thinking, she was going to be the one in control.

She bolted toward the kitchen. Ned ran after, catching her by the arm. "Ellie, please . . ."

She spun wildly in his grasp. "Goddammit, Ned, what the hell are you doing here?"

"Guess I thought, given all the publicity"—he held back a smile—"your office just didn't seem the place to meet."

Ellie tried to pull away one more time, but he

held her firmly, but not too hard. "I need to talk to you, Ellie. Just hear me out."

She felt an urge to try and throw him, to go for the gun, but she had to admit that a tiny part of her was actually pleased, pleased that he was all right, anyway. That he was there. In her skintight suit, with his hand on her, she felt a little embarrassment take hold. She was blushing now. "What the hell are you doing, Ned?"

"I'm trusting you, Ellie. That's what I'm doing. I'm showing you the new look. So what do you think?"

"I think when you get out of prison, you'll be a helluva candidate for *Extreme Makeover*." She pulled against him.

Ned relaxed his grip. "What I meant was, maybe you could start to trust me, too."

She stood there, glaring at him. Part of her still wanted to make a run for the gun. The other part knew he wouldn't even try to stop her. "It's hard to trust you, Ned. Every time I do, someone else you're connected to seems to turn up dead. You don't just show up here like this. I'm a federal agent, not your AOL buddy. What the hell makes you think I won't arrest you?"

"One thing," he said, still holding her arm.

"What?" she asked, glaring back at him.

He let go of her arm. "I think you believe me, Ellie."

Ellie took another quick glance toward the gun, but she knew it didn't matter. She wasn't going for it. Ned was right. She did believe him. She felt her body coil up with frustration. Then she finally gave in, staring into his eyes. "Did you kill that woman, Ned?"

"Tess?" He shook his head. "No."

"And your brother? What happened to him?"

"All I did was go see him. That was after I met with my father. Ellie, my brother was dead when I got there. My *brother,* Ellie. Whoever did it was waiting for me. Nearly killed me, too. Someone sent him, Ellie. He thought I had the paintings. I still don't even know who he was."

"His name was Anson. He was a two-bit enforcer from south Florida with a record a mile long."

"So, don't you see . . . that proves it. Someone sent him from *here.*"

Ellie narrowed her eyes. "*You* live in south Florida, don't you, Ned?"

"You really think I knew him, Ellie?" He reached into his pocket and came out with a folded-up piece of paper. "Look, I have something to show you."

She recognized it instantly. The page ripped out of the art book. Van Gogh's *Dr. Gachet.*

"Dave was trying to show me this when he was killed. He wasn't trying to turn me in. He was trying to *help* me, Ellie." Ned's eyes were like some helpless, pleading child's. "I've got nowhere to go, Ellie. *Gachet's real.* You have to help me find him."

"I'm a federal agent, Ned. Don't you get it?" She touched his arm. "I'm sorry about your brother. I truly am. But the only way I can help is for you to turn yourself in."

"I think we both know it's a little late for that." Ned leaned back against the porch rail. "I know everyone figures I took the art. Tess, Dave . . . my prints are all over the place. You want the truth, Ellie? It's not about that anymore—clearing myself. Whoever sent that sonuvabitch to kill Dave was looking for the art. We both know that no one's going to continue looking if they have me."

"Will you please get real, Ned." Ellie felt tears of frustration biting at her eyes. "I *can't* join up with you. I'm with the FBI."

"Get real, huh, Ellie?" Ned seemed to sink. "You don't think every day I wake up and wish this wasn't real. . . ." He backed off to the edge of the porch. "I made a mistake coming here."

"Ned, please, you can't go back out there now."

"I'm gonna find out who set us up, Ellie."

Ned jumped off the deck and Ellie realized her heart was beating wildly. She didn't want him to leave. What could she do? Make a play for the gun. Was she going to shoot him?

He stood on the ground and winked up at her on the porch in her dripping wetsuit, his gaze drifting to the kayak. "Nice board. What is it, a Big Yak?"

"No," Ellie said, shaking her head. "A Scrambler."

He nodded approvingly. The lifeguard, right. Then he started to back away into the night.

"Ned!" Ellie called.

He turned around. For a second they stood staring at each other.

She shrugged. "For what it's worth, I liked you better blond."

Chapter 53

WHEN DENNIS AND LIZ STRATTON threw a party, the A-list people came, or at least the people who thought they were A-list.

Ellie had no sooner walked through the door than a fashionably clad waiter put a tray of caviar canapés in front of her and she was face-to-face with some of the prominent people in Palm Beach art society, or so they would tell you. Reed Barlow, who owned a gallery on Worth Avenue, was leading around a gorgeous blonde in a low-cut red dress. Ellie recognized a stately white-haired woman who owned one of the more ostentatious collections in town, with a tanned man half her age on her arm, a "walker."

Ellie felt a little uncomfortable just to be there. All the women were dressed in designer gowns with major-league jewels, and she was in an off-the-rack black dress with a cashmere cardigan wrapped around her shoulders. Her one accommodation was the diamond solitaire studs her grandmother had left her. But in this room no one would notice.

She waded deeper into the house. Champagne seemed to flow at almost every turn. Magnums of Cristal, which Ellie knew cost hundreds of dollars a bottle. And caviar—a huge bowl rested in the hand-carved body of a swan sculpted in ice. In the den a quintet of string players from a Florida symphony. A photographer from "The Shiny Sheet" getting the ladies to jut a hip, angle a leg, turn on their brightest, whitest smiles. All this for charity, of course.

Ellie caught a glimpse of Vern Lawson, the Palm Beach head of detectives, standing stiffly on the edge of the crowd, wearing an earpiece. Probably racking his brains over what she was doing there. And along the walls stood at least five barrel-chested men in tuxedos, hands behind their backs. Stratton must have hired half the off-duty cops in Palm Beach as security.

A small crowd was buzzing in the corridor leading to Stratton's living room. Ellie went over to see what all the commotion was about.

Her jaw dropped.

She was staring at Matisse's *Still Life with Violin,* one of the most famous examples from his cubist stage. Ellie had seen it once at the MoMA in New York. She'd heard it had changed hands recently in a private sale. But seeing it there on Stratton's wall, suddenly she felt angry. That's why he had invited her. The SOB was trying to rub it in her face.

"So, I see you found the Matisse, Agent Shurtleff." A haughty voice startled her from behind.

Ellie turned. Stratton was wearing a collarless white shirt and a cashmere blazer, a smug, self-satisfied expression on his face. "Not a bad example, on such short notice. Perhaps not as explosive as the Picasso, but what can one do. . . . A collector has to fill his walls. Even if I had to overpay."

"It's lovely," Ellie said, unable to hide her appreciation of the painting itself.

"There's much more. . . ." Stratton took her by the arm and led her to a group of admirers staring at a well-known Rauschenberg on another wall. That one must've gone for ten million alone. And on the steps leading into the great room, on two wooden easels, were stunning El Greco drawings: studies, she recognized, from his famous *The Opening of the Fifth Seal of the Apocalypse*.

Masterpieces.

"Whoever's advising you on your art is doing a better job," Ellie said, looking around.

"So glad you approve." Stratton smiled, clearly enjoying himself. "And all dressed up, I see. Come, have some champagne. There must be a nephew of someone rich and famous floating around here who would find what you do for a living completely refreshing."

"Thanks," Ellie sniffed up at him, "but not tonight. I'm working."

"*Working?*" Stratton seemed amused. "Well, that will set you apart in this crowd. Let me guess, you think that Ned Kelly character is in the house?"

"Kelly . . . no." Ellie looked at him. "But I was wondering if the name Earl Anson means anything to you."

"Anson?" Stratton shrugged and took a deep, thoughtful breath. "Should it?"

"He was the man killed along with Kelly's brother up in Boston. Turns out he was a hood from around here. I thought it might ring a bell."

"Why would it?" Stratton said, nodding across the room to a familiar face.

"Because he was up in Boston looking for your three paintings."

Stratton waved across the room to his wife, greeting guests in an off-the-shoulder gown that looked like Prada. Liz Stratton smiled when she saw Ellie.

"You keep forgetting," Stratton said, barely shifting his gaze, "it's four. There were four paintings stolen. You always seem to overlook the Gaume."

"An innocent man was killed up there, Mr. Stratton. A law student," Ellie came back at him.

"One less lawyer," Stratton said, and laughed at his own tasteless joke. "Now, I'm afraid I have other guests."

"And what about Tess McAuliffe?" Ellie said, grabbing Stratton at the elbow. "Am I confused about her, too?"

Stratton's face grew taut.

"I know you were seeing her." Ellie stared at

him. "I can tie you to the Brazilian Court. You were having an affair with Tess."

Stratton's gaze suddenly hardened. "I think we should have that champagne now, Ellie." He latched on to her arm. "Out on the veranda."

Chapter 54

MAYBE SHE SHOULDN'T have said what she did. She knew she had gone too far. But she wanted to throw it in his face and watch the haughty smile disappear.

Stratton dragged her through large French doors leading onto the vast terrace off the ocean. They were outside before she could resist. He'd dug his fingers into her arm.

"Get your hands off me, Mr. Stratton." Ellie tried to pull away without making a scene—like taking him down in the middle of this crowd.

"I thought you might like to see the Fratesi marbles out here," Stratton said as they passed a couple wandering on the terrace. "I shipped them from a villa outside Rome. Seventeenth century."

"I'm a federal agent, Mr. Stratton," Ellie warned him. "Twenty-first century."

"A federal fucking bitch is what you are,"

Stratton said, muscling her over to a remote section overlooking the sea.

Ellie looked around for someone she could yell to if things got really bad. A band was starting to play inside. If this got back to Moretti, she'd be toast.

"It seems our talk the other day didn't impress." Stratton yanked her across the tiles to a fieldstone ledge.

"You're a pretty little girl, Ellie. You know how pretty little girls have to be careful in today's world. Even when they're with the FBI."

"You don't want to take this any further," Ellie said, trying to pull away. "You're threatening a federal agent. . . ."

"Threats? I didn't make any threats, Agent Shurtleff. All the threats came from you. Tess was private. I liked to fuck the little bitch, that's all. I don't know how she died. I don't much care. But as an observation, when pretty little girls do things, like, say, jog on the beach, or better yet, sea-kayaking . . . Look, Ellie . . . You never can tell how rough it gets out there in the surf."

"I'm going to tie you to Earl Anson." Ellie glared back at him.

Her cardigan fell off. Stratton had her by the arm, a grin on his face she didn't like, staring at her shape and her bare shoulders. "You must look cute in a wetsuit, Ellie. Maybe I'd like to see some more of you myself."

Chapter 55

WHAT WAS THIS?

I was out on the jetty, overlooking Stratton's house, when I saw it all unfold. I'm not sure why I was even there. Maybe because that was where it all began; where Mickey and Bobby and Barney had been set up—and I was out of answers. Or because it burned me that Stratton could be in there celebrating about something while my life was falling apart.

Or maybe because it seemed that I'd been watching parties like this from the outside my whole life.

Whatever it was, I watched this guy in a navy blazer dragging a girl onto the terrace, maybe fifty yards away. He forced himself against her on the stone ledge. *Shit, Ned, you've hit the bottom now,* I groaned. I figured I was in for some peep show of the idle rich doing it under the stars.

Suddenly I realized the girl was Ellie.

I went closer. *It was Ellie!* And the guy in the blazer, Dennis Stratton. I'd seen his picture in the papers. But I was wrong. There was nothing amorous going on. He had her by the arm and they were arguing. Ellie tried to pull away.

I inched closer, crouching near a rock wall. Their words started to come clear. Something about Tess . . . something about this being a private matter. Was I hearing this right? What did Tess have to do with Stratton?

Then Ellie said, "I'm going to nail you for fraud—and murder!"

That was all I needed to hear, but the bastard started threatening her. Ellie was trying to twist away. "You're *hurting* me."

I hoisted myself up the concrete seawall and onto the ledge of the terrace.

Then I jumped down off the ledge onto the terrace a few feet behind the two of them. It all happened quickly after that. I jerked Stratton away and nailed him with a solid right. He went down hard on the terrace.

"You want to put your hands on somebody," I said over him, "c'mon, how 'bout me?"

Stratton looked up as if he were dreaming. He rubbed his jaw. "Who the hell are you?"

I turned to Ellie and did a double take. She was beautiful. In a cute black dress, shoulders exposed. All made up. And diamond studs sparkling in her ears, nice ones. She was staring at me with her mouth open.

I was hoping I hadn't shocked her so much that she'd say my name.

She didn't. Instead, Ellie took hold of my arm. "I was wondering where you were. Let's get out of here." She looked at Stratton, who was slowly getting to his feet. "Love your party, Dennis. I'll be seeing you soon. Count on it."

Chapter 56

"THAT WAS BAD, NED," Ellie said, hustling around the side of Stratton's house. "You could've been caught."

"I thought that was the plan," I said, guiding her past a couple of parking attendants at the front gate. "I get caught."

She made a right turn onto the beach. I was half expecting her to stop, pull out her gun, and arrest me right there. Then it hit me, what I had heard up on the terrace.

"You think it's Stratton?" I looked at her, a little dazed.

Ellie didn't answer.

I stopped walking. "You said you were going to bust him for murder and fraud. You think it's Stratton?"

"You got a car, Ned?" Ellie said, ignoring me.

I nodded vacantly. "In a manner of speaking . . ."

"Then go get it. Now. I don't want to know you here. Meet me back in Delray."

I blinked. She wasn't arresting me.

She glared impatiently. "I don't think you need directions, do you, Ned?"

I shook my head, and as I started down the street, a grin spread across my face. "You believe me, don't you?" I called.

Ellie stopped at a navy sedan. "You believe me," I called again.

She opened her car door. "That was stupid, Ned. What you did." She softened. "But thanks . . ."

The whole drive to Delray, I wasn't sure what Ellie really meant back there. The new, paranoid me was sure I was going to come face-to-face with a roadblock of cops and flashing lights. All she had to do was turn me in and Ellie could make a career for herself.

But there were no roadblocks. No cops jumping out at me when I pulled around the corner from her house near the beach in Delray.

By the time I knocked on the front door, Ellie had changed. Her makeup was off, the diamond earrings gone. She had on a pair of jeans, white tee, a pink waist-length sweatshirt. You know what, though, she still looked beautiful.

"Let's get one thing straight," she said as I stood in the doorway. "You're going to jail. You were involved, Ned, whether you killed those people or not. I'm going to help you with the guy who killed your friends, and then you turn yourself in. You understand? You got it?"

"I understand," I said. "But there's something I have to know. You and Stratton on the terrace . . . You were talking about Tess."

"I'm sorry you had to hear that, Ned." She sat on a stool at the kitchen counter. She shrugged. "She and Stratton. They were seeing each other. They were lovers."

Those words slammed into me.

Tess . . . and Dennis Stratton. A hollow feeling rose in my chest. I guess I'd kidded myself a bit. Why someone like Tess would want someone like me. *But Stratton?* I sank onto the couch. "For how long?"

Ellie swallowed. "I think until the day she was killed. I think he was with her after you."

The sinking feeling was starting to simmer now—into anger. "The police know this? They know, Ellie, and they're after *me?*"

"Seems nobody wants to take on Stratton. With the possible exception of, say, *me.*"

All of a sudden things started to become clear. What I'd heard up on Stratton's terrace. Why Ellie hadn't turned me in. Why I was there. "You think he did it, don't you? You think he set up my friends? That's he's Gachet?"

Ellie came over and sat on the coffee table in front of me. "What I'm starting to think, Ned, is if your friends didn't steal Stratton's art, *who did?*"

A smile crossed my lips. I felt this weight draining out of my shoulders. For a moment I wanted to take Ellie by the hand, or hug her. But the joy quickly faded. "But why Tess?"

"I don't know yet." Ellie shook her head. "Did she ever say anything to you? Maybe she knew about you and your friends beforehand. How did the two of you meet?"

"On the beach. Near where I worked . . ." I thought back. I was the one who had gone up to her. Could it be possible that she was in on it? That I'd been set up? No, that was crazy. It was all crazy. "Why would Stratton want to steal his own art?"

"The insurance maybe. But it's not like he needs the money. Maybe to cover up something else?"

"But if that's the case, where was the art when Mickey and the guys went to take it?"

A light blinked in Ellie's eyes. "Maybe someone beat them to it."

"Someone else? Who? Tess?" I shook my head defiantly. "No way." But one thing I couldn't put away, and it didn't make any sense to me. "If Stratton set up his own heist, if he has the paintings—why did he need to send a guy to kill Dave? Why is he still coming after me?"

We looked at each other. I guess we came to the answer at the same time.

Stratton didn't have the art. *Someone had double-crossed him.*

Chapter 57

I HAD A SUDDEN sinking feeling. This was going to be bad. "Listen, Ellie," I said, "I haven't been entirely truthful with you."

Her eyes narrowed. "Oh no. What is it?"

I swallowed uneasily. "I think I might know someone who was involved."

"Okay," she said, "and you were going to share this with me when, Ned? Another old friend?"

"No." I shook my head. "Actually . . . my father."

Ellie blinked a couple of times. I could see her trying to remain calm. "*Your father!* I know he has a record, Ned. But just how in the hell is he involved with seven murders?"

I cleared my throat. "I think it's possible he knows who Gachet is."

"Oh," Ellie grunted, staring incredulously at me, "I thought it was something important, Ned.

Is it possible you could maybe have told me this, say, *before* I threw my career away by bringing you here?"

I told her how Mickey never made a move without him, my conversation with him at Fenway Park.

"Your father knew you were going to visit Dave?" Ellie asked, wide-eyed.

"No," I said. The thought was too gruesome. Even for Frank.

"You know, from what you're telling me," Ellie said, "we're going to have to bring him in."

"It won't do any good," I said. "First, the guy's a pro, Ellie. He's spent a quarter of his life in prison. Second, there's nothing to play against him. He's sick, Ellie. Dying of some kidney disorder. He's not going to roll over. He was willing to let his own son take the fall.

"Anyway, he'd never have killed them. Mickey was like a son to him. Now he's lost two because of his messes." The image of Dave's body came back to me. "Not to mention me."

Ellie kept surprising me. She reached out and took hold of my hand. "I'm sorry, Ned, I truly am, about your brother."

I wrapped my fingers around hers. I looked into her face and braved a smile. "You know I don't have those paintings, don't you, Ellie? You know I didn't kill any of those people. Mickey, Tess, Dave . . ."

"Yes," Ellie said, nodding, "on all counts."

Something changed for me as I looked into those soft blue eyes. Maybe it was the way I had seen her at Stratton's party. Adorable but so brave, standing up to him. Or what she was doing for me now. The risk she was taking. It felt so good, after so long, to have someone on my side.

"Ellie?" I said.

"Yes," she murmured. "What now?"

"Don't arrest me for this. . . ."

I placed a hand on her cheek and kissed her gently on the lips.

Chapter 58

I KNEW THAT wasn't the smartest thing to do. I half expected her to jump up and shove me away: *Have you lost your mind?*

But she didn't. Ellie just sort of lifted her chin and parted her mouth, and her tongue danced around mine a little, soft and warm. The whole thing took both of us by surprise. Suddenly I had my arms around her and I was pulling her against me, until I could feel her heart beating against my chest. You know, sometimes it takes just one kiss to find out if the sparks are really there. They were.

I held my breath as we let go. I was scared of what she was going to say. I brushed a wisp of hair out of her eyes.

Her eyes were sort of blinking—as though maybe she wasn't sure about what had just happened, either.

"It's not right, Ned."

"I know. I'm sorry, Ellie. It was just that it was so good to finally hear that you believe me. And you were looking so cute up on that terrace. I guess I was overwhelmed."

"Not that." She looked at me and curled a little smile. "*That* part was great. I was just thinking about Stratton. He's got these amazing new acquisitions. If he did this theft for the insurance, why press finding the stolen art? He's got what he wanted."

"Maybe he wants them back," I said. "You know, have his cake and eat it, too."

"Listen," she said, focusing herself, "don't get attached to *this*, Ned. This was basically a handshake. To reflect our new working agreement."

I tried to pull her close again. "I was hoping we might take it straight to contract form?"

"Sorry," she sighed. "Call me old-fashioned, but you're a wanted man and I'm the FBI. Besides, there's work to do." She reached out and pulled me up. I was surprised at how strong she was. "You gotta go. You won't be offended, will you, if I ask you to leave by the back door?"

"No," I laughed, "it's become part of my regular routine."

I went to the porch door and slid it open. I looked back at Ellie. I didn't know if it was a mistake, what we'd done. Or if it would happen again. I understood the risk she was taking with me. Our eyes met.

I smiled from the door. "Why are you doing this, Ellie?"

"I don't know." She shrugged. "Let's just say I'm boxing, Ned."

"Boxing?"

"I can't explain right now. You gonna be okay?"

I nodded. "Well, whatever it is, thank you, Ellie."

"I told you, it was just a handshake," she said with a wink.

I shook my head. "I meant for believing in me. Nobody has in a long while."

Chapter 59

THE TALL MAN was hunched down in the front seat of the tan Ford, resting the Nikon on his lap, about fifty feet from Ellie Shurtleff's house. He was getting too old for this. And these cars were too cramped. He was thinking about the old days, when you could really stretch out your legs in a Cougar or a Grand Am.

He saw someone leaving Ellie Shurtleff's house from the back. *Okay,* he thought, angling the Nikon, *time to shift into gear.*

Holy shit! He jumped up, did a double take. That was Ned Kelly walking into the street.

It was *definitely* Kelly. He clicked off a few frantic shots. *Click, click, click.* He felt as if he were having a heart attack.

All he was supposed to do was keep tabs on sweet little Ellie. He never expected anything this good. He followed Kelly down the street and zoomed in with the lens.

Click, click.

Of course, he knew the schmuck was innocent. Obviously the FBI gal felt that way, too. Or she was in cahoots with him.

He started thinking about what he should do. He could run up and arrest Kelly. Build a whole career on this. Get his face on the front page of *USA Today.* Course, then he'd have to explain what he was doing keeping tabs on Ellie.

He zoomed in and took a last shot of Ned Kelly climbing into some old clunker. Close-up of the North Carolina plates. Another shot of Kelly's face. Guy didn't look too bad for the wear and tear.

Oh, you got balls, honey, the tall man had to admit. The whole world was out looking for him, and look where he was—*at your house.*

The tall man put down the camera and, flicking a matchbook deftly through the fingers of his right hand, watched Kelly drive away.

Diminutive, he thought, nodding to himself, *but ballsy.*

Chapter 60

BY THE TIME I got back to Champ's cycle shop it was close to midnight. To my surprise, I spotted a light on inside. Then I saw Champ's Ducati parked by the Dumpster.

"Late night?" I heard him say as I slipped in through the door connected to the garage bay. Champ was sitting down with his feet up on the counter, his chair angled back, and the omni-present bottle of beer. The TV was on. Jay Leno interviewing Nicole Kidman.

"National Pride Night?" I said, taking a seat in a chair next to him.

"She's an Aussie, mate. I'm Kiwi," Geoff replied, a little peeved. He offered me a beer. "I don't assume you know last night's curling results just 'cause you were born up near Canada, do I?"

"Guilty," I said, and clinked my bottle to his. I leaned back next to him with my feet up, too.

"So, how was the party, mate? Any good women?"

"One," I said.

"These tall bitches..." Geoff ignored me, nodding toward Nicole on the TV screen. "Always found them a little difficult to handle myself. Legs get in the way. I know this one gal—"

"Champ," I interrupted, "do you want to hear about what happened tonight?"

"Actually," he said, lowering his chair and facing me, "if you must know, I want to tell you what a well-formed decision you made when you signed me up. This gal I was mentioning is a real night owl. She's a clerk twice a week. At the Brazilian Court."

I brought down my feet and stared. "Okay."

"First, you may have to accept, mate, that that pretty Aussie girlfriend of yours wasn't all she led you to believe."

"I think I'm past that," I said.

He pivoted and faced me, forearms on knees. "Seems that she had some frequent visitors to her room there. Some prominent ones. How does the name Stratton sound to you, Neddie-boy?"

"Like old news," I said with a sigh of disappointment. "Dennis Stratton. He was seeing Tess. I'm already there."

"You're barely in the neighborhood." Geoff shook his head with a smile. "I'm not talking the old man, mate. I'm talking Liz Stratton. *Dennis's wife.*"

He saw my shock and rocked back, taking a self-satisfied swig of his beer. "Whadya think, I got a knack for this sort of work, or what, Neddie-boy?"

Chapter 61

A LOT OF THINGS had shocked me since I left Tess's suite at the Brazilian Court and thought my life was about to take off. But what could Stratton's wife have to do with Tess?

Ellie and I had settled on a code if I needed to contact her at the office. I'd use the name Steve, as in McQueen. And I did, first thing the following morning. I told her what Champ had told me.

"I think we have to talk to Liz Stratton, Ellie."

"First," she said, "I think we have to find out who Liz Stratton really is."

I had a trump card I'd been holding back, and I was thinking now might be the time to use it. "I may have a way."

"No, you don't do anything," Ellie shot back. "You stay put. I'll get you when I know something. You *comprende*, Steve?"

So I played it like a good little fugitive. I

spent the day holed up in the small room above
Geoff's garage, picking through some mi-
crowave lasagna and his John D. MacDonald
crime novels, watching the news on TV. The
next day, too. Ellie didn't return my calls. I felt
like Anne Frank hiding from the Germans. Except it wasn't just the Germans who were after
me, it was the whole world. And it wasn't some
doctor's family who was protecting me, or
Brahms I was hearing through the walls, but
some loony cycle racer blaring U2, revving up
his Ducati.

Late that afternoon, Geoff banged on the floor.
"Team meeting," he yelled. "Coming up the
stairs. You decent, mate?"

I figured "decent" meant my T-shirt and box-
ers, and "team meeting" was "beer time, four
P.M." I swung open the door.

To my surprise, there was Ellie, and Geoff
hanging back with a grin.

"I want to thank you, mate, for your keen
sense of discretion in keeping it just between us,
and the fucking FBI, that you are here."

"Guess you two have met," I said, kicking
open the door. I scrambled around for a second,
putting my legs into a pair of jeans.

Ellie peeked around the disgusting storage
room—boxes of spare parts, cycle catalogs strewn
all over the floor, the unmade cot I'd slept in—trying to find a place to sit. "Nice digs . . ."

"Thanks," Geoff said, kicking a box of
twisted rims out of the way. "Used it many times
myself. And I have to admit," Champ said, nod-

ding approvingly at me, "when you said FBI agent, Neddie, I wasn't exactly thinking Jodie Foster."

She did look cute in a black suit and pink top, but not very cheery. "What'd you find out about Liz?"

"Not much." She took a beer and tipped it obligingly toward Geoff. "The woman's untouchable. Her maiden name's O'Callahan. An old Florida family. Lawyers and judges, mostly. About as private and influential as you can get. She went to Vanderbilt, worked for a while at her daddy's law firm. She married Stratton about eighteen years ago. I'm told she was his access into the circles that financed many of his business deals."

"We have to talk to her, Ellie."

"I tried," Ellie sighed. "I wanted to question her without drawing the attention of my office. But I hit a wall with the family lawyer. Only with Stratton present, and even then only with a pre-submitted list of questions."

"Christ, the tart's tighter than a nun in a condom factory," Geoff said, then gulped a swig of his beer.

"Nice." Ellie scrunched up her nose. "Stratton keeps her totally under wraps. She doesn't even go out for lunch without guards. I don't have enough to bring her in for questioning."

"Jesus, Ellie, you're the FBI. . . ."

"What do you want me to do, run this by my boss? What we need is someone in her circle.

Someone who can get to her. Make her talk. And I don't have any contacts there."

As I said, I had a trump card. And it wasn't worth holding any longer. I rolled the beer bottle around in my hands. "I may have a way."

Chapter 62

SOMEONE SAYS HE'S your friend, but you never really know. Life has taught me that there are always barriers that get in the way. Like the rich siding with the rich, whatever side they're on. What is it I hear the English say? There are no lifelong friends, or lifelong enemies. Only lifelong interests. And I guess you never know what those interests are until you try.

So the next morning I made the call. I might as well have been a sixteen-year-old asking a girl out for the first time. I was never so nervous dialing a number in my life.

"It's me, Neddie." My mouth went dry as soon as I heard him answer.

I waited. No reply. I started worrying I had made a mistake. I could be getting us all in an awful lot of trouble.

"You sure dropped the hose in the deep end—for a pool boy," Sollie Roth finally sighed.

I didn't laugh. He didn't mean for me to. That was Sollie's way of being dead-on serious. "You said something, Sollie, as I drove away. You said a man doesn't run off in the middle of the night. That no problem was too big to solve. Maybe I should've listened to you. I know how things look now. What I need to know is, do you still mean that, Sollie?"

"I never turned you in, son, if that's what you're looking for. I said I was sleeping when you took off."

"I know that," I said, feeling a little ashamed. "Thanks."

"No thanks needed," he said matter-of-factly. "I know people, kid. And I know you didn't do those crimes."

For a second I hung my head away from the phone. I swallowed thickly. "I didn't, Sollie. I swear to God. But I need some help to prove it. Can I trust you, Sollie?"

"You can trust *this,* Ned," the old man said. "I've been where you are now, and I learned that the only thing that's gonna keep you from spending the rest of your life in prison comes down to the quality of your friends. You have those kinds of friends, Neddie-boy?"

"I don't know," I answered. My lips were dry. "What kind are you, Sollie?"

I heard him chuckle. "In matters like this," Sol Roth said, then paused, "the highest, kid. *The highest.*"

Chapter 63

"SO WHO ARE WE meeting here?" Geoff pulled the bike into the parking lot across the street from St. Edward's Church and cut the ignition.

Green's was a luncheonette/pharmacy situated on North County, a sleepy throwback to a bygone time. When JFK was president and Palm Beach held the Winter White House, Kennedy and Washington staffers would party all night, attend early mass at St. Ed's, then spill into Green's for a jolt of joe and some waitress sass while still in their tuxes.

The man we were meeting was sitting in his corner booth, under the window, wearing a powder blue V-necked sweater and golf shirt, a Kangol hat next to him, his thinning white hair plastered tight against his scalp. He had the *Wall Street Journal* open and wore a pair of reading glasses. He looked more like some retired accountant checking his stocks than the man who was going to save my life.

"So, you got some kind of ringer, mate?" Champ elbowed me, his eyes sweeping the room for the person we were going to meet. "That's why you're holed up with me. Someone really on the inside."

"I told you, Champ, trust me."

I shuffled over to the table. The man seated there took a sip of coffee and folded the *Journal* into an even square.

"So you never turned me in," I said with a grateful smile.

"Why would I want to do that?" He looked up. "You still owe me two hundred dollars from gin."

I grinned broadly. He did, too. I put out my hand.

"It's good to see you, son," Sol said, shaking my hand and cocking his head a bit at how I'd changed. "Seems you went to an awful lot of trouble just to cut your hair."

"Time for a change," I said.

"You want to sit down?" He moved his hat and looked at Geoff. "This is the fellow you were speaking about?" He squinted a bit uncomfortably at Champ's striking orange hair.

"Either of you mind cutting me in?" Champ stared blankly, wondering what the hell was going on.

I grinned. "The pit just got a little more crowded, Champ. Say hello to Sollie Roth."

Chapter 64

"SOL ROTH!" Geoff did a double take, eyes wide. "Like in the Palm Beach Downs Sollie Roth? And the dog track? And that hundred-foot Gulf Craft docked at the marina over there?"

"Hundred and forty," Sol said, "if you're counting. And the Polo Club and the City Square Mall and American Reinsurance, if you need the entire résumé. Who are you, son, my new biographer?"

"Geoff Hunter." Champ stuck out his hand and sat across from Sol. "Of the single-lap, 1000cc superpole speed record. Two hundred fifteen miles per hour. Two twenty-two, if they could ever fix on the blur. Face to the metal, ass to the air, as they say."

"And who says that, son?" Sollie took Geoff's hand a little tepidly.

A waitress wearing a Simpsons T-shirt came up. "What can I get you boys? Mr. Roth?"

I did my best to hide my face. Two other tables were calling for her. She rolled her eyes at Sollie. "Now you know why I drink, Mr. Roth."

I ordered scrambled eggs with a little cheddar thrown in. Champ ordered some kind of elaborate omelet with peppers, salsa, Jack cheese, and tortilla chips sprinkled in. A short stack of pancakes, home fries. Sollie, a soft-boiled egg on whole-wheat toast.

We chatted for a few minutes in soft voices. About how I'd made the right move by calling him. He asked how I'd been holding up and said he was really sorry to hear about my brother. "You're dealing with very bad people, Ned. I guess you know that now."

Our breakfast arrived. Sollie watched as Champ dug into his thick omelet. "Been coming here thirty years, never saw anyone order that before. That any good?"

"Here"—Champ pushed the plate across—"it would be an honor. Try some, Mr. Roth."

"No, thanks," Sol said. "I'm trying to live past noon."

I put down my fork and huddled close to him "So, you make any progress, Sol?"

"Some," he said with a shrug. He mopped his toast in the goopy egg. "Though some of what you hear is going to hurt you, kid. I know you were keen on that girl. I did a little checking around with my own sources. I'm afraid it's not quite what you think, Neddie. Dennis Stratton wasn't using Tess. It was the other way around."

"The other way around," I said. Liz was setting *him* up. "What do you mean?"

Sol took a sip of coffee. "Liz Stratton was actually behind her husband's affair with this girl. More than behind it, Neddie, she orchestrated it. Set him up. She had the girl on a retainer."

I blinked back, confused. "Why would she be doing that?"

"To discredit him," Sol replied, spooning another packet of Cremora into his mug. "Everyone knows this Stratton marriage isn't exactly what it seems. Liz has wanted out for a long time. But he's got a stranglehold on her. Most of the money's in his name. She was going to set him up and walk away with everything he's got."

"You know I heard about these tarts who . . ." Geoff gobbled a forkful of omelet.

I held him back. "So, what are you saying, Sollie? Tess was hired? Like some kind of actress . . . Or scam artist?"

"A little more than that, kid." Sol pulled out a folded piece of paper from the pocket of his sweater. "I'm afraid she was a professional."

It was a faxed copy of a police rap sheet. From Sydney, Australia. I was staring at Tess's face. Her hair was pulled back, her eyes downcast. A different girl. The name on the rap sheet was Marty Miller. She'd been arrested several times, for selling prescription drugs and for prostitution in King's Cross.

"Jesus Christ." I blinked, and sank back in the booth.

"She was a high-class call girl, Ned. She was

from Australia. That's why there was nothing on her around here."

"New South Wales," I muttered, recalling our first day on the beach.

"Hmmph," Geoff snorted, taking the sheet from my hand. "An Aussie. Not surprised . . ."

A call girl. Paid to screw Dennis Stratton. Hired to do a job. My blood started to simmer. All that time I'd been thinking there was no way I deserved her—and it had all been just a sham.

"So, he found out about her," I said, clenching my jaw, "and had her killed."

"Stratton's got people who work for him who would do just about anything, Ned," Sol said.

I nodded. I thought of Ellie's doubts about the local cop, Lawson. The one who always seemed to be around Stratton. "That's why the police are dragging their heels. They knew there was a connection between them. He owns them, right?"

"If you want to catch him, Neddie," Sol said, looking at me earnestly, "I own a few things, too."

I smiled gratefully at Sollie. Then I stared at the rap sheet again. Poor Tess. Such a beautiful face. She probably thought this was the payday of her life, too. That shimmering, hopeful look came back to me, the one I couldn't understand. How she felt that her luck was about to change as well.

I'm going to get him, Tess, I vowed, looking at her face. Then I dropped the rap sheet onto the table. "Marty Miller," I said, smiling at Sol. "I didn't even know her name."

Chapter 65

DENNIS STRATTON left his office in one of the financial buildings along Royal Palm Way a little after five.

His Bentley Azure pulled out of the garage and I started up my dingy Impala.

I'm not entirely sure why I had the urge to follow him, but what Sollie had told me really pissed me off. I had seen Stratton in action on the terrace with Ellie. I guess I just wanted to see firsthand what this asshole was about.

Stratton swung around at the light and continued over the bridge into West Palm. I followed, a few car lengths behind. He was busy talking on the phone. I figured even if he noticed, there was no way a guy in an old clunker like mine would register on his mental radar.

His first stop was Rachel's out on 45th Street, a steakhouse where you can wolf down a large porterhouse and watch strippers on the stage. A bouncer greeted him as if they were old friends. All the pretension of class with his big house and the fancy art. Why was I not surprised?

I pulled into a Rooms to Go parking lot across from Cracker Barrel and waited. After fifty minutes I almost decided to call it a night. Maybe half an hour later Stratton came out with another man: tall, ruddy, white-haired, a navy blazer and lime green pants. One of those "I can trace my roots back to the *Mayflower*" kind of faces. They were laughing and smirking.

They both climbed into the Bentley, put the top down, and lit up cigars. I pulled out behind them. *Blue bloods' night out!* They headed down to Belvedere, past the airport, and turned into the Palm Beach Kennel Club. VIP parking.

It must've been a slow day, because the attendant rolled his eyes jeeringly at my wheels, but he seemed happy to take my twenty and slip me a clubhouse pass. Stratton and his buddy headed up on an elevator to the fancy seats.

I took a table on the other side of the glass-enclosed clubhouse. I ordered a sandwich and a beer and felt obliged to go up to the window every once in a while with a couple of two-dollar bets. Stratton seemed to be into it, though. He was loud and garrulous, puffing on his cigar, peeling off multiple hundreds from a huge wad on every race.

A third person came to the table: a fat, balding guy, suspenders holding up his pants. They kept betting wildly, ordering bottles of champagne. The more they lost, the more they laughed, throwing big tips to the stewards who took their bets.

About ten, Stratton made a call on his cell phone and they all stood up together. He signed for the bill—it must've been in the thousands. Then he put his arms around the other two and headed back downstairs.

I paid my check and hurried after them. They piled into his Bentley. They had the top down and were all smoking cigars. The Bentley was weaving a bit.

They crossed back to Palm Beach over the middle bridge. Stratton wrapped around to the right and turned the Bentley into the marina.

Partytime, huh, boys?

A gate rose and a guard waved them through. No way I could follow. I was definitely curious, though. I parked the car on a side street and climbed back up onto the walkway of the middle bridge. I headed up the ramp. An old black guy was fishing off the bridge farther ahead. The spot gave us a bird's-eye view of the marina.

Stratton and his cronies were still winding around the dock. They walked to the next-to-last berth and climbed aboard this enormous white yacht, *Mirabel,* the kind of gleaming white beauty you couldn't take your eyes off. Stratton acted as if he owned it, greeting the crew, taking the others around. Trays came out—food, drinks. The Tres Assholes had the party thing going: booze, cigars, sitting around on Stratton's yacht as though they owned the world.

"Oooh-wee," the black fisherman up the way whistled.

Three long-legged model types were making their way in high heels along the dock. They climbed aboard the *Mirabel*. For all I knew, they might've been the same girls who were performing at Rachel's that night.

Stratton seemed pretty familiar with one of them, a blonde in a short red dress. He had his arm around her, introducing the others to his friends. They started passing around drinks and pairing off. The fat one started dancing with a thin redhead in a waist-baring T-shirt and denim skirt.

Stratton dragged Red Dress onto a bench seat. He started kissing her and feeling her up. She wrapped a long leg around him. Then he got up and took her in one arm, a bottle of champagne in the other, and with a joke to his buddies disappeared below.

"Some show," I said to the fisherman.

"Many the night," he said. "Sure beats the red tail this time of year."

Chapter 66

"WHERE DID YOU GET THIS?" Ellie rose from her kitchen table, staring at Tess's rap sheet.

"I can't tell you that, Ellie." I knew how pathetic that sounded. "But it's from someone with clout."

"*Clout?*" She shook her head. "This isn't clout, Ned. The police don't even have this information. I'm risking everything by getting involved, and you can't tell me who else you're talking to?"

"If it makes you feel any better," I said sheepishly, "I didn't tell him about you, either."

"Oh, great, Ned," Ellie chortled, nodding, "that just makes everything swell. I always knew this was an inside job. Now I have no goddamn idea whose." I saw her thinking. "If Liz set up her husband on this affair . . ."

"I know," I said, finishing the thought for her, "she could've set him up on the art, too."

Ellie sat back down, an expression that was part

realization, part puzzlement. "Could we be all wrong about Stratton?"

"Let's say she did set up her husband on this." I sat down next to her. "Why go after my buddies? And why did they have to kill Dave?"

"No," Ellie said, shaking her head, "that was Stratton. I'm sure of it. He was double-crossed. He thought it must've been you."

"So who the hell is Gachet, Ellie? Liz?"

"I don't know. . . . " She took out a pad of paper and scribbled some notes at the counter. "Let's just stick with what we have. We're pretty certain Stratton had a hand in killing Tess. Clearly, he found out about the scam. And if he did, chances are good he knows his wife was behind it, too."

"Now we know what all the bodyguards are about," I snorted. "They're not so much to protect her. They're there to make sure she doesn't run."

Ellie curled one leg under the other, yoga-style. She picked up the rap sheet. "I figure we can either take this and hand it over to the PBPD, who knows what *they'll* do with it. . . . "

"The person who gave it to me didn't want me to do that, Ellie."

"Okay, Ned." Ellie looked at me a little crossly. "I'm game. What *did* he want you to do?"

"Clear myself, Ellie."

"Clear yourself, huh? Meaning what, you and me?"

"This woman's in a shitload of danger, Ellie. If

we could get to her . . . If she could help us prove a connection between Stratton and Tess, maybe even the art, that would be enough, right?"

"What do you want to do, kidnap her? I told you, I already tried—"

"You tried your way, Ellie. Look—" I spun around and faced her—"don't ask me how I know this, but I was told Liz Stratton has a standing lunch date on Thursdays down at Ta-boó on Worth Avenue. That's the day after tomorrow."

"Who told you this?" Ellie stared at me, a little angry now.

"Don't ask." I took her hand. "I told you, someone with clout."

I searched her eyes. I knew what a risk she was already taking. But maybe this could clear me. Liz Stratton obviously knew some things.

Ellie smiled fatalistically. "This person you know has enough clout to get me out of the jail cell next to you when all of this comes out?"

I squeezed her hand. I smiled a thank-you.

"You know there's still the little matter of the bodyguards, Ned. They're always around her. And we can't exactly have you coming out in public, can we? At Ta-boó."

"No," I agreed, shaking my head, "but fortunately, Ellie, I know just the guy."

Chapter 67

"SO HOW DO I LOOK?" Geoff grinned, peering coolly over his Oakleys. "Clean up pretty well for an outback grease monkey, if I say so myself. Credit the Polo store in town."

The well-appointed front room and bar at Taboó was filled with the in crowd of Palm Beach. Blondes, blondes everywhere, women in pastel-colored Polo cashmere with Hermès bags; men in their Stubbs & Wootton slippers and sunglasses, Trillion sweaters draped over their shoulders, picking at stone crabs and Caesar salads, some of the best grub in Palm Beach. Several patrons looked as if they had stepped in out of the mansions on Ocean Drive.

"George Hamilton's got nothing on you," Ellie said, glancing over Geoff's shoulder across the room.

Liz Stratton was seated at a corner table, having lunch with three girlfriends. Her two bodyguards were at the bar, one eye on Liz, the other drifting to another slender blonde who had just climbed out of a Lamborghini.

"Just soaking up the view," Geoff said, smiling, "until I spring into action. Never know when I'll get invited back here to the island."

Ellie sipped her Perrier and lime. Her stomach had a riot going on inside. Just to be sitting in Taboó, she must be out of her mind. Up till now, she could make the case that she was doing her job. In a few minutes, though, if things didn't go so well, "aiding and abetting" would be a gift plea for her.

The key was to get Liz Stratton out of the restaurant and keep the bodyguards there. Ned was waiting in back with the car. They would whisk her away, and hopefully Liz would be as eager to talk as they were to hear her.

"Jesus," Geoff said, craning his neck and nudging Ellie with his elbow, "tell me that's not Rod Stewart at the bar."

"That's not Rod Stewart. But I think I see Tommy Lee Jones."

A waiter named Louis came up and asked if they were ready to order. "Stone crabs for me," Geoff said, closing the menu as though he did this every day. Ellie ordered a chicken salad. She had a receiver in her ear, wired to Ned in back. They just had to wait for the right time to make a move. *Oh, brother* . . .

A few minutes passed. The waiter came with their meals. All of a sudden, Liz Stratton stood up with one of her friends. They headed toward the ladies' room.

"It's happening *now,* Ned," Ellie said into the wire. She cast a cautious eye at the bar. "Watch my back, Champ."

"Just my luck. Food looks great," Geoff groaned, looking at his just-arrived crab claws.

Ellie got out of her seat and made a beeline to Liz, intercepting her in the back of the restaurant. Liz blinked back a vague look of recognition.

Ellie leaned in as if to give her a kiss. "You know who I am, Mrs. Stratton. We know about you and Tess McAuliffe. We have to talk to you. There's a back door straight ahead. We have a car outside. We can do this real smoothly if you come now."

"Tess . . . ," she said hesitantly. Then a quick eye to her guards. "No, I can't. . . ."

"Yes, you can, Liz," Ellie said. "It's either this or you go down for extortion and accessory to murder. Just don't look behind, and follow me out the door."

Liz Stratton stood there, unsure what to do.

"Believe me, Mrs. Stratton, no one's looking to lay any of this on you."

Liz Stratton twitched back a nod. "Suz, you go ahead," she told her friend. "I'll be in in a second."

Ellie put her arm across Liz's shoulders and quietly tried to propel her forward. "Ned, we're coming out," she said.

One of the bodyguards got up. He stood there, watching for a second, trying to gauge what was going on.

Ellie pushed Liz through the door. *C'mon, Champ, now! Do your thing.*

"G'day, mates." Geoff stepped up to the bar,

blocking their way. "Either of you know where a guy might find a ticket to the Britney Spears Dance America concert at the Kravis? I *think* it's at the Kravis."

"Fuck off," the bodyguard with the ponytail said, attempting to push past him.

"*Fuck off?*" Geoff blinked, stunned. He kicked the legs out from under the big one with the ponytail, knocking him to the floor. "I take my Britney very seriously, mind you, and I don't care for anyone making her seem like some cheap passed-around tart." He grabbed the second guy by the arm and hurled him up against the bar. A tray of drinks toppled, glass shattering.

A pretty brunette bartender with the name tag Cindy yelled, "Hey, cut it out!" Then, to the other bartender, "Andy! Need a little help here. Bobby! Michael!"

Suddenly, Ponytail reached inside his jacket and pulled out a gun.

"On the other hand, mate," Geoff said, backing away, palms up, "anyone who sticks her tongue down Madonna's throat for the whole world to see is a bit of a slut in my book."

He pushed a barstool at the startled bodyguards, then made a dash for the front door.

"It *is* you!" he said, knocking into Rod Stewart at the bar. "Loved the last album, mate. Very romantic. Didn't know you had it in you."

Chapter 68

"THIS IS NED KELLY," Ellie said, pushing Liz Stratton into the backseat of her FBI car.

Liz stared, shocked and confused at what she was hearing.

"He's an innocent man, Mrs. Stratton, who's being framed for murders we think your husband committed."

I turned from behind the wheel and peered into Liz Stratton's eyes. They didn't look outraged or angry at what was going on. Only a little afraid.

"He'll kill me," Liz said. "Can't you tell—I'm scared to death of him. But I can't hold this together anymore."

"We're going to put him away, Mrs. Stratton." Ellie squeezed into the rear seat next to her. "But to do it we need your help."

I hit the gas and gunned the car as soon as I heard the door slam in back. I went around the block and stopped on a side street.

Ellie turned and faced Mrs. Stratton. This was it, I knew. What Liz said in the next two minutes could save, or doom, me. "We know you set up Marty Miller to pose as Tess McAuliffe to have an affair with your husband."

Liz swallowed, knowing there was no point keeping up the pretense anymore. "Yes, I set him up," she said. Part of her seemed to smile while admitting it; another part seemed on the verge of tears.

"And, yes, I know he found out and had her killed. I know it was wrong, terribly wrong. But my husband's a dangerous man. He won't let me go anywhere without those goons."

"I can make that end," Ellie said, placing her hand on Liz's shoulder. "I can tie him to the murder scene at the Brazilian Court. I just need to prove he found out about what you were doing."

"Oh, he knew about it," Liz Stratton sniffed. "He ran a security check on Tess. He traced a bank wire of mine to an account under her real name. He confronted me two days before the art was stolen."

Liz pulled down her sweater and showed us two dark bruises around her neck. "This proof enough for you?"

I couldn't wait any longer. I spun around. Liz knew enough that she could change everything that had happened to me. "Please, Mrs. Stratton, who stole the art? Whoever did murdered my friends and my brother. *Who is Gachet?*"

She placed her hand on my arm. "I promise you, Mr. Kelly, I had nothing to do with whatever happened to your brother. Or any of the others who died. But I wouldn't put anything past Dennis. He's crazy over his art. He wants it back more than anything I've ever seen."

I looked at Ellie. She seemed as surprised to hear these words as I was. If Dennis Stratton didn't steal his own paintings, then who did?

"Someone double-crossed him, Mrs. Stratton. I think you may know who. Who took the art? Who set this in motion? Was it you?"

"Me?" Liz's mouth twisted into an amused smile. "You want to know what a prick my husband is, well, you're about to find out. *The art wasn't stolen.*" A glimmer of revenge flared in her eyes.

"Only *one* painting was."

Chapter 69

ONLY ONE PAINTING was stolen. Ellie and I blinked at her, perplexed. "What are you saying?"

Suddenly I heard the roar of an engine coming from down the block. Champ, bent over the bars of his Ducati, was gunning the cycle straight for us. He decelerated in a flash, screeching to a stop next to our Crown Vic. "Time to go, Kemo Sabe. Posse's on our tail. About a block behind."

I looked up the street and saw a black Mercedes making the turn, speeding directly toward us.

"It's me they want," Liz said, looking at Ellie. "You don't know these terrible people. They'll do anything for my husband." She turned to me. "You've got to go!"

She pushed open the car door and, before we could stop her, climbed out and started to back away. "Here's what I'll do. Come to the house," she said. "Around four. Dennis will be there. Then we'll talk."

"Liz," Ellie said, starting after her, "just tell me what you meant, only one painting was stolen? There were four."

"Think about it, Agent Shurtleff," Liz Stratton said with a smile, backing farther away. "You're the art expert. Why do you think he calls himself Gachet?"

The black Mercedes veered toward Liz and started to slow down. "Come to the house," she said again with a thin, fatalistic smile. "At four."

Two men jumped out on the run and grabbed Liz Stratton. They glared angrily at us, stuffing her roughly into the backseat. I didn't like leaving her, but we didn't have a choice.

"Uh-oh, Neddie." Champ glanced back up the street. He revved the Ducati. "We've got trouble."

There was a second vehicle behind the Mercedes—a black Hummer—speeding directly for us. And this one showed no signs of slowing.

"Ned, get out of here." Ellie started to push me out the door. "They're after *you*, remember."

I squeezed Ellie's hand. "I'm not leaving you."

"What can they do to me?" Ellie said. "I'm with the FBI. But I *can't* be here with you. Go!"

"Ned, c'mon," Geoff urged, revving the Ducati to a deafening pitch.

I jumped out of the driver's seat of the Crown Vic and hopped on the back of Geoff's cycle. Ellie waved. "I'll call you when we're clear."

"Don't worry about her, mate," Champ said. "Worry about us!"

I locked my arms around his waist. "Why?"

"You ever been in an F-15?"

"No." I looked behind. The Hummer was bearing down on us. It wasn't slowing. In about three seconds it would be right on top of us.

"Neither have I," Champ said, redlining the Ducati, "but hold on. I'm told it feels something like *this*."

Chapter 70

THE FRONT WHEEL kicked up, the g-force threw my head back, and with what seemed like a supersonic blast, the Ducati rocketed away.

I felt as though I were being dragged by a jet taking off, holding on for dear life. I pressed myself into Geoff's back, certain that if I loosened my arms for a second, I'd be hurled onto the concrete like a bouncing ball.

We flew down the street in a tuck, headed in the direction of the lake. I took a glance behind. The Hummer didn't even stop. It was coming after us for sure.

"Get out of here! They're coming!" I shouted above the roar into Champ's ear.

"Your wish is my command!"

The Ducati's engine exploded and I was thrown back hard as we shot past homes at a hundred miles an hour. My poor, abused stomach tightened in a knot. A stop sign was coming up pretty quick. Cocoanut Row. The last intersection before the lake. There was only one way to go down here, *north*. Champ slowed just a little. The Hummer was barreling fast behind.

"Which way?" Champ shouted, glancing back.

"*Which way?* There *is* only one way," I said. *Right*. We were still only a block or two from the poshest shopping street in all of Florida. There could be cops around.

"That's what you think," he said.

I felt this monstrous downshift and Champ's Ducati slid into the intersection—and hairpinned sharply to the *left*.

I think my stomach was left somewhere behind. We were leaning so low, my jeans scraped against the pavement. We barely managed to avoid a head-on with a Lexus driven by some tourist with his bug-eyed family.

All of a sudden we were zigzagging down Cocoanut.

"How's that for an exit, mate?" Geoff flashed back a grin.

It was as if we had jumped through the woods on some ski trail, and now we were on another trail, skiing against the flow. I looked around for a cop, exhaling with relief that one wasn't in sight. Then I looked behind. The Hummer had screeched to a stop at the intersection. I thought for sure he'd yank a right and get out of there. But he didn't! He swerved to the left—and was coming after us again.

"Jesus," I shouted, squeezing Champ's ribs, "he's still on us!"

"Damn"—he shook his head—"those bastards have no respect for the law."

He pressed the throttle, but now we were coming up on Palm Beach's busiest shopping street, Worth Avenue. We slowed for half a second.

"Always wanted to try this . . ." Champ gunned the bike again.

He jerked the Ducati to the left. Suddenly we were heading up Worth Avenue. *Against traffic.*

The wrong way!

Chapter 71

THIS WAS THE craziest yet!

We were zigzagging through oncoming cars, swerving out of people's way. Tourists and other shoppers on the sidewalk pointed as if it were some kind of show. We cut between two cars, people pointing, their heads craning. I was praying I didn't hear the sound of a police siren.

We dodged a man loading an SUV, then side-swiped an antique pedestal. It shattered into pieces on the ground. Oh shit . . . We drove past the Phillips Galleries. I glanced behind. Amazingly, the Hummer had made the turn and was still behind us, horn blaring madly at anyone blocking the way. It was as if the driver knew he had immunity if he got caught.

"Champ, we have to get out of here," I said. "Get *off* this street."

He nodded. "I was thinking the same thing."

We made a sharp right, zipping into an entrance to the Poincietta Country Club. I glanced behind. The Hummer had made its way through the obstacle course of traffic. It was still following us.

Champ hit the accelerator and we picked up speed, approaching a golf course. Through hedges I could see golfers on a fairway. The Hummer was still closing.

I gripped Champ's waist. "I'm up for ideas."

"How's your golf game, buddy?"

"My what?"

"Hold on!" He jerked the Ducati at a sharp right angle, sparks slashing up from the pavement. We blasted right through an opening in the hedges, branches whipping my face.

Suddenly we were off the road and in the middle of a perfectly manicured golf fairway!

Ten yards in front of us some poor guy with a five iron was about to play his shot to the green.

"Sorry, playing through!" Champ shouted as the Ducati sped past. Two golf partners in a cart looked on, as if they were in someone else's crazy nightmare. Maybe they were. "Dogleg a bit to the right," Geoff said. "I'd play a fade."

He crossed the wide emerald green fairway, the Ducati picking up speed, every golfer standing agog. I yelled, "Champ, are you crazy, man?"

Suddenly we slipped through another hedge and were in the middle of someone's backyard. There was a beautiful pool, a cabana, and a startled woman in a bathing suit reading on a chaise longue.

"Sorry," Geoff said, waving as we weaved by, "wrong turn. Carry on."

The gal immediately reached for a cell phone. I knew that in about two minutes the Hummer was going to be the least of our worries. The Palm Beach police would be on our tail. Whatever element of slapstick comedy this scene had was fading into full-fledged panic, fast—*very* fast.

We ducked through another opening in a hedge and emerged on South County. "All clear," Geoff said with a wink. No way the Hummer could have followed us.

Problem was, the island of Palm Beach is parallel to an inlet, and if you happened to be running from certain death, there are only a few ways off. We headed toward the South Bridge. I figured we were safe now, unless someone radioed the bridge. We passed a few mansions. Dennis Stratton's house, too. I was starting to exhale.

Then I glanced behind.

Oh, man!

The Hummer was back on our tail. And so was a black Mercedes. Only this time it was worse. *Way worse.* A projectile zipped by my ear with this piercing whine. Then another.

The bastards were shooting at us.

I clutched Champ tightly by the waist. *"Geoff, hit it!"*

"Aheadaya, mate!"

The Ducati jerked, righted itself, then blasted forward into some kind of kited-up supergear.

We shot by more big-time mansions, the wind

and the salt from the ocean breeze lashing at my eyes. I saw the speedometer hit ninety, a hundred, a hundred ten . . . one twenty. We both tucked our bodies as far forward as we could. Face to the metal, ass in the air. We put some distance between us and the two cars.

Finally we approached the end of a brief straightaway. Trump's place, Mar-a-Lago, was on our right. We rounded a steep curve, and then . . .

The South Bridge was in sight.

I took a last look behind. The Hummer was about a hundred yards back. We were going to be okay.

Then I felt the Ducati go into a giant downshift. I heard Geoff yell, "Oh, shit!"

I looked forward and I couldn't believe it.

A Boston Whaler was putt-putting its way up the Intercoastal. My heart was going putt-putt, too—only really fast.

The bridge was going up.

Chapter 72

THE BRIDGE BELL was clanging. The guardrail was already going down. A line of cars and gardeners' trucks was starting to back up.

The Hummer was coming up behind us.

We had seconds to decide what to do.

Geoff slowed, falling in at the end of a line of cars. The Hummer slowed as well, seeing that we were squeezed in—caught.

We could do a 180 and try to get past them, but they had guns. Maybe we could zip around the circle and head farther south, past Sloan's Curve, but there was no way off the island until past Lake Worth, miles.

"Okay," I yelled over the sputtering bike. "I'm taking ideas here, Geoff."

But he had already made up his mind. "Hold on," he said, staring ahead, gassing the engine hard. *"Tight!"*

My eyes widened as I saw what he had in mind. "You know what you're doing?"

"Sorry, buddy"—he glanced behind one more time—"this one's new even for me. . . ."

He jerked the Ducati out of line and gunned the huge bike forward, right under the guardrail. My stomach started to crawl up toward my throat. The bridge was opening now. First a couple of feet, then five, ten.

The bike started to climb up the slowly rising platform. "Stay bloody *low!*" Geoff yelled.

We zoomed up the ramp with the engine blasting, the g-force slamming my ribs. I had no idea how much space separated us from the other side of the bridge. I was tucked into a crouch, and I was praying.

We lifted off the edge of the road and into the air at about a sixty-degree angle. I don't know how long we stayed airborne. I kept my face pressed to Geoff's back, expecting to feel some out-of-control, spinning panic, then free fall, and finally the crash that would separate my body into parts.

But all there was, was this amazing sensation. How a bird must feel—soaring, gliding, weightless. No sound. Then Champ's voice, whooping: "We're going to make it!"

I opened my eyes just in time to see the tip of the oncoming bridge coming toward us, and we cleared it, our front wheel perfectly elevated. We careened off the pavement, my stomach lurching. I expected to fly off and braced for the crash, but Geoff held the landing.

We bounced a few more times, then he sort of touched the brakes and the bike glided down the platform. *We'd made it!* I couldn't believe it.

"How's that!" Geoff hooted, coasting to a stop in front of a backup of cars on the other side of the bridge. We were in front of a woman in a minivan, her eyes as large as dinner plates. "Eight-five on the dismount, maybe, but I'd say the landing was a perfect ten. . . ." Geoff turned around and gave me a shit-eating grin. "Sweet! Next time, think I'd like to give that one a try at night."

Chapter 73

ACROSS THE STREET from Ta-boó, the man in the tan car had watched the whole scene unfold, and he didn't like one thing about it.

The first Mercedes pulled up, the doors flung open, and one of Stratton's men dragged Liz Stratton into the backseat.

He squinted into the camera. *Click, click.*

Then Stratton's boys in the Hummer peeled out after Ned Kelly and that Kiwi cowboy on the show-off bike.

"Dangerous folks," he muttered to himself, clicking off one more shot. *That son of a bitch better be able to really ride.*

Then two of Stratton's goons got out of their car and went up to Ellie Shurtleff.

For a second, that made him reach for his gun. Didn't know if he should interfere. Some kind of argument took place. They started to get a little

rough with her. The Shurtleff gal flashed her
badge, standing up pretty tall in the saddle.

She had spunk, the man in the car had to
admit. He'd give her that.

Setting up this scheme to get to Liz Stratton.
Cavorting with a murder suspect.

"Spunk," he chuckled, but not exactly a lot of
shrewdness. All he'd have to do was pass along a
print to the feds across the street and it wouldn't
exactly be a gold star for her career. Or the rest of
her life, for that matter.

Stratton's men backed off. Flashing the badge
seemed to work, because after some jostling, they
got back in their car. They drove the Mercedes
close to the other car, then sped away. He took his
hand off his gun. He was glad he'd decided to
wait. This could get even bigger.

Maybe he *should* just pass along these prints.
The guy was a wanted killer. She was taking a hell
of a risk. What if she was involved in some way
herself?

He watched the FBI gal get back in her car and
drive away. "Not shrewd," he said to himself
again, tucking away his camera. He flicked a
matchbook between his fingers.

But a shitload of spunk.

Chapter 74

ABOUT 3:30 that afternoon, Ellie met us back at Champ's garage.

I was happy to see that she was okay and gave her a hug. I could tell by the way she held on to me, she'd been worried about me, too. We told her about the motorcycle chase.

"You're crazy." Ellie shook her head at Geoff.

"I don't know," he said with a shrug, as if reflecting on it. "I've often found the line between crazy and physically irresponsible to be quite blurred. Anyway, I thought it was a far cry better than having to party up with those guys in the Hummer. Given the circumstances, I actually thought things went pretty well."

I shot a glance to the clock on Champ's garage wall. It was getting to be that time. A lot could play out for us in the next hour or so. We could find out who stole Stratton's art. I could be cleared of the murders. "You ready to go to Liz's?

Ready to nail Dennis Stratton?" I asked. Ellie seemed nervous, though—for her, anyway.

"Yeah," she said. She caught my arm, her expression tight. "Just so you understand, that's not the only thing that's going to happen at Stratton's today."

She opened her jacket. A set of handcuffs dangled from her waist.

I felt my stomach shift. I'd felt strangely free for the past few days, following up on the crimes, maybe getting closer to catching a killer. I'd almost forgotten she was an FBI agent.

"If it all goes like we hope in there," she said, that law-enforcement look back in her eye, "you're going to turn yourself in. You remember the deal?"

"Sure." I looked at her and nodded, but inside I was dying. "I remember the deal."

Chapter 75

WE CROSSED OVER the middle bridge to Palm Beach mostly in silence. My stomach was twisting inside. Whatever happened at Stratton's, I knew my freedom was about to end.

The town was eerily quiet for a Thursday in mid-April. There were only a few tourists and shoppers on or around Worth Avenue seeking out the late-season sales. A white-haired doyenne crossed in front of us at a light, in a fur wrap despite the April heat, her poodle in tow. I looked at Ellie and we smiled. I was holding on to anything I could right now.

We turned onto Stratton's private street, just off the ocean. That's when I realized something was wrong.

Two police cars were blocking the road, their lights flashing. Others were parked all around Stratton's gate.

At first I thought that the reception was for me,

and I was scared. That Liz had set me up. *But no* . . . An EMS truck was pulling through the gate.

"Get down," Ellie said to me, turning around. I sank down in the backseat, my face tucked under my cap. Ellie lowered her window and flashed her shield to a policeman blocking traffic. "What's happened?" she asked.

The cop took a quick glance at her ID. "There are a couple of bodies in the house. Two people shot. Never seen anything like what's been happening lately."

"Stratton?" Ellie asked.

"No," the officer said, shaking his head. "One's a bodyguard, they're telling me. The other's Mr. Stratton's wife."

He waved us through, but I felt my blood drain and a feeling of panic grip me from head to toe.

Liz was dead. Our case against Stratton was dead, too. We had no way to prove he knew that his wife had set him up. But worse, we had lured poor Liz into this.

"Oh, Jesus, Ellie, we got her killed," I said, feeling as if it were Dave all over again.

Ellie turned in through the gates onto the long pebbled driveway. Three more patrol cars were parked in front of the house, as well as a second EMS van, its doors open.

"You wait here," Ellie said, pulling up in front. "Promise me, Ned, you won't run."

"I promise," I said. "I'm not going anywhere." Ellie slammed the door and ran inside. I felt as though something inevitable was about to happen. I knew it, in fact.

"I promise, Ellie," I said, reaching for the door, "I'm not running anymore."

Chapter 76

STRATTON WAS IN THERE.

Ellie spotted him in the foyer. Sitting in a chair, rubbing his ashen face, mirroring shock. Carl Breen, the detective Ellie had met in Tess's suite, was sitting with him. And Ponytail, the pock-marked asshole who'd taken off after Ned and Champ, was standing smugly by.

"I can't believe she would do this," Stratton muttered. "They were having an affair. She told me. She'd been angry with me. I'd been working too hard. Ignoring her . . . *But this . . .*"

Ellie looked ahead into the sunroom. Her stomach sank. She immediately recognized one of the muscular bodyguards she'd seen at Stratton's party lying faceup on the floor. There were two bullet holes in his chest. But worse, so much worse, was the sight of Liz Stratton, lying back on the floral love seat across from him, still dressed in the same white pantsuit she'd had on that afternoon. A trickle of blood ran down one side of her forehead. Vern Lawson was kneeling beside her.

Ellie had heard a cop talking on the way in. It was supposed to be a murder-suicide.

Like hell. Ellie felt her blood grow hot. She looked at Lawson, then Stratton, then back at Liz. *What a complete sham!*

"I knew she was upset," Stratton continued to Detective Breen. "She finally told me about the affair. That she was going to end it. Maybe Paul wouldn't let her go. *But this* . . . Oh, God . . . She seemed so happy just a few hours ago." Stratton caught Ellie's eye. "She went out to lunch with friends. . . ."

Ellie couldn't hold back. "I know you killed her," she said to Stratton bluntly.

"What?" He looked up, startled.

"You set this up," Ellie went on, teeming with anger. "There was no affair. The only affair was *yours,* with Tess McAuliffe. Liz told us everything. How she set you up. But you found out. *You* did this, Stratton, or had it done."

"*You hear this?*" Stratton yelled, and rose from his chair. "You hear what I have to defend myself against? From this bullshit art agent!"

"I was with her," Ellie said, looking at Breen, "only a couple of hours ago. She told me everything. How she arranged an affair to discredit her husband and he found out. How he was implicated in stealing his own art. Check at the Brazilian Court. Run the photos. You'll see. Stratton was with Tess McAuliffe. Ask him what Liz meant, that only *one painting* was stolen."

There was thick silence in the room. Breen peered at Stratton. Stratton looked around edgily.

"Maybe Liz did know something about the art," Lawson said. He was holding a gun in a plastic Baggie. "It's a Beretta .32," he said. "Same kind of gun used in the killings over in Lake Worth." He looked at Breen.

Stratton sat down again. His face turned a blank, shaken white.

"You're not buying this?" Ellie said. "You think Liz Stratton stole the art? That she killed all those people?"

"Or her boyfriend." Lawson shrugged. He raised the evidence Baggie. "We'll see . . ."

"You got it all wrong," Ellie said, eyeing the smirk creeping onto Stratton's face. "Liz asked us here. She was going to lay it out for us. That's why Liz Stratton's dead."

"You keep saying *us,* Special Agent Shurtleff," Lawson finally said. "You mind telling us who you mean?"

"She means *me,*" a voice came from the entranceway. Everyone spun around.

Ned had entered the room.

Chapter 77

"THAT'S NED KELLY!" Lawson's eyes popped.

Two Palm Beach policemen grabbed me and slammed me onto the tiled floor. A knee drove into the small of my back, and my arms were pinned behind me. Then my wrists were twisted into cuffs.

"I turned myself in this afternoon to Agent Ellie Shurtleff," I said, my cheek pressed to the floor. "She met with Liz Stratton today. She was about to testify against her husband. Liz no more killed herself than I killed Tess McAuliffe. Agent Shurtleff brought me here to confront Stratton with the information, and turn myself in."

I looked up at Ellie with a resigned expression as one of the cops patted me down. She looked back at me with a blank stare. *Why, Ned?* The policemen dragged me to my knees, hands behind my back.

"Radio it in," Lawson barked to a young

plainclothesman. "The FBI, too. Tell 'em we just apprehended Ned Kelly."

I was taken to a patrol car, pushed inside, the door slammed shut. I took one last look over my shoulder at Ellie. She didn't wave. Nothing.

Less than fifteen minutes later I was at the holding cells in the Palm Beach police station. I was stripped, searched, photographed, and tossed into one of the cells. The place was really buzzing. Cops craned their necks for a look.

They didn't charge me with anything right away. I guess the police were waiting to sort things out. I knew they had no direct evidence linking me with anything—other than the guy who killed my brother in Boston.

They were actually taking it easy on me. The Palm Beach cops were pretty good guys, and I eventually made a phone call up to Boston, looking for my father. My mother answered. He wasn't home. "Listen, Mom, you have to tell him to come clean. My life is in the balance." She hesitated a little, then started to cry. "Just ask him, Mom. He knows I'm innocent."

Then I sat back and waited—for whatever was going to happen next.

In that cell, it all started to sink in. Mickey and Bobby, Barney and Dee. The horrible way they had died. I thought of Tess, poor Tess. So many victims. All killed by Gachet? Who the hell was he? There I was in jail—and he was out there, free.

It just didn't seem right somehow.

Part Five

ART'S BOOMING

Chapter 78

THEY FED ME a meal. They gave me blankets and a sheet. I sat down on the cot and passed a lonely night in a cell. I figured this would be the first of many. There was a lot of noise down the hall—the clang of cell doors, someone throwing up.

It wasn't until the next morning that somebody finally came for me. A heavyset black cop from the day before. With two others.

"Free to go, I guess?" I said with a fatalistic smile.

"Oh, yeah, right," he chuckled. "They're waiting for you up in the spa. Don't forget your robe."

They took me upstairs to a small interview room. Just a table and three chairs, a mirror on the wall that I figured was two-way. I waited alone for about ten minutes. The nerves were starting to go. Finally the door opened and two cops stepped in.

One was the tall white-haired detective who was there when I surrendered at Stratton's. Lawson. Palm Beach PD. The other was a short, barrel-chested guy in a blue shirt and tan suit. He flicked me his card as if I were supposed to be impressed by the initials.

Special Agent in Charge George Moretti. FBI. Ellie's boss.

"So, Mr. Kelly," Lawson said, squeezing into a wooden chair across from me. "What are we going to do with you?"

"What am I being charged with?" I asked.

He spoke in a slow, relaxed drawl. "What do you think we *should* charge you with? You left us about the whole criminal statutes book to choose from. The murder of Tess McAuliffe? Or your friends?" He consulted a sheet. "Michael Kelly, Robert O' Reilly, Barnabas Flint. Diane Lynch?"

"I didn't do *any* of that. . . ."

"Okay, plan B, then," Lawson said. "Burglary. Interstate traffic of stolen goods, resisting arrest . . . The death of one Earl Anson, up in Brockton . . ."

"He killed my brother," I shot back. "And he was trying to kill me. What would you have done?"

"Me, I wouldn't have gotten into this mess in the first place, Mr. Kelly," the cop replied. "And just for the record, it was *your* prints off that knife, not his. . . ."

"You're in a shitload of trouble," the FBI man

said, pulling up a chair. "You got two things that can save your ass. One, where are the paintings? Two, how was Tess McAuliffe connected to any of this?"

"*I don't have the paintings,*" I said. "And Tess wasn't connected. I met her on the beach."

"Oh, she was connected," the FBI man said, and nodded knowingly, leaning close, "and, son, you don't come straight with us now, your whole life as you knew it is going to be a memory from this point on. You know what it's like in a federal prison, Ned. No beaches there, son, no pools to tend."

"I *am* being straight with you," I interrupted. "You see a lawyer here? Did I ask for one? Yes, I got involved to steal those paintings. I set off alarms around Palm Beach. *Check.* You got reports of several break-ins around town prior to the theft that night, didn't you? I can give you the addresses. And I didn't kill my friends. I think you know that by now. I got a call from Dee that the art wasn't there. That someone had set them up. Someone named Dr. Gachet. She told me to meet them back at the house in Lake Worth, and by the time I got there they were dead. So I freaked. I fled. Maybe that was wrong. I'd just seen my lifelong friends carried out in bags. What the hell would anyone do?"

The FBI man blinked. He sort of narrowed his eyes at me, like, *Enough of the yuks, kid. You don't even know the trouble I could cause you.*

"Besides," I said, turning to Lawson, "you're not even asking the right questions."

Chapter 79

"OKAY," THE COP SAID with a shrug, "so tell me the right questions."

"Like, who else knew the art was going to be stolen?" I said. "And who was in Tess McAuliffe's suite after me? Who sent that punk up to Boston to kill my brother? *And who is Gachet?*"

They looked at each other for a second, then the FBI man smiled. "You ever stop to think that's because we know the answers to those questions, Ned?"

My gaze hardened on him. I waited for him to blink. *They knew.* They knew I didn't kill anybody. They had me in there, grilling me, and they knew I didn't kill Tess or Dave. They even knew who Gachet was. The longer he waited to answer, the more I was sure he was going to say, *Your father is Dr. Gachet.*

"The ballistics matched," the Palm Beach detective said, grinning. "The gun we found at

Stratton's. Just like we suspected. It belonged to Paul Angelos, the Strattons' bodyguard. Same gun was involved in the Lake Worth murders. He was sexually involved with Liz Stratton. Another of Stratton's men confirmed it. He was doing her dirty work. She was setting up her husband. Seems pretty clear to us. She wanted the money; she wanted to get away from Dennis Stratton. She was linked to Tess McAuliffe. You want to know who Gachet is, Ned? You want to know who sent that guy to Boston? It was Liz. Special Agent Shurtleff said she basically admitted as much at the restaurant."

Liz . . . Gachet? I looked at them incredulously. Waiting, as though they were going to crack big smiles.

Liz wasn't Gachet. Stratton had twisted this, set her up. He had maneuvered the whole thing. And they were buying it!

"Actually, there's only one question we still have for *you*," Lawson said, leaning in close.

"What the hell happened to the art?"

Chapter 80

I WAS BROUGHT BEFORE a judge and charged with burglary, resisting arrest, and interstate flight.

For once, they got the charges right. I was guilty of all three.

The public defender they assigned me advised me to plead not guilty, which I did, until I figured I could call Uncle George in Watertown and have him get me one of his fancy lawyers, as he had offered. I sure needed one now.

They set my bail at $500,000.

"Can the defendant post bail?" The judge looked down from the bench.

"No, Your Honor, I can't." So they took me back to my cell.

I stared at the cold, concrete walls, thinking this was going to be the first day of many like it.

"Ned."

I heard a familiar voice from outside. I shot up on my cot.

It was Ellie.

She looked *so good,* in a cute print skirt and a short linen jacket. I ran over to the bars. I just wanted to touch her. But I felt so ashamed in my orange jumpsuit, on the wrong side of the bars. I don't know, but *that* might have been the most depressing moment of all.

"It's going to be all right, Ned." Ellie tried to look upbeat. "You're going to answer all their questions. Tell them everything, Ned. I promise, I'll see what we can do."

"They think it was Liz, Ellie," I said, shaking my head. "They think she was Gachet. That she set everything up, with her bodyguard. The art . . . *They got it all wrong.*"

"I know." Ellie swallowed hard, clenching her jaw.

"He's gonna get away with murder," I said.

"No"—she shook her head—"he's not. Listen, though. Cooperate. Be smart, okay?"

"That would be a shift." I gave her my best self-effacing smile. I searched her eyes. "So, hey, how's it going for you?"

Ellie shrugged. "You made me a big hero, Ned. The press is all over me."

She put her hand next to mine on the bar and glanced down the hall to see if anyone was watching. Then she wrapped her little finger around mine.

"I feel pretty ashamed, in here like this. Just like my father. I guess everything's changed."

"Nothing's changed, Ned." Ellie shook her head.

I nodded. I was a felon, about to plead guilty and go to prison. And she was an agent for the FBI. *Nothing's changed.* . . .

"I want you to know something. . . ." Her eyes were glistening.

"What's that?"

"I'm going to get him for you, Ned. I promise. For your friends. For your brother. You can count on it, Ned."

"Thanks," I whispered. "They put my bail at five hundred thousand dollars. Guess I'm gonna be in here for a while."

"At least there's one good thing that can come out of this. . . ."

"Yeah, what's that?"

She smiled coyly. "You can go back to being blond." That got me to smile, too. I looked in Ellie's eyes. God, I wanted to hug her. She squeezed my hand once more and gave me a wink. "So, I'll have Champ crash through the wall at, say, 10:05?"

I laughed.

"Take it easy, Ned." Ellie brushed her thumb tenderly against my hand. She started to back away. "I'll see you. Before you even know."

"You know where to find me."

She stopped. "I meant what I said, Ned." She looked me in the eye.

"About Stratton?"

"About all those things, Ned. About *you.*"

She gave a one-fingered wave and backed

down the corridor. I sat back and took a look around at the small, cramped place that was going to be my home for a while. A cot. A metal toilet, bolted to the floor. I was psyching myself up to spend some quality time.

Ellie had been gone for only a couple of minutes when the heavy black cop appeared in front of the cell again. He inserted a key.

"The spa, right?" I pulled myself up. Guess they weren't done with me yet.

"Not this time," he laughed. "You just made bail."

Chapter 81

THEY LED ME to the Intake Center and handed back my clothes and my wallet. I signed a couple of forms and looked beyond the desk to the outer room. They hadn't told me who had bailed me out.

Standing on the other side of the glass, outside the Intake area, was Sollie Roth.

The door buzzed open, and clutching my bundle, I stepped through. I put out my hand.

Sollie took it, smiling. "Like I said, kid, about your friends . . . the highest, kid, the *highest*."

He put his arm around me and led me down the stairs into the garage. "I don't know how to thank you," I said. And I meant it.

Sol's latest car pulled up—a Caddie. The driver hopped out.

"Don't thank *me* so much," he said as the driver opened the rear door, "as *her*."

Ellie was sitting in the backseat.

"Oh God, you're great," I said. I jumped in beside her and gave her a hug. Best hug of my entire life. Then I looked at those deep blue eyes and kissed her on the lips. I didn't care whether anybody saw, whether it was wrong or right.

"If you two lovebirds don't mind," Sol said, clearing his throat in the front seat, "it's late, I'm a few thousand poorer on account of you, and we have work to do."

"Work?"

"Why am I under the impression there was someone you wanted to nail for murder?"

I couldn't contain the grin spreading across my face. I squeezed Sol's arm. It was hard to explain how warm I felt inside—these two people standing up for me.

"I figure we can beat the press by going out the back way," Sol said, nudging his driver. "You mind your old room back at the house?"

"You mean I can just go back to the house?"

"You're free to go where you want, Ned," Ellie said. "At least, until your trial. Mr. Roth here took responsibility for you."

"So, don't get any ideas." He shot a stern look back at me. "Besides, you still owe me two hundred bucks. And I aim to collect."

I couldn't believe what was happening. I was numb. I'd felt hunted for so long. Now I had people who believed in me, who would fight for me.

We got back to Sol's house in a few minutes. The gates to his estate swung open and the Caddie pulled into the bricked courtyard in front. Sol turned to me. "I think you'll find the place like when you left. In the morning, we'll see about hooking you up with a good lawyer. That sound okay?"

"Yeah, Sol, that sounds great."

"In that case, I'm going to bed," he sighed. He said good night with a wink, and I was left with Ellie, staring up at my old place above the garage, realizing that for a few amazing moments, nobody was chasing me.

Ellie stood there, staring at me. There was an ocean breeze warming us through the swaying palms. For a second I drew her close and cupped her face in my hands. I wanted to tell her how much I appreciated what she'd done, but no words came out.

I bent and gave her another kiss. Her mouth was warm and moist, and this time there was nothing hesitant about it. When I was out of breath I pulled away. I let my hand linger on her breast. "So, Agent Shurtleff, what happens now?"

"Now," Ellie said, "maybe we go upstairs, go over a few details about the case."

"I thought that was wrong," I said, taking her gently by the hand. I drew her close, felt her heart beating, felt her tight little body fit into mine.

"Way wrong," Ellie said, looking up at me, "but who's counting now?"

Chapter 82

THERE WAS NO holding back this time. It was a struggle just to drag ourselves up the stairs. Our mouths were locked and we were pawing at each other's clothing the second we stumbled through the door.

"What was it you wanted to discuss?" I said, and grinned, undoing the buttons on Ellie's jacket.

"I don't know . . . ," she said. She wiggled out of her blouse. She had a wonderful body. I had seen it the day I caught her kayaking. This time I wanted all of it. I pulled her close to me.

"I want you to know," she said, pulling at my belt, then tunneling her hand down my jeans. I was as hard as granite. "You're still going to jail. No matter how good this is."

"That's not much incentive," I said. My hands traveled down her spine and into her skirt. I eased the zipper down and helped her slink out of the skirt, until it fell to the floor.

"Try me," Ellie said.

I picked her up in my arms and laid her softly on the bed. I kicked off my pants. She arched her back, slithered gracefully out of her panties, and smiled.

I held myself over her, our eyes locked. Every muscle in my body, every cell, was exploding with desire for this incredible girl. Her skin was smooth and soft; mine was sweaty and on fire. She was taut, cut; small, tight muscles in her arms and thighs rocked against me with willowy restraint. She arched her spine.

"I can't believe we're really doing this," I said.

"Tell me about it," Ellie said.

I eased inside her. Ellie let out a whimper, a beautiful sound, and held on tight to my arms. She was so small and light, I could almost lift her. We rocked like the steady rhythm of the surf outside. I couldn't help thinking, *This is what it's about, you lucky SOB. It's about this wonderful gal who risked everything for you, who looked inside and saw what no one else was willing to see.*

Now what are you going to do about it? How are you going to hold on to Ellie Shurtleff?

Chapter 83

THE WINDOW WAS OPEN, the moon was bright, and a breeze coming off the ocean was softly brushing us like a fan. We curled up against the pillows, too exhausted to move.

Not just from each other, from the three times Ellie and I had made love, but from the stress of all that had happened. And now, being there with Ellie. For a moment, feeling a million miles away from the case, I leaned my head against her shoulder.

"So, what do we do now?" I asked, Ellie balled up in my arms.

"You do what Sol said," she answered. "You get yourself a great lawyer. You stay out of trouble for a change. Tend to your case. With what they have on you, Ned, with a clean record, you're looking at maybe a year—eighteen months, max."

"You'll wait for me, Ellie?" I tickled her, teasing her with pillow talk.

She shrugged. "Unless another case turns up and I meet someone else. This kind of thing, you just never know."

We laughed, and I drew her in to me. But I guess it was dawning on me that I was thinking about something else. I was going to jail. And Stratton had manipulated everything. Perfectly.

"Answer me something—you trust the Palm Beach cops to see this through? Lawson? What about your own outfit, Ellie? Moretti?"

"There may be someone I can trust," she said. "A Palm Beach detective. I don't think he's under Lawson's thumb. Or Stratton's."

"I still have a chip to play," I said. She looked at me, eyes wide. "My father . . ."

"*Your father?* You didn't give him up to the police?"

I shook my head. "Nope. You?"

Ellie stared blankly. She didn't answer, but I could see in her still face that she hadn't.

She stared into my eyes. "I'm thinking we're missing something. What Liz said in the car. Only one painting was stolen. And, 'You're the art expert. Why do you think he calls himself Gachet?'"

"What is it about this Gachet? What's so special?"

"It was one of the last paintings van Gogh ever did. In June 1890, only a month before he killed himself. Gachet was a doctor who used to stop in on him, in Auvers. You saw the picture. He's sitting at a table, in his cap, head resting in his hand.

The focus of the painting is those sad, blue eyes . . ."

"I remember," I said. "Dave left me a picture of the painting."

"His eyes are so remote and haunting," Ellie went on. "Full of pain and recognition. The painter's eyes. It's always been assumed it foretold van Gogh's suicide. It was bought at auction by the Japanese in 1990. Over eighty million. It was the highest price ever paid for a work of art at the time."

"I still don't get it. Stratton didn't have any van Goghs."

"No," Ellie said, "he didn't." Then I saw this ray of awareness. "Unless . . ."

"Unless what, Ellie?" I sat up and faced her.

She chewed on her lip. *"Only one painting was stolen."*

"You gonna let me in on what you're thinking, Ellie?"

Ellie smiled at me. "He hasn't won yet, Ned. Not entirely. He still doesn't have his painting." She threw the sheets off her. Her eyes brightened into a smile. "Like Sollie said, Ned. We have work to do."

Chapter 84

TWO DAYS LATER I got permission to fly to Boston. But not for the reason I had hoped. Dave's body had finally been released by the police. We were burying him, at our local church, St. Ann's, in Brockton.

A federal marshal had to accompany me on the trip. A young guy just out of training named Hector Rodriguez. The funeral was out of state, therefore out of my bail agreement. And I was a flight risk, of course. I already had. Hector was stapled to my side the whole way up.

We buried Dave in the plot next to my brother, John Michael. Everyone was huddled there, cheeks streaming with tears. I held my mom by the arm. It's what they say about the Irish, right? We know how to bury people. We know how to hold up. We got used to losing people early in the Bush.

The priest asked if anyone had any last words.

To my surprise, my father stepped forward. He asked for a moment alone.

He stepped up to the polished cherry casket and placed his hand on the lid. He muttered something softly. What could he be saying? *I never wanted this to happen to you, son? Ned shouldn't have gotten you involved?*

I glanced at Father Donlan. He nodded. I stepped down to the gravesite and stood next to Frank. The rain started to pick up. A cold breeze blew in my face. We stood there for a moment. Frank ran his hand along the casket, never even glancing at me. He took a deep swallow.

"They needed a go-between, Ned," my father said, and gritted his teeth. "They needed someone to organize a crew, to do the heist."

I turned to him, but he kept staring straight ahead. "Who, Pop?"

"Not the wife, if that's what you mean. Or that other chump they killed."

I nodded. "I already knew that, Pop."

He shut his eyes. "It was supposed to be a layup, Ned. No one was supposed to get hurt. You think I would put Mickey onto anything that was dirty? Bobby, Dee . . . Jesus, Ned, I've known her dad for thirty years. . . ."

He turned to me, and in the thinness of his face, I could see tears. I had never seen my father cry. He looked at me, almost angry. "You think for a second, son, I would've ever let them take you?"

Something cracked in me at that moment. In the pit of my chest. In the rain. With my brother lying there. Call it the loathing that had been building up. My resolve to see him as I did. I felt this powerful salty surge in my eyes. I didn't know what to do. I reached out and wrapped my hand gently over his, on the casket. I could feel his bony fingers tremble, the terror in his heart. In that moment I felt what it must be like to be scared to die.

"I know what I've done," he said, straightening, "and I'll have to live with it. However long that is. Anyway, Neddie"—I saw a hint of a smile—"I'm glad you ended up okay."

My voice cracked. "I'm not okay, Pop. Dave's dead. I'm going to prison. Jesus, Dad, who?"

He tightened his fist into a hard ball. A breath slowly leaked out, as if he were fighting some oath or vow he'd kept for many years. "I knew him from years ago in Boston. He moved away, though. The move did him good. They needed a crew from out of town."

"*Who?*"

My father told me the name.

I stood there for a moment, my chest tight. In a second, everything was clear to me.

"He wanted a crew from out of town," my father said again, "and I had one, right?" He finally looked at me. "It was just a payout, Ned. Like going to the bank and they hand you a mil. Split aces, Ned. You know what I mean?"

He massaged his hand across the polished casket lid, slick with rain. "Even Davey would've understood."

I moved close and put my hand on his shoulder. "Yeah, Pop, I know what you mean."

Chapter 85

PALM BEACH Detective Carl Breen was sipping a Starbucks on a bench facing the marina across the bridge off Flagler Drive. Ellie turned to him. "I need you to help me, Carl."

They stared at the fancy white yachts across the lake, beauties, crews in white uniforms hosing them down.

"Why me?" Breen asked. "Why not go to Lawson? You and he seem to be buddies."

"Great friends, Carl. Stratton, too. That's why I'm here."

"Slip's okay," the Palm Beach detective said, and smiled, speaking of Lawson. "He's just been here a long time."

"I'm sure he's okay," Ellie said. "It's who he works for I don't trust."

A gull cawed from a mooring a few feet away. Breen shook his head.

"You've sure come a ways in a couple of weeks

since you stumbled into my crime scene. The most sought after suspect in America falls in your lap. Now you're making accusations against one of the most important people in town."

"Art's booming, Carl. What can I say? And I wouldn't have exactly called it 'falling into my lap.' I was abducted, remember."

Breen raised his palms. "Hey, I actually meant it as a compliment. So, what's in all this for me?"

"Biggest bust of your career," Ellie said.

Breen let out an amused laugh. He took a last gulp of the coffee and crumpled the cup into a ball. "Okay, I'm listening. . . ."

"Stratton had Tess McAuliffe killed," Ellie said, eyes fixed on him.

"Knew you were going to say that," Breen sniffed.

"Yeah? Well, what you probably didn't know was that Tess McAuliffe wasn't her real name. It was Marty Miller. And the reason you haven't been able to find out a thing about her is that she's from Australia. She was a hooker down there. She was hired to do a job. *Stratton.*"

"And where did you get this?" Breen faced her.

"Doesn't matter," Ellie said. "You can have it, too. What *does* matter is that Dennis Stratton was having an affair with her, and that *your own department* knows about this and hasn't done shit. And that he killed his wife in retaliation and pinned the whole mess on her and the body-guard."

"Killed her?" Breen's eyes shone. "In retaliation for what?"

"In retaliation for conspiring with Tess. Liz wanted out. She was coming clean with us. Stratton did it. To get rid of her and get the heat off himself."

"One thing I still don't get," Breen said, nodding cautiously. "You said my department already knew about this relationship, between Tess and Stratton. You want to explain?"

"Dennis Stratton was seen there, at the Brazilian Court, with Tess on several occasions. I saw a golf tee in his home that matched one found at the murder scene. I ran his picture by the staff of the hotel myself. The PBPD has all this."

Breen's blank expression took Ellie by surprise.

"This shouldn't come as a surprise, Carl. You didn't get this information passed along?"

"You think if we had, we wouldn't have followed up on something like that? You don't think we would've been all over Stratton? Lawson, too. I assure you, he hates the arrogant SOB as much as you do." Breen screwed his eyes into her. "Just who was it that supposedly passed along this information?"

Ellie didn't answer. She stared back at him just as blankly. A hollow, sick feeling had swelled in her chest. Everything changed. She had the sensation she was sliding, slowly at first, then faster, against her will.

"Forget it, Carl," she muttered, rewinding everything she knew about this case, back to its very first moments.

Everything had just changed.

Chapter 86

IT WAS A LONG, quiet flight back to Florida. Agent Rodriguez and I barely exchanged a word. I had buried my brother. I'd maybe seen my father for the last time. And I was bringing something back with me as well. Something pretty earth-shaking.

The name of the person who'd killed my brother and my closest friends.

As I came through the Jetway at the Palm Beach airport, I spotted Ellie waiting for me. She was standing apart from the usual crowd of giddy family members welcoming their relatives to the Florida sunshine. She was still on duty, I guess, dressed in a black pantsuit, her hair tied back in a ponytail. She smiled as she saw me, but she looked as though it were the end of a stressful day.

Hector Rodriguez bent down and took off the monitoring device strapped to my ankle. He shook my hand and wished me luck. "You're back to being the FBI's problem now."

For a second, Ellie and I just stood there. I could see her reading the stress in my eyes. "You okay?"

"I'm okay," I lied. I checked around to see if anyone was watching, then I folded her into my arms. "I have some news."

I could feel her face brushing against my chest. For a second, I wasn't sure who was holding whom. "I have news, too, Ned."

"I know who Gachet is, Ellie."

Her eyes grew moist and she nodded. "C'mon, I'll drive you home."

I guess I expected her to be completely stunned when on the way back to Sollie's I told her the name my father had given me. But she just seemed to nod, turning onto Okeechobee.

"The Palm Beach police never followed up the lead on Stratton," she said, pulling over and putting the car in park.

"I thought you informed them," I said, a little dazed.

"I did," Ellie said. "Or I thought so."

It took me a second to see where she was going.

I think until that moment, hiding from the law, trying to prove my innocence, I'd never focused on just how angry I felt. But now I felt it coming on like some storm I couldn't hold back. Stratton always had someone on the inside. He held all the cards.

"How do we handle this?" I asked Ellie, cars shooting by.

"We can get a deposition from your father, but these are law enforcement people, Ned. It's going to take more than an accusation from a guy who's got a grudge and whose history isn't exactly unimpeachable. That's not exactly *proof*."

"But *you* got proof."

"No, all I got was that someone covered up on the Tess McAuliffe case. If I brought that to my boss, it would barely raise an eyebrow."

"I just buried my brother, Ellie. You don't expect me to just sit here and let Stratton and these bastards get away with it."

"No, I don't expect that, Ned."

I saw a look of resolve in her soft blue eyes. The look said, *I need you to help me prove this, Ned.*

And all I said was "I'm in."

Chapter 87

IT TOOK ELLIE two days to get the proof.

It was like looking at a painting from a different angle, the prism turned upside down. Every image, every piece of light refracted differently. She knew that whatever she came up with, everything depended on this. She'd better be sure.

First, she went into the PBPD file on the murder-suicide involving Liz Stratton. There was a NIBIN search in there, tracing the history of the gun. As Lawson had said, it matched up positively as one of the weapons used in the massacre of Ned's friends in Lake Worth. It also made the case against Liz and the bodyguard appear pretty airtight.

She flipped the page.

The Beretta .32 had been confiscated in a drug bust two years before by a joint operation of the Miami–Dade County Police Department and the FBI. It had been held in a police evidence bin in

Miami and had been part of a weapons cache that had mysteriously disappeared a year before.

Paul Angelos, the murdered bodyguard, was a former Miami cop. Why would someone on Stratton's payroll be carrying a dirty gun?

Ellie looked back for the officers who had been assigned to the Miami case. She figured Angelos's name would be there, but it was the name at the bottom of the page that made her freeze.

This could be happenstance, she told herself. What she needed was solid *proof*.

Next, she started digging into the background of Earl Anson, the guy who had killed Ned's brother up in Brockton. How would he find his way to Stratton?

Anson had been a longtime criminal from down in Florida. Armed robbery, extortion, trafficking in drugs. He'd spent time in Tampa and Glades prisons. But what puzzled her was that for both prison stints, despite a spotty record, he was bumped up for early parole. A four-to-six for robbery bargained down to fourteen months. A second-offense felony tossed to time served.

Anson knew someone on the inside.

Ellie called up the warden's office at Glades, a max to medium institution about forty miles west of Palm Beach. She managed to get Assistant Warden Kevin Fletcher on the line. She asked him how Earl Anson had qualified twice for early release.

"Anson," Fletcher said, punching up his record, "didn't I read he just got waxed up in Boston?"

"You won't be seeing him a third time, if that's what you mean," Ellie confirmed.

"No loss there," the assistant warden sighed, "but someone seemed to be pretty tight with him. He had a sugar daddy."

"Sugar daddy?" Ellie said.

"Someone who was protecting him, Agent Shurtleff. And not for what he was giving up in here. My guess? He was someone's CI."

Someone's informant.

Ellie thanked Fletcher, but now she felt stymied. Finding out who was handling a CI would be impossible without running up a bright red flag.

So she tried another tack. She called a friend, Gail Silver, in the Miami District Attorney's Office.

"I'm looking into an ex-con named Earl Anson. He was a hit man in this art heist I'm working on. I was hoping you could get me a list of trials he was a testifying witness at."

"What is he, some kind of rent-a-witness?" Gail kidded her.

"CI," Ellie said. "I'm trying to see if he had any connections to fences or art rings that I could track these paintings through." Not entirely a lie.

"What are you looking for?" the ADA replied, seeming to treat her request as routine.

"Defendants, convictions . . . ," Ellie said casually. She held her breath. "Case agents, Gail . . . if you're able to provide that, too."

Chapter 88

THE FOLLOWING AFTERNOON Ellie knocked on Moretti's office door. She caught her boss leafing through a file, and he grudgingly waved her in. "Something to report?"

Things had gone from bad to worse with Special Agent in Charge Moretti. Clearly, he felt upstaged, shown up after Ned's arrest, by the little art agent who was suddenly getting all the publicity.

"I've been looking into something," Ellie said at the door. "Something's come up I'm not sure what to do with. On the art."

"Okay." Moretti leaned back, shifting a file.

"Ned Kelly mentioned something," Ellie said, sitting down, a file on her lap. "You know, he went to Boston for his brother's funeral."

"Right, I've been meaning to talk to you about him." Moretti crossed his legs.

"He talked to his father up there. It's a little

out of the blue, sir, but he indicated he knew who this Dr. Gachet is."

"*Who* did?" Her boss sat up.

"Kelly's father," Ellie said. "More so, he seemed to imply it was someone in law enforcement. *Someone down here.*"

Moretti narrowed his gaze. "How would Ned Kelly's father have any idea who was behind the heist?"

"I don't know, sir," Ellie said, "that's what I want to find out. But I started wondering why the Palm Beach police had never acted on that Stratton thing with Tess McAuliffe I laid out for you. You did pass it along?"

Moretti nodded. "Of course . . ."

"You know Lawson, who heads the detectives unit up there? I've always had some doubts about him."

"Lawson?"

"I've seen him at Stratton's house all three times I've been there," Ellie went on.

"You don't stop trying to put two and two together, do you, Special Agent Shurtleff?"

"So I checked into the .32 that Liz Stratton used," she said, ignoring him. "You know where it came from? It was stolen from a police evidence bin."

"You don't think I know where you're headed with this? You get to take a big bow to the press for bringing in Ned Kelly, then you say so long to playing Mrs. Kojak. Wasn't that our agreement? As far as the Bureau is concerned, these murders are solved. Ballistics. Motive. *Airtight.*"

"I'm talking about the art," Ellie said, looking right back at him. "I thought I might go up there and hear the old man out. If that's okay?"

Moretti shrugged. "I could send a local team. . . ."

"A local team's not familiar with fences, or what to ask about the art," Ellie countered.

Moretti didn't answer. He hid his face behind a steeple of his hands. "Just when do you plan to go?"

"Tomorrow morning," Ellie said. "Six A.M. If the guy's as sick as I've heard, it might be good to get up there now."

"Tomorrow morning." Moretti nodded sort of glumly, as if he were thinking something over. Then, a second later he shrugged, as if he had made up his mind.

"Try to be careful this time," he said, and smiled. "You remember what happened the last time you went up there?"

"Don't worry," Ellie said. "What are the chances of something like that happening two times in a row?"

Chapter 89

THAT NIGHT Ellie put on an old wrinkled T-shirt, cleaned her face, and slid into bed about eleven.

She was tired, but also wired. She didn't turn on the TV. For a while she leafed through a book on van der Heyden, a Dutch painter from the seventeenth century, but mostly found herself staring off into space.

She'd found out what she needed to know; now it was just a question of what to do next. She finally flicked off the lights and lay in the dark. No way she could sleep.

Ellie pulled the covers up over her shoulders. She glanced at the clock. Twenty minutes had passed. She listened to the silence in the house.

Suddenly she heard a creaking sound from out in the living room. Ellie froze. *The floor groaning, or maybe someone sliding through the window.* She usually left it open for the breeze.

She listened some more, eyes stretched wide, not moving a muscle. She waited for a second sound.

Nothing.

Then she heard the creaking sound again.

This time Ellie lay completely silent for a full twenty seconds. She wasn't imagining anything. It was unmistakable.

Someone was in the house.

Jesus Christ. Ellie sucked in a breath. Her heart was racing. She reached under the pillow and wrapped her fingers around the gun that she usually kept on the coatrack but tonight, just to be sure, had by her side. Ellie carefully switched off the safety and eased the pistol out from under her pillow. She told herself to be calm, but her mouth was completely dry.

She hadn't read it wrong. This was happening tonight!

The creaking sounds came closer. Ellie could feel someone advancing in the dark toward her bedroom. She wrapped her fingers around the gun.

You can do this, a voice said inside. *You knew it was going to happen. Just wait a little longer. C'mon, Ellie.*

She peeked above the covers at the door as a shape slipped through.

Then the sound that sent a tremor down her spine. The click of a gun.

Oh shit. Ellie's heart nearly stopped. *The bastard's going to shoot me.*

Ned . . . now!

The bedroom lights shot on. Ned was standing on the other side of the room with a gun pointed at the intruder. *"Put it down, you sonuvabitch. Now!"*

Ellie bolted upright with her own gun, leveling it, two-handed, at the man's chest.

He stood there, blinded by the sudden light, his gun suspended somewhere between Ellie and Ned.

Moretti.

"Put it down," Ellie said again. "Or if he won't shoot, I will."

Chapter 90

I HAD NO IDEA what was going to happen next. What would Moretti do? We were in some kind of standoff. I'd never shot anyone before. Neither had Ellie.

"One last time," Ellie said, straightening up on her bed. *"Put it down. I will shoot you!"*

"Okay," Moretti said, eyeing both of us. He was acting calm, as though he'd been in this situation before. He slowly lowered the gun to a non-threatening angle, then placed it gently on Ellie's bed.

"We've had the house under surveillance, Ellie. We spotted Kelly coming in. Thought he might be up to something. We were worried. I know what this looks like, but I thought it would be best if I—"

"It doesn't wash, Moretti." Ellie shook her head, climbing out of bed. "I told you, I traced Liz's gun. I know where it came from. A bust *you* were an agent on. What about *this* one? Was it stolen out of the Miami office, too?"

"Jesus," the FBI man said, "you're not actually thinking—"

"I'm totally thinking that, you slimy son of a bitch. *I know!* I know about you and Earl Anson. I know you ran him as a CI. It's too late to bullshit your way out of this. I don't have to go to Boston. Ned's father—he already talked. He told Ned he knew you from your days up in Boston." Moretti swallowed hard. "You had me under surveillance? So, where's your backup, Moretti? Be my guest. Call them in."

Tightness crept onto the FBI agent's face. Then a shrug of resignation.

"Is this how you killed Tess McAuliffe?" Ellie picked up his gun. "Sneaking up on her in the bath, stuffing her head under?"

"I wouldn't know," Moretti said. "I didn't kill Tess McAuliffe. Stratton's man did that."

I tightened my fist on the gun. "But my friends, in Lake Worth . . . You did that, you sonuvabitch."

"Anson did." Moretti shrugged coolly. "Sorry, Neddie-boy, didn't your mother ever tell you what happens when you take something that doesn't belong to you?"

I started to move toward Moretti. Nothing would've made me happier than to break his jaw.

Ellie held me back. "You don't get off that easily, Moretti. There were *two* guns used in Lake Worth. The .32 and a shotgun. One person didn't do that killing."

"Why?" I stared at him, my hand tightening on

the gun. "Why did you have to kill them? We didn't take the art."

"No, you didn't take the art. Stratton did that himself. In fact, he had the art sold before you ever heard of the job."

"Sold?" I looked at Ellie. I was hoping she could make some sense of this.

Moretti smiled. "You had it pegged all the time, didn't you, Ellie? Ned's big score, it was just a cover. How does it feel, your buddies ending up getting killed for a scam?"

Moretti was grinning at me as if he knew the answer to the next question would hurt even more. "A scam for what? Why did you need to come after us—if the art was already sold? Why Dave?"

"You still don't know, do you?" Moretti shook his head.

Tears were burning in my eyes.

"Something else got taken," Moretti said. "Something that wasn't part of the original deal."

Ellie was staring at me now. "The Gaume," she said.

Chapter 91

"CONGRATULATIONS." Moretti clapped. "I knew if we stayed here long enough, somebody would say something smart."

Ellie's eyes drifted from Moretti to me. "The Gaume's barely collectible. Nobody would kill for that."

Moretti shrugged. "I'm afraid it's lawyer time now, Ellie." The FBI man's haughty grin returned. "Nothing I said will be admissible. You'll have to prove it all, if you can, which I doubt. The gun, Anson . . . everything you brought up before is circumstantial. Stratton will protect me. Sorry to ruin the bust, but I'll be drinking margaritas and you'll still be filling out case sheets for your pension."

"How's *this* for circumstantial, Moretti?" I nailed him as hard as I could in the mouth. He almost went down, blood flowing from his lip.

"That's for Mickey and my friends," I said. I

hit Moretti again, and this time he did go down. "That one was for Dave."

It took about five minutes for two police cars responding to the 911 to screech to a halt in front of the house. Four officers rushed in as Ellie explained who it was and what had happened. She was already on the phone to the FBI. Lights were whirling everywhere. The policemen led Moretti down the front steps. Such a sweet moment.

"Hey, Moretti," Ellie called. He turned on the lawn. "Not half bad," she said with a wink, "for an art agent, huh?"

I watched them take him away and I was thinking that the whole thing had to break now. It couldn't hold together. Moretti would talk. He'd have to.

That's when a whole new picture of horror began to unfold for me.

A man with a hand inside his jacket stepped out of a car down the street, walking onto Ellie's lawn.

I saw what was happening. The man just walked past the flashing police cars; his hand came out of his sports jacket. He got close to Moretti, in the arms of the cops.

Two loud shots into the FBI man's chest.

"No!" I screamed, starting to run. Then my voice got softer as I came to a horrified halt. "Pop, *no* . . ."

I had watched my father kill Special Agent in Charge George Moretti.

Part Six

ONE THING PENDING

Chapter 92

FBI SUPERVISOR Hank Cole stared out at the view of the Miami skyline from his office window. Behind it, nothing but gorgeous blue sea. Sure beat the hell out of Detroit, the ADIC reminded himself. Or Fairbanks! He wondered if they even had golf courses in Alaska. Cole knew he had to salvage something out of this mess. And fast. If he wanted to keep that fancy title in front of his name, if he wanted to keep seeing this delicious view every day.

First, his office had spearheaded an all-out, national manhunt for the wrong man. Okay, that happens. Anyone could see how Kelly fit the bill. But then the lead FBI investigator on the case accuses her own boss of trying to kill her in her home *to cover up that he was the trigger man in the whole thing*. Then Moretti gets gunned down as the cops are taking him away.

And by whom? Cole crumpled a piece of paper

tightly in his fist. By the father of the original suspect!

Oh, he was going down! ADIC Cole clenched his teeth. The press was going to have a field day. There'd have to be an internal investigation. The Bureau would tear flesh out of his throat. Cole felt a pain in his chest, thought maybe it was a heart attack. *A heart attack . . . I should be so lucky.*

"Assistant Director Cole?"

Cole turned away from the window and back to the meeting in his office.

Sitting around his conference table were James Harpering, the Bureau's chief local counsel; Mary Rappaport, Palm Beach County DA; and Art Ficke, the new agent in charge.

As well as his own private career torpedoer herself, Special Agent Ellie Shurtleff.

"So, what do we have," Cole tried to ask calmly, "to back up Special Agent Shurtleff's allegations against Moretti?"

"There's the gun trace," Ficke proposed. "And Moretti's prior connection to Earl Anson. Adds up to some good detective work." He nodded to Ellie Shurtleff. "But all about as circumstantial as you can get."

"There's Frank Kelly's testimony," Ellie said.

"The admission of a career felon? With a grudge against the deceased?" Harpering, the lawyer, shrugged. "It could stand up, if we could establish a prior connection between the two."

"We have about forty-eight hours," Cole sniffed, "before someone from Washington takes over. So, giving some credence to Special Agent Shurtleff's claim, how do we stand on Stratton? Can we tie him to Moretti in any way?"

"Contact between Moretti and Stratton would have been understandable," Harpering injected. "He was the agent in charge on his case."

"What about prior to the art being stolen?"

"Moretti was a pro, sir," Ficke said.

"Goddammit." Cole pushed back his chair. "If Moretti was dirty, I want it out. Stratton, too. So, for the sake of this group, Special Agent Shurtleff"—he looked at Ellie—"and your career, would you please tell us again how Special Agent in Charge Moretti happened to end up at your house?"

Chapter 93

ELLIE CLEARED HER THROAT. She was nervous. No, *nervous* didn't even begin to describe how she felt. She told them again about Ned's coming back from his brother's funeral and what his father had said. What Liz Stratton had told them, too. How she and Ned had set up Moretti after she traced the gun.

Crazy as it was, she felt they believed her. Sort of, anyway.

"And just how long have you and this Kelly character been . . . *cooperating* on this case?" ADIC Cole asked.

"Since he turned himself in," Ellie answered, swallowing. She dropped her head. "Maybe a little before."

"*Maybe a little before.*" Cole tightened his jaw and glanced around the table as if for some kind of explanation.

Ellie cleared her throat. "I can bring him down," she said apprehensively. "Stratton."

"You're on such incredibly thin ice already, Special Agent Shurtleff, your knees must be freezing cold." Cole glared at her.

"I can bring him down, sir," she said, more firmly.

Cole narrowed his gaze at her. She checked Harpering and Ficke to see if they were smirking. They weren't.

"All right," the ADIC sighed, "how?"

"He thinks we have something he wants," Ellie said.

"This painting," Cole said, nodding. "The . . . Gaume? What is it about this thing?"

"I don't know yet," Ellie said, "but Stratton doesn't know we don't know, either."

Cole looked at Harpering and Ficke. There was stiff, evaluating silence around the table.

"You're trained as an art investigator, aren't you, Special Agent Shurtleff?" Cole inquired.

"Yes, sir." Ellie nodded. He knew she was.

"So, you would think"—Cole placed his palms together—"knowing that, I'd have to be pretty much suicidal to let you run something like this after what you've done. We screw this up, you could basically sweep whatever's left of my career into the trash."

"Mine, too, sir." Ellie looked him in the eye.

"Right," the ADIC said. He cast a glance to Ficke and Harpering.

"The way things are right now," the lawyer said, "Stratton walks away and we're left with the biggest cleanup mess since the *Exxon Valdez.*"

Cole rubbed his temples hard. "Just for the sake of conversation, Special Agent Shurtleff, what exactly would you need to do this job?"

"I'd need it leaked that Moretti didn't talk. That he didn't say a word about Stratton. And that I've been taken off the case. That I'm under investigation."

"That won't be hard," Cole said.

"And something else," Ellie went on, since she was on such a hot streak.

"What's that?" The ADIC rolled his eyes impatiently.

"This could get a little unorthodox, sir. . . ."

"Oh, and it's been going along so 'by the book' up to this point." Cole couldn't help but smile.

Ellie sucked in a breath. "I'll need Ned Kelly, sir."

Chapter 94

I WAS PLAYING GIN at the house with Sollie.

We were outside, in the covered cabana by the pool. I'd been confined to Sollie's until my role in what happened at Ellie's house was fully resolved.

A little matter of having violated my bail agreement—possession of a firearm.

I knew Ellie was in trouble. I knew what we did could cost her her job. Everything was out now: my dad's involvement, what Ellie had found out about Moretti, our conversations with Liz. *Me*.

With Liz and Moretti dead, we didn't have much to hang on Stratton. He had orchestrated everything perfectly. That made me the angriest of all. That, and my father. Frank thought he was squaring things with the Man, but the irony was that by pulling the trigger, he had let Stratton go free.

"You keep throwing me hearts, I keep taking them," Sol said with an apologetic sigh.

"I guess I'm not much competition today," I said, drawing a card.

"Competition? This is rehabilitation, Ned. I promised the judge. Besides, at this rate I'll have made back your bail by tomorrow afternoon. Then you can get the hell out."

I smiled at the old guy. "I'm worried about Ellie, Sol."

"I can see that, kid, but you know, I think it'll be all right. The girl can handle herself fine."

"She tried to help me, and I got her in trouble. I want to get Stratton, Sollie. I was sure we had him nailed."

"I know you do, kid." Sol laid down his hand. "And my guess is, you'll still get your chance. Let me tell you something about guys like Dennis Stratton. You know what their weakness is? They always think they're the biggest fish in the pond. And trust me, Ned, there's always one a little bigger." He was looking straight at me. "But first, there's something more important you got to do, Ned."

"What's that?" I grinned. *"Deal?"*

"No, I'm talking about your father, kid. . . ."

"My illustrious father is the reason we're in this mess," I said, picking my hand back up. "Without him, we'd have someone to testify against Stratton. Don't think for a second he was acting nobly."

"I think he was doing things the only way he

knew how. The guy's sick, Ned. Jesus, kid, *fours.* . . ."

"Huh?"

"You passed on my four of spades. You're not thinking, Ned."

I looked at my hand and saw the jumbled mess I was playing and realized my mind was a million miles away.

"Take care of your own business, son," Sol said, still talking about my dad. "This Stratton thing, it'll work itself out. But while we're on it," he said, fanning out his cards and catching my eye, "I might be able to help you a bit."

"What are you talking about, Sol?"

"Discard, kid. . . . It's all about the fish. We'll talk later."

I tossed out a ten of diamonds.

"*Rhythm!*" Sollie's eyes lit up, laying down his cards. "This is too easy, kid." He pulled in the score sheet. His third straight gin. "If this is the way it's gonna be, I'm gonna let you go back to jail."

Winnie, Sollie's Filipina housemaid, came out, announcing that we had a visitor.

Ellie followed a few steps behind.

I jumped up out of the chair.

"Your ears must be burning, dear." Sollie Roth smiled. "Look at your boyfriend. He's so worried about you, he can't keep score."

"He's right," I said, and gave her a hug. "So, how'd it go?"

She shrugged, sitting down at the table. "Between getting Moretti killed and hanging out

with you, I'm what you call an Agent's Manual
disaster. The ADIC took the appropriate action.
Until we work this out, I'm on disciplinary review."

"You get to keep your job?" I asked hopefully.

"Maybe." Ellie shrugged. "Pending one
thing . . ."

"What's that?" I swallowed, figuring it was
some sort of drawn-out procedural review.

"Us," she said. "Taking down Dennis Stratton."

I didn't know if I had heard her right. I sat
there, looking at her a bit quizzically. "You said
us?"

"Yeah, Ned," Ellie said, the tiniest of smiles
peeking through. "You and me. That would be
us."

Chapter 95

ELLIE HAD some digging to do first. In the art world, of all places. What the hell was it about this piece? The Gaume.

There were countless ways to do research on a painter, even one she had barely heard of, who had died a hundred years before.

She went online, but she could find hardly a thing on Henri Gaume. The painter had lived a totally unremarkable life. They were no biographies. Then she looked him up in the Benezit, the vast encyclopedia of French painters and sculptors, translating from the French herself. There was virtually nothing. He was born in 1836 in Clamart. He painted for a while, in Montmartre, exhibiting between 1866 and 1870 at the prestigious Salon de Paris. Then he disappeared off the artistic map. The painting that was stolen—Stratton hadn't even put in an in-surance claim on it—was called *Faire le ménage* (Housework). A housemaid gazing into a mirror over a basin. She couldn't find a provenance on it; it wasn't listed.

Ellie called the gallery in France where Stratton claimed he had bought it. The owner could barely remember the piece. He said he thought it came out of an estate. An elderly woman in Provence.

It can't be the painting; Gaume is as ordinary as they come.

Was there something in it? A message? Why did Stratton want it so badly? What could be worth killing people for?

Her head began to ache.

She pushed away the large books on nineteenth-century painters. The answer wasn't there. It was somewhere else.

What was it about this worthless Gaume?

What is it, Ellie?

Then it struck her, not with a wallop but like a little bird lightly scratching away at her brain.

Liz Stratton had told her as Stratton's men took her away. That resignation in her face, as if they would never see her again. *You're the art expert. Why do you think he calls himself Gachet?*

Of course. The key was in the *name.*

Dr. Gachet.

Ellie pushed back from her desk. There had always been rumors, apocryphal, of course. Nothing had ever turned up. Nothing in van Gogh's estate. Or when his brother went to sell his work. Or the artist's patrons, Tanguy or Bonger.

One of the art books on her desk had van Gogh's portrait of the doctor on the cover. Ellie pulled it in front of her and stared at the country doctor—those melancholy blue eyes.

Something like this, she was thinking, *would be worth killing for.*

Suddenly Ellie realized she was talking to the wrong people, looking in the wrong books.

She stared at van Gogh's famous portrait.

She'd been poring over the wrong painter's life.

Chapter 96

"YOU READY?" Ellie made sure, handing me the phone.

I nodded, taking it as though someone were handing me a gun that I was going to use to kill somebody. My mouth was as dry as sand, but that didn't matter. I'd been dreaming of doing this since I first got that call from Dee and an hour later found Tess and my buddies dead.

I sank into one of Sollie's chairs out on the deck. "Yeah, I'm ready. . . ."

I knew Stratton would speak to me. I figured his heart would be pounding as soon as he heard who it was. He was sure I had his painting. He had killed for it, and this was clearly a man who operated on the assumption that his instincts were right. I punched in the number. The phone started to ring. I leaned back and took a deep breath. A Latina housekeeper answered.

"Dennis Stratton, please?"

I told her my name, and she went to find him. I told myself that it was all going to end soon. I'd made promises. To Dave. To Mickey and Bobby and Barney and Dee.

"So, it's the famous Ned Kelly," Stratton said when he finally came on the line. "We get a chance to speak. What can I do for you?"

I'd never talked to him directly. I didn't want to give him a second of phony bullshit. "I have it, Stratton," was all I said.

"You have *what*, Mr. Kelly?"

"I have what you're looking for, Stratton. You were right all along. I have the Gaume."

There was a pause. He was evaluating just how to react. Whether I was telling the truth, or screwing with him. Setting him up.

"Where are you, Mr. Kelly?" Stratton asked.

"Where am I?" I paused. This wasn't what I expected.

"I'm asking where you're calling from, Mr. Kelly. That too difficult for you?"

"I'm close enough," I replied. "All that matters is, I have your painting."

"Close enough, eh? Why don't we put that to the test? You know Chuck and Harold's?"

"Of course," I replied, looking nervously at Ellie. It wasn't supposed to go like this. Chuck & Harold's was a bustling, people-watching watering hole in Palm Beach.

"There's a pay phone. Near the men's room. I'll be calling it in, let's say, four minutes from now. And I mean exactly, Mr. Kelly. Are you that 'close enough'? Make sure you're there to pick it up when it rings. Just you and me."

"I don't know if I can make it," I said, glancing at my watch.

"Then I would *scoot*, Mr. Kelly. That's three minutes and fifty seconds from now, and counting. I wouldn't miss my call if you ever want to discuss this matter again."

I hung up the phone. I looked at Ellie for a split second.

"Go," she said.

I ran through the house and into the front courtyard. I hopped into Ellie's work car. She and the two FBI agents ran behind, climbing into another car. I shoved it into gear and took off through the gate, screeching in a wide arc onto County. I sped the six or seven blocks down to Poinciana as quickly as I could. I took the corner at about forty and screeched to a stop right in front of the place.

I glanced at my watch. *Four minutes on the nose.* I knew the way to the men's room. I used to hang out at the bar.

Just as I got there, the phone started ringing.

"*Stratton!*" I answered.

"I see you are resourceful," he said, as though he were enjoying the hell out of this. "So, Mr. Kelly, just you and me. No reason to have other people listening on the line. You were saying something about a painting by Henri Gaume. Tell me, what do you have in mind?"

Chapter 97

"I WAS THINKING of handing it over to the police," I said. "I'm sure they'd be interested in a look." There was silence on the other end. "Or we could strike a deal."

"I'm afraid I don't deal with suspected murderers, Mr. Kelly."

"That gives us something in common already, Stratton. Usually, neither do I."

"Nice," Stratton chuckled. "Why the sudden change of heart?"

"I don't know. Just sentimental, I guess. I heard somewhere it was your wife's favorite."

This time Stratton didn't make a sound. "I am looking for a piece by Henri Gaume. How do I know that what you claim to have is even the right one?"

"Oh, it's the one. A washerwoman staring into a mirror over a sink. Wearing a simple white apron." I knew anyone could have gotten ahold of the police report. That description wasn't exactly proof. "It was in your bedroom hallway the night you had my friends killed."

"The night they robbed me, Mr. Kelly. Describe the frame."

"It's gold," I said. "Old. With filigree trim."

"Turn it over. Is there anything written on the back?"

"I don't have it in front of me," I said. "Remember, I'm at Chuck and Harold's?"

"Now that wasn't very smart, Mr. Kelly," Stratton said, "for the kind of discussion you have in mind."

"There's writing on it," I said. I knew I was about to reveal something good. *To Liz. Love forever, Dennis.* Very touching, Stratton. What a crock."

"I wasn't asking for your commentary, Mr. Kelly."

"Why not? It comes with the piece. Same price."

"Not a very savvy strategy, Mr. Kelly. To piss off the person you're trying to sell to. Just to hear you out, what sort of price is it that you have in mind?"

"We're talking five million dollars."

"*Five million dollars?* That piece wouldn't sell for more than thirty thousand to Gaume's own mother."

"Five million dollars, Mr. Stratton. Or else I drop it off with the police. If I remember right, that was the sum you and Mickey had originally agreed to."

Stratton went silent. Not the kind that suggested he was thinking. The kind where he wanted to wring my neck. "I'm not sure what it is you're talking about, Mr. Kelly, but you're in luck. I do have a reward out on that piece. But just to be completely sure, there's something *else* on the back. In the right-hand corner of the frame."

I closed my eyes for a second. I tried to remember everything I'd been told about this painting. He was right. There was something else on the frame. I was about to reveal something that made me feel dirty. As if I had betrayed people. People I loved.

"It's a number," I whispered into the phone. *"Four-three-six-one-oh."*

There was a long pause. "Well done, Ned. You deserve that reward for how you've handled everybody. Including the police. I'll be at a charity function tonight, at the Breakers. The Make-A-Wish Foundation. One of Liz's favorite causes. I'll take a suite there under my name. How about if I excuse myself from the party, say, around nine?"

"I'll be there."

I hung up the phone, a dull beat thudding in my chest. When I walked out of the restaurant, a black car was waiting at the curb. Ellie and two FBI agents were looking at me expectantly.

"We're in business," I said. "Nine o'clock tonight."

"We got some work to do before then," one of the agents said.

"Maybe later," I said, "there's something I have to do first."

Chapter 98

A GUARD SEARCHED ME and led me back into the holding cells in the Palm Beach County Jail. "What is it with you Kellys?" he asked, shaking his head. "In the blood?"

My father was lying on a metal cot in a cell, staring off into space.

I stood watching for a while. In the dingy light, I could almost make out the faded facial lines of a younger man. A scene from my childhood flashed: Frank, arriving home with this grand entrance, carrying a big box. Mom was at the sink. JM and Dave and I were sitting around the kitchen table after school, eating snacks. I was maybe nine.

"*Evelyn Kelly . . .*" My father spun Mom around, and said like the game show announcer, "*Come on down!*"

He thrust out the box, and I'll never forget the look on my mother's face as she opened it. Out

came this gorgeous fur coat. Frank draped it on
her and twirled her around like a dancer. My
mother had this flushed, shocked look on her
face, something between elation and disbelief.

My father dipped her back like a ballroom
dancer, winking to us. "Just wait till you see
what's behind door number three!" My father
could charm the gun off a beat cop when he
wanted to.

"Hey, Pop," I said, standing there by his cell.

My father rolled onto his side. "Neddie," he
said, and blinked.

"I didn't know what to bring, so I brought
these. . . ." I showed him a bag filled with Kit Kat
chocolate bars and Luden's wild cherry cough
drops. My mother used to bring them every time
we visited him in prison.

Frank sat up, grinning. "I always told your
mom, I'd put a hacksaw to better use."

"I tried. Those metal detectors make it a
sonuvabitch, though."

He smoothed down his hair. "Ah, these new
times . . ."

I looked at him. He was thin and slightly yellow, but he seemed relaxed, calm.

"You need anything? I could probably get Sollie to fix you up with a lawyer."

"Georgie's got it covered," he said, shaking his
head. "I know you think I messed up again," my
father said, "but I had to do it, Ned. There's a
code, even among shits like me. Moretti broke it.
He killed my flesh and blood. Some things, they
don't go unattended. You understand?"

"You wanted to do something for Dave, it was Dennis Stratton you should've shot. He ordered it done. What you did messed up our best chance to get him."

"So how come I'm feeling like I finally did some good?" My father smiled. "Anyway, I've always been a small-picture guy. I'm glad you're here, though, Ned. There's some things I want to say."

"Me, too," I said, my palms resting on the bars.

Frank reached over and poured himself a glass of water. "I've never been very good at seeing you for who you are, have I, son? I never even gave you what you deserved after you got cleared on that prep school thing. Which was just to say, I'm sorry, Ned, for doubting you. You're a good kid—a good man."

"Listen, Pop. We don't have to go over those things now. . . ."

"Yes, we do," my father said. He struggled to his feet. "After John Michael died, I think I couldn't face up to the truth that it was me that got him killed. Some part of me wanted to say, *See, my boys are the same, the same as me.* It's the Kelly way. When you got that job at Stoughton, the fact was, I was pretty goddamn proud."

I nodded that I understood.

"That day, back home . . . that was the worst day of my life." My father looked in my eyes.

"Burying Dave." I nodded, then exhaled. "Me, too."

"Yeah." His eyes rounded with sadness. "But I

was talking about that day at Fenway. When I let you walk away and take the heat for what I'd done. That's when I think I realized what a mess I'd made of my life. How big a man you were, and how small I'd become. Nah, how much of a punk I'd always been. I was always a two-bitter, Neddie. But *you* aren't."

Frank shuffled, weak-kneed, over to the bars. "This is long overdue, Ned, but I'm sorry, son. I'm sorry for the way I've let everybody down." He clasped his hand over mine. "I know it's not enough to say that. I know it doesn't make anything right. But it's all I have."

I felt tears burning at the back of my eyes. "If Dave's up there watching," I said, trying to laugh, "I bet he's thinking, *Man, I sure could've used that particular bit of wisdom a few days earlier.*"

Frank grunted a laugh, too. "That was always the rap on me—big ideas, shit timing. But I've left things okay. For your mother. And you, too, Ned."

"We're going to get this guy, Pop." I squeezed him back. Now I *was* crying.

"Yeah, son, you get him good." Our eyes met in a wordless, glistening embrace. And Sol was right. I forgave him there. For everything. I didn't even have to say a word.

"I gotta go, Pop." I squeezed his bony fingers. "You may not see me for a while."

"I definitely hope not, son," he chuckled. "Not where I'm going, at least." He let go of my hand.

I took a step back down the cell row. "Hey, Pop," I said, and turned, my voice catching.

Frank was still standing at the bars.

"Tell me something. Mom's fur coat. The one you brought home that day. It was stolen, right?"

He fixed on me a second, the sunken eyes suddenly hardening, like, *How can you ask me something like that?* Then a smile creased his lips. "Course it was stolen, kid."

I backed down the corridor and smiled at my father for the last time.

Chapter 99

THE FBI MAN fitted a wire around me.

"You'll be miked at all times," Ellie said. We were at Sol's, which we'd been using as a sort of base. "Our people will be all around. All you have to do is say the word, Ned, and we'll be all over Dennis Stratton."

There was a whole team of agents now. Moretti's replacement was a thin-lipped guy with slick, dark hair and horn-rimmed glasses who was calling the shots. Special Agent in Charge Ficke.

"Here are the ground rules," Ficke said. "First, you don't make a move without Stratton. No intermediaries. You don't bring up Moretti's name. I don't want him to think there's a chance he divulged anything. Don't forget, Stratton probably never met Anson. He never met your father. Get him talking about the heist if you can. Who set it up? Ask to see the check. The check is enough to get him. Are you up to doing this?"

"I'm up to it, Agent Ficke. How do we handle the painting?"

"Here . . . Check it out."

A female agent brought out a bundled, heavily taped package. "What's in it?" I asked.

"A lot of trouble for you if they get to open it," Ficke replied. "So, ask to see the check before they do. If they give you a hard time, we're coming in to get you."

I looked at Ellie. "You'll be there?"

"Of course I'll be there."

"There'll be backup on every level," Ficke said. "Once you get what we need, or they open the goods, we'll break down the door. You'll be okay."

I'll be okay. I eyed him. Like some expendable private being waved out to test a minefield. *Go ahead, you'll be okay.* One thing everyone in the room knew: Stratton had no intention of letting me leave that hotel room alive.

"I want to talk to Ellie," I said.

"She's not running this show," Ficke said rather sharply. "Any questions, address them to me."

"I don't have any questions. I need to talk with Ellie. And not here. Alone. Outside."

Chapter 100

WE WENT OUT on the pool deck. I saw Ficke watching us through the blinds, so I led her down the steps to the beach, *my office,* as far away from him as possible.

Ellie rolled up her pants and left her shoes on the stairs. Then we walked out onto the sand. The sun was starting to set. It was going on six.

I took Ellie by the hand. "Nice out here, huh? Kind of makes me miss my old lifeguard days. Didn't know how good I had it then."

I held her by the shoulders, and brushed a wisp of hair out of her eyes. "You trust me, Ellie, don't you?"

"You don't think it's a little late to be asking me that question, Ned? I didn't arrest you when I had the chance. We stole a car. Withheld information, kidnapped a material witness . . . In my book, that goes as trust."

I smiled. "You should've gotten out of that car

when I told you to. Things would be a whole lot different."

"Yeah, you'd probably be in jail, or dead. And I'd still have pretty good job security. Anyway, as I recall, I didn't have much choice at the time. You did have a gun."

"And as I recall, the safety was on."

I pulled her close and I could feel her heart beating forcefully against my chest. Neither of us knew what was going to happen tonight. And afterward, the whole world would be different. I had felony charges waiting for me. I'd have to do time. Afterward, I'd be a felon and she'd still be an FBI agent.

"What I'm asking, Ellie, is for you to keep trusting me. Just for a while longer now."

She eased away from me and tried to read what was in my eyes. "You're scaring me, Ned. We can nab him. This whole thing'll be over. Please, just for once, play this one by the book."

I smiled. "You gonna be there for me, Ellie?"

"I told you," she said, looking at me with resolve in her eyes, "I'll be right outside. I wouldn't let you go in there alone."

I know you wouldn't. I pulled her against me again and looked beyond her at the setting sun.

I didn't have the heart to tell her I meant *afterward.*

Chapter 101

JUST TURNING ONTO the long drive leading up to the Breakers took you back to another world.

The twin majestic towers awash in glowing light, probably Palm Beach's best-known sight. The stately loggia of arches welcoming visitors to the lobby, the rows of light-kissed palms. Once, Flaglers and Mellons and Rockefellers went there in lavish private rail cars. Now it was people who were trying to act like them.

Tonight I was going to crash it for a while.

I pulled Ellie's Crown Vic behind a Mercedes SL 500 and a Rolls in the redbrick circle leading to the lobby doors. Couples stepped out in tuxes and fancy gowns, adorned with glittering jewels. I was in a pair of jeans and a green Lacoste shirt, which was hanging out. Even the parking attendant gave me a look as if I didn't belong.

I'd heard about these society galas, even waited

at a couple when I first came down. They were near the center of the Old Guard social life down there. For this and that charity, the invitations read. More like so a few doyennes could show off their jewels and parade around in stylish gowns, eating caviar and sipping champagne. Who knows how much actually made it to the "cause" being celebrated? I remembered hearing somewhere that a woman whose husband died suddenly kept him on ice for weeks until the party season ended.

Here goes nothing, Ned. . . .

I tucked the thick wrapped bundle the feds had given me under my arm and went inside the lobby. Lots of people were milling about, some in formal attire, others in the red jackets of hotel personnel, a few in casual wear. I figured any of them could be Stratton's men watching me. Or FBI.

The FBI was probably freaking out about now, wondering what the hell was going on.

I glanced at my watch—8:40. I was twenty minutes ahead of schedule.

I headed straight to the front desk. An attractive desk clerk named Jennifer greeted me. "I think there's a message for me," I said, "under Stratton."

"Mr. Kelly," she said with a smile, as if expecting me. She came back with a sealed hotel envelope. I showed her ID and ripped open the flap. Written on a hotel notecard were just two words: *Room 601.*

Okay, Ned. Let's get it done. I held my breath for a second and tried to calm my nerves.

I asked Jennifer where the Make-A-Wish dinner was being held, and she pointed toward the Circle Ballroom, down the ornate lobby corridor and to the left.

I tucked the wrapped package, "the Gaume," under my arm and followed two couples in formal dress, who I was sure were headed to the ballroom.

Suddenly a voice scratched in my earpiece. Ficke, and he was pissed. "Goddammit, Kelly, what are you doing? You're twenty minutes ahead of the plan."

"Sorry, Ficke. *Plan's changed.*"

Chapter 102

I PICKED UP MY PACE until I could see the Circle Ballroom up a set of stairs beyond the lobby bar.

There was a small crowd gathered at the door, people in tuxedos and evening gowns giving their names and presenting their invitations. Not exactly airline security. The kind of band music you swear you'll never dance to was coming out of the ballroom. I just sort of melted in behind.

A white-haired woman looked at me as if I were SpongeBob SquarePants. The diamond pendants in her ears were about as large as Christmas ornaments. I squeezed past her, and then I was inside. "Sir!" I heard, but I ignored it.

You better make this work, Neddie.

The room was actually breathtaking, filled with fresh flowers, and this incredible chandelier hung from the coffered ceiling. The band was playing "Bad, Bad Leroy Brown," done cha-cha style. Every woman I passed was dripping in diamonds—necklaces, rings, tiaras. The men wore crisply pressed tuxedos, with white kerchiefs folded perfectly. One man was in a kilt.

I started looking feverishly for Stratton. I knew I looked about as out of place as a Maori tribesman at the queen's tea party.

Suddenly someone lifted me by the arm from behind, edging me away from the crowd. "Deliveries are in the back, Mr. Kelly," the person spat into my ear.

I spun around. It was Champ, grinning. "Had you going for a second, didn't I, mate!"

He was dressed like the perfect waiter, holding a silver tray of caviar blinis. Except for the orange hair, he fit right in.

"Where's Stratton?" I asked him.

"In the rear—where else would the asshole be?" Champ nudged me. "He's the one wearing the tux. . . . Relax, mate"—he put up his palm apologetically—"just trying to ease the mood."

I caught a glimpse of Stratton through the crowd. Then I checked around for his goons.

"Ned," Champ said, putting down his tray and squeezing my shoulder, "this is gonna work. Course, I say that before every jump and I've got a couple of permanently rearranged vertebrae that might tend to disagree." He gave me a wink and knocked his fist against mine. "Anyway, no worries, mate. . . . Friends are in the house. I've got your rear."

"Ned!" A voice crackled in my earpiece. *Ellie.* "Ned, what're you doing? *Please . . .*"

"Sorry, Ellie," I said, knowing she must be panicking now. "Just keep tuned in. *Please.* You're gonna get your man."

In the crowd, I spotted faces I recognized. Henry Kissinger. Sollie Roth, chatting with a couple of prominent business types. Lawson.

Then I spotted Stratton in back. He was holding a champagne glass and chatting up some blonde in a low-cut gown. A few people around him were laughing. The joke was, Liz was barely in the ground and now he was the most celebrated bachelor in Palm Beach.

I sucked it up and started toward him.

As Stratton caught me approaching, his eyes grew wide. There was a sudden moment of surprise, then his composure returned, a nasty little smirk appearing on his face. Stratton's friends looked at me as if I were delivering the mail.

"You're a little early, Mr. Kelly. Weren't we supposed to meet up in the room?"

"I'm right on time, Stratton. Plan's changed. It occurred to me, why waste this wonderful event? I thought you and your friends might be interested to hear us conduct our business right here."

Chapter 103

UPSTAIRS IN ONE of the hotel suites, Ellie was panicking. She kept shouting into the microphone, "Ned, what're you doing?" but Ned wasn't answering.

"Abort," Ficke was saying. "We're calling this fiasco off."

"We can't do that," Ellie said. She pulled herself up from her listening post. "Ned's in the ballroom. He's meeting with Stratton. He's going through with it, *now*."

"If we go down there, Special Agent Shurtleff," Ficke said, glaring at her, "you can be damn sure it'll be to pick him up, not help him. Show's over." He ripped off his headset. "I'm not getting the Bureau dragged down over this cowboy." He nodded to the ops man. "Cut it off."

"No," Ellie said, shaking her head. "Give me two guys. We can't just walk away from him. We promised. He'll still need backup. He's going through with it. He's meeting with Stratton."

"Then by all means stay and listen, Special Agent Shurtleff," the agent in charge said at the door. "Tape's rolling."

Ellie couldn't believe it. He was just folding it all up. Ned was down there. With no backup.

"He said he was going to bring us Stratton, and he's doing it," Ellie said. "We promised. We can't just walk away from him. We're going to get him killed."

"You can take Downing," Ficke said. "And pick up Finch in the lobby." He looked at her sort of indifferently. "He's your asset, Special Agent Shurtleff. He's your problem."

Chapter 104

"DO OUR BUSINESS *HERE?*" Stratton said with that smug, unflappable smile of his, even though I knew he must be wondering what the hell was going on.

I met his smile with one of my own. "You killed my brother, Stratton. You didn't think I was going to let you off without a little pain?"

A few heads turned. Stratton glanced around, clearly off guard.

"I have no idea what you're talking about, Mr. Kelly, but for a man who's currently under arrest and facing federal charges, I don't see how you're in any position to be hurling accusations at me."

"He killed Liz, too," I said, loud enough so that anyone nearby turned to hear. "And covered it up in that ridiculous affair because she was about to turn him in. He stole his own art and resold it, then had those people killed in Lake Worth to make it seem like a theft gone bad. But he's been searching for something. Something that wasn't supposed to be taken. Right, Mr. Stratton?"

I held out the wrapped shipping box.

Stratton's eyes widened. "Oh, Mr. Kelly, whatever in the world do you have there?"

I had him. I had him nailed. I could see that always-in-control veneer begin to crack and sweat form on his brow.

I spotted Lawson edging closer through the crowd. And worse, Stratton's henchman, Ponytail.

"Too bad, then, that Moretti was killed by your own father," Stratton said. "Why not tell everybody that? I think it's *you* who's doing the covering up. *You're the one out on bail.* You don't have the slightest proof."

"The proof . . ." I looked at him and smiled. "The proof's in the painting." I held out the package. "The one you asked me to bring here tonight, Mr. Stratton. The Gaume."

Stratton eyed the bundle, wetting his lips, a damp, nervous sheen bubbling up on his brow.

Hushed whispers trickled through the gathering crowd. People were crowding closer, trying to hear what was going on.

"This . . . this is absurd," he started to stammer, searching for a friendly face. People were waiting for an answer. I was almost gleeful.

Then he turned back to me, but instead of unraveling, his face began to regain its accustomed control. "This pathetic act might actually work," he said, his eyes lighting up, "if you actually *had* that painting in the box. Right, Mr. Kelly?"

The ballroom was suddenly silent. I felt as if every eye had turned to me. *Stratton knew.* He knew I didn't have the goods. *How?*

"Go on, open it. Show the world your evidence. Somehow, I don't think this is going to play very well when it comes to your sentencing."

How did he know? In that instant I flashed through the possibilities. Ellie . . . no way! Lawson . . . he wasn't in the loop. Stratton had another mole. He had someone else in the FBI.

"I warned you, Mr. Kelly, didn't I," Stratton said, smiling icily, "not to waste my time?"

Ponytail grabbed hold of my arm. I noticed Champ pushing through the crowd, wondering what he could do.

I glared back at Stratton. All I could do was spit out one helpless question: "*How?*"

"Because *I* told him, Ned," said a voice in the crowd.

I recognized it instantly. And my heart began to sink. Everything I trusted, every certainty, fell away from me.

"Ned Kelly," Stratton said, grinning. "I believe you know Sol Roth."

Chapter 105

"SORRY, NEDDIE-BOY," Sol said, and slowly stepped out of the crowd.

It was as if I had been slapped in the face. I know I turned white, stunned, taken totally by surprise. Sol was my secret weapon, my ace in the hole tonight.

All I could do was stare at the old man, dumbfounded, dazed—a massive weight crashing floor by floor through the planks of my heart. I'd seen my brother killed. My best friends brutally murdered. But until that moment I didn't really know what I was fighting. The rich banding with the rich. It was a club. I was on the outside. I felt my eyes sting with tears.

"You were right," Sol sighed guiltily, "I brokered a private sale between Dennis and a very patient Middle Eastern collector. He has the art safely in a vault where it will sit quietly for twenty years. Quite lucrative, if I may say so my-self. . . ."

I couldn't believe what I was hearing. Every word out of his mouth was like a lance jabbed deeper. *I hope you appreciate it, Sol. And that you spend it well. That money bought the deaths of my brother and best friends.*

Stratton nodded to Ponytail. I felt a blunt object jab me in the ribs. A gun.

"But what I never counted on, you greedy son of a bitch"—Sol's tone suddenly changed and he turned toward Stratton—"was that all those people were going to die."

Stratton blinked, the smirk on his lips gone.

"Or that you were capable of killing Liz, whose family I've known for forty years, you sick, conspiring fuck."

Stratton's jaw tightened, uncomprehending.

"We sat by while you sucked the life out of her, you monster. We watched you, so all of us bear some blame. If I'm ashamed of anything in this godforsaken mess, it's that. Liz was a good woman."

Sollie reached inside his jacket pocket. He came out holding a Baggie. In it there was some kind of key. A hotel key. The Brazilian Court. Just as we had planned. Tess's key. He turned to Pony-tail, who still had a gun stuck in my ribs. "You left this in your pocket, big fella. Next time, you oughta be more careful who goes through the wash."

Stratton stared, mesmerized by the key, his face turning a shade of gray. Every person in the Cir-

cle Ballroom could see comprehension forming
on his face.

Liz.

Liz had found Tess's key. She had screwed him
from the grave.

I don't know which was better, watching Stratton start to come apart in front of his society
friends or thinking how Dave and Mickey would
have loved how we set him up. Sol shot me a
wink, like, *How's that, Ned?* But all I was thinking was *Jesus, Dave, I hope you're watching. I
hope you're eating this up.*

Then Sollie turned around. Not to me, but to
Lawson. "I think you have the evidence you
need. . . ."

The detective stepped forward and took Stratton by the arm. No one in the room was more
shocked than I was. Ellie and I were sure he was
Stratton's man.

"Dennis Stratton, you're under arrest for the
murders of Tess McAuliffe and Liz Stratton."

Stratton stood there, lips quivering at Sollie,
totally aghast.

Then everything started to come apart. Ponytail took the gun off my ribs and, grabbing me as
cover, thrust it toward the Palm Beach cop.
Champ dove out of the crowd and barreled into
him, sending the punk reeling across the room.
They wrestled for a second, Geoff rolling him
onto his back.

"Hate to do this to you, mate, but you owe me
a chrome side grille for my Ducati." Champ

head-butted Ponytail in the forehead. With a loud crack, the thug's head went back.

That was when his gun went off.

At first there were screams, people pushing frantically toward the entrance. *"Someone's shooting!"*

I looked at Stratton, Lawson, Sollie. . . . As a last resort, my eyes drifted to Champ. He hung there, straddled over Ponytail. A disbelieving smile slowly crept onto his lips. At first I thought he was saying, *See, I told you I had your back, mate.* But then I could see it was more like shock. Blood began to seep through his white shirt.

"Geoff!" I yelled. He had started to reel. I lunged and caught him, bringing him gently down to the floor.

"Shit, Neddie," he said, looking at me, "bastard owes me a whole new bike for this one."

Another crack rang out, and then mayhem. Stratton's other bodyguard was shooting. I saw Lawson go down. Everyone else hit the floor.

A slug ripped into the bodyguard's chest and he fell back through a window, dragging embroidered curtains off giant rods and onto the floor. Then I caught sight of Stratton, free of Lawson's grasp. He was backing away, slinking toward the kitchen door.

I was shouting into the mike for Ellie. *"Champ's down. He's hit!"* But she wasn't answering. I had changed the plan on everyone. Now what?

"Jesus, mate, go," Champ said. He wet his lips.

"For God's sake, I've got everything under control down here."

"You hold on." I squeezed his hand. "Cops'll be here soon. Pretend you're waiting for a goddamn beer."

"Yeah, I could use one of those about now."

I reached for Ponytail's gun. Then I headed after the man who had ordered my brother killed.

Chapter 106

THE SHOOTING WAS OVER when Ellie and the two other FBI agents got down to the ballroom. Shell-shocked people in tuxes and gowns were milling about outside. Seeing the FBI jackets, everyone pointed inside. "There's been a shooting. Someone's been hit."

Ellie ran into the ballroom, gun drawn. Hotel security personnel were already on the scene. The room was mostly cleared of people. Chairs and tables were overturned, flowers on the floor.

This was bad.

She saw Lawson propped against a wall, a red stain on his shoulder. Carl Breen was kneeling next to him, shouting into a radio. Three other bodies were down. Two looked like Stratton's men. One was wrapped in a curtain, and looked dead. The other was Ponytail, the pig who had chased Ned. He was out cold and wasn't going anywhere.

The third Ellie recognized by his orange hair.
Champ!

"My God," Ellie said, and rushed over. Geoff
was lying on his back, with a knee raised. His left
side was matted with blood; his face was white,
his eyes a little glassy.

"Oh, Jesus, Champ . . ." Ellie knelt down.

A security man was barking into a radio, calling for EMS. Ellie leaned over and looked Geoff
in the eye. "Hang on. You're gonna be all right."
She put her hand on the side of his face. It was
sweaty and cold. She felt her eyes glisten with
tears.

"I know, there's gonna be hell to pay," Geoff
said, managing a smile, "me impersonating a
waiter and all."

Ellie smiled back. She gently squeezed his
hand. Then she looked around the ballroom.

"He went after him, Ellie," Geoff whispered.
He shifted his eyes in the direction of the kitchen.
"Ned took Ponytail's gun."

"Oh, shit," Ellie said.

"He had to, Ellie." The Kiwi wet his lips.

"That's not what I meant," Ellie said. She
checked her weapon, then squeezed Champ's
hand one more time. "I've seen Ned with a gun."

Chapter 107

I BOLTED THROUGH the ballroom's kitchen doors. The frightened kitchen staff, hearing gunshots outside, were just about hugging the walls, staring at me, unsure who was chasing whom.

I looked at a black guy in a chef's hat. "A man went through here in a tuxedo. Which way did he go?"

"There's a door in back," the chef finally said, pointing. "It leads into the lobby. And upstairs. The main hotel."

Room 601, I remembered.

I found the stairs and started up. It was worth a chance. Two teenagers appeared, coming down.

"You see a man in a tuxedo, running?" I asked.

They both pointed up the stairs. "Guy has a fricking gun!"

Six flights up, I pushed open a heavy door and came out in a red plush-carpeted hallway. I listened for Stratton's footsteps. *Nothing.* Room

601 was to the left, toward the elevators. I headed in that direction.

I turned the corner and saw Stratton myself. He was down at the end of the hall, struggling to jam a plastic key into a door. I didn't know what was inside. Maybe more help.

"*Stratton!*" I yelled, pointing the gun at him. He turned and faced me.

One thing almost made me smile, his cool, always-in-control demeanor twisted into a frantic glare. Stratton's arm jerked upward and he fired his gun. Flashes careened off the wall near my head. I pointed my gun but didn't fire. As much as I hated him, I didn't want to kill him.

But Stratton saw my gun—and he ran down another corridor.

I went after him.

Like cornered prey, Stratton started trying doors around the elevator landing. They were locked. There was a balcony there, but it led nowhere but outside.

Then a door finally opened—and he disappeared.

Chapter 108

THE STRANGEST THOUGHT flashed through my mind as, gun in hand, I made my way up a darkened concrete staircase, following Dennis Stratton.

Years ago. Back in Brockton. I was wrestling with Dave.

I think I was fifteen; he must've been ten. He and one of his goofy buddies had been making idiotic chimp noises while I was trying to make out with this girl, Roxanne Petrocelli, in Buckley Park, just down from our house. I chased him down by the jungle gyms, and had him pretty good, maybe the last time I could ever take Dave. I had his arms and neck pinned back in a kind of full nelson. I kept saying, "Uncle? Uncle?" hoping he'd give up. But the tough guy wouldn't budge. I kept pushing harder, watching him grow redder in the face. I thought if I pushed any more, I would kill him. Finally Dave cried out, "Okay, Uncle," and I let him go.

For a second he just sat there, breathing heavily, the color coming back to his cheeks; then he charged at me with all his might and knocked me on my back. As he rolled on top of me, Dave was smirking. "Uncle Al thinks you're a dumb sonuvabitch."

I don't know why that popped into my head as I climbed after Stratton. But it did. One of those weird connections in the brain when you feel in danger.

The stairs rose right up into one of the Breakers' enormous towers. The stairwell was dark, but outside, huge floods sent chasms of brilliant light shooting into the night. I didn't see Stratton anywhere—but I knew he was up there.

I kept hearing, like a distant drumming in my head, *Uncle Al thinks you're a dumb sonuvabitch.*

I pushed open a metal door and came out onto the concrete floor of the hotel roof. The scene was almost surreal. Palm Beach laid out all around. The lights of the Biltmore, the Flagler Bridge, apartment buildings over in West Palm. Huge floods, arranged like howitzers, channeled massive beams of blinding light at the towers and the hotel's facade.

I looked around for Stratton. Where the hell was he? Tarps and storage sheds and TV dishes, all in shadow. I felt a chill shoot through me, as though I were exposed.

Suddenly a gunshot rang out, a bullet ricocheting off the wall just over my head. It had missed me by inches.

"So what is it, Mr. Kelly? Have you come for revenge? Is it sweet?"

Another shot cracked into the tower wall. I squinted into the beams of light. I couldn't find him anywhere.

"You should've done what you promised. We'd both be in a better spot. But it's that thing about your brother, isn't it? That's what you Kellys seem to have in spades. Your stupid pride."

I crouched low and tried to find him. Another shot rang out, clipping the tarp above my head.

"Getting closer to the end," Stratton cackled, almost laughing. "Seems we did have one thing in common, though, right, Ned? Funny how our conversation just never got around to her."

My blood started to boil. *Tess.*

"She was one sweet piece of ass. Now, those friends of yours and your brother—that was just business. *But Tess* . . . That one I regret. You, too, I bet. Ahhh, she was just another whore."

If he was trying to get me mad, it was working. I jumped out from behind the cover and fired two angry rounds in the direction of Stratton's voice. A floodlight shattered.

A shot rang back. I felt a searing pain lance my shoulder. My hand shot to the wound. The gun slid out of my hand.

"Oh, jeez, Ned"—Stratton showed himself from behind a light trestle—"careful there, buddy."

I stared at the bastard. He had that supercilious

grin I'd grown to detest, along with his shiny bald brow.

And that was when I heard it. The faintest *thwak-thwak-thwak* beating in the distance. Coming closer, getting louder.

Then off in the sky, a set of flashing lights was approaching, pretty fast. A chopper.

"Wrong again, Mr. Kelly." Stratton smiled. "Here comes my ride."

Chapter 109

ELLIE CLIMBED the stairwell leading from the kitchen doors.

She ran into a waiter hurrying down, babbling about this guy who was chasing some lunatic, headed up to the sixth floor. *Ned.* Ellie told him to grab the first cops or FBI agents he could find and send them after her. Exiting on six, she encountered a freaked-out concierge, shouting into a phone for security. She said that two men with guns were up on the roof!

Ellie checked her weapon one more time and stepped into the stairwell tower.

What the hell are you doing, Ned?

Ellie brushed beads of sweat off her cheek. She heard voices on the roof. She clutched her Glock with both hands.

Ellie quickly made her way to the top of the stairs. She looked out. Floodlights illuminated the tower ceiling. The lights of Palm Beach stretched

out below. She leaned against the heavy door.
Now what? She knew Stratton and Ned were
outside. *Stay calm, Ellie,* she exhorted herself. It's
like training. You stay out of the line of fire. You
size up the situation. You wait for backup.

*Except in training, you didn't have some guy
you probably loved screwing up the situation.*

She told herself she knew how to do this. She
twisted the handle on the door and took a deep
breath.

Then she heard two sharp bangs echoing on
the rooftop. That changed everything.

Shots were being fired.

Chapter 110

I HAD SCREWED UP things like the complete amateur I was. The thought that Stratton would get away after murdering Mickey, Dave, his own wife, was killing me more than anything else.

"Don't be so glum, Ned," Stratton said expansively. "We're both going on a trip. Unfortunately, yours will be a little shorter."

He shot a glance at the chopper's progress and motioned me along the roof with a wave of his gun. I didn't want to give in to him, to give him the satisfaction of seeing me afraid—but I knew my only chance was to go along. The FBI *was* in the building. Someone had to be up there soon. Just wait him out somehow.

There was a narrow stone ledge in front of me, all that separated us from a six-story drop.

"Come on, Mr. Kelly," Stratton said with derision in his voice. "Time to take your big bow. This is how you'll be remembered."

The wind kicked up and now I was starting to get really scared. Stratton's helicopter was executing a narrowing circle, angling in toward the roof. The lights of Palm Beach stretched out before me.

Stratton stood five feet behind me. His gun was pointed at my back. "How does it feel, Ned—knowing you'll be dead while I'll be sipping mai-tais in Costa Rica, reading over that fancy nonextradition treaty? Almost doesn't seem fair, does it?"

"Go to hell, Stratton."

I heard the chilling click of his gun.

I clenched my fists. *No way. No way you're going over for him.* If he wanted to kill me, he'd have to pull the trigger. If he could.

"Come on, Neddie-boy, be a man." Stratton moved in closer. The deafening *thwak-thwak* of the chopper echoed against the hotel walls. I heard Stratton's voice, mocking me: "If it makes you feel any better, Ned, with the kind of clout I have, I would've beaten it in court, anyway."

He took a step closer. *Don't make it easy on him, Ned.*

Now!

I clenched my fists and was about to spin, when I heard a voice shouted above the copter's roar.

Ellie's voice.

"Stratton!"

Chapter 111

WE BOTH TURNED. Ellie was about twenty feet away, partly hidden by the glare of lights on the roof. She had her arms extended in a firing stance.

"You're going to put the gun *down*, Stratton. *Now*. Then I want you to move away from Ned. Otherwise, I'll put a bullet in your head. So help me God."

Stratton paused. He still had the gun pointed at me. A stream of sweat started to trickle down my temples.

Man, I stood perfectly still. I *knew* he wanted to kill me. All he had to do was nudge me and I'd go over the edge.

He glanced sideways at the copter. It was hovering about thirty feet above. A side door opened and someone threw down a rope ladder.

"I don't think so," he shouted to Ellie. He grabbed me by the back of the collar and jammed the gun against my head. "I don't think you want your boyfriend to take a bad spill. Anyway, Ellie, you're an art investigator. I doubt you could put a bullet in *The Last Supper* if they stretched it out on the side of a barn."

"I said *put the gun down, Stratton.*"

"I'm afraid I'm the one giving the orders," Stratton said, shaking his head. "And what we're going to do now is make our way over to that ladder. You're going to let us, because it's the only chance you have of keeping him alive. And while all this is happening, I want *you* to be very careful, Ellie, *very careful,* that no one in the copter up there takes a shot at you."

"Ellie, get back!" I shouted.

"He's not going anywhere," Ellie said. "The second you move a foot away from him—for any reason—I'm going to blow his head off. And, Stratton, just so you know—MFA and all—I could put a bullet through a disciple's *eye* on *The Last Supper* from this distance."

For the first time I felt Stratton become nervous. He glanced around, evaluating how he was going to pull this off.

"This way, Ned," he barked in my ear, the gun pressed into my skull, "and don't do anything foolish. Your best chance is to let me get to that rope."

We took two steps back, skirting along the ledge. The chopper was veering in closer, the roar deafening, dangling the ladder about ten feet above our heads.

I was looking at Ellie, trying to read in her eyes

what she wanted me to do. I could try to barrel into him. Give Ellie some firing room. But we were really close to the ledge.

Stratton had his gaze fixed on the swaying ladder. It was only a few feet out of his grasp.

"Ellie," I said, looking at her, thinking, *God, I hope you get what I'm doing now.*

I edged a step to the left, and Stratton had to move, too. Suddenly he was in the beam of one of the powerful floods. He grabbed for the ladder, now only inches away.

"Ellie, *now!*"

I pushed him, and Stratton spun, gun extended, blinded by the full glare of the floodlight. He screamed, "Aagh . . . !"

Ellie fired! An orange spark in the night. A *thud* in Stratton's chest. *Ya!* Stratton staggered back, the impact jerking him close to the ledge. He teetered for a second, looking down. Then somehow he caught himself and reached. The ladder seemed to find him, his fingers desperately wrapping around the lowest rung.

The chopper lifted away.

Stratton swayed there for a second. Then miraculously, he began to hold on. There was a smirking grin on his face, like, *See, Ned, I told you, didn't I?* He raised his free arm. I was so mesmerized by what had happened, I almost didn't see what was happening.

He was leveling his gun at me. The bastard was going to kill me after all.

A shot rang out. Stratton's white tuxedo shirt exploded into bright red. His gun fell away. Then his fingers slipped, grasping frantically for rope, clutching only darkness.

Stratton fell. His garbled, frantic scream faded into the night. I hate to admit it, but I liked that scream a lot.

I ran to the ledge. Stratton had come to rest on his back in the parking circle at the hotel's front entrance. A crowd of people in tuxedos and hotel uniforms rushed over to him.

I looked back at Ellie. I couldn't tell if she was all right. She was sort of frozen there, her arms extended. "Ellie, you okay?"

She nodded blankly. "I never killed anyone before."

I wrapped my good arm around her and felt her gently sink into my chest. For a second we just stayed motionless on the Breakers' roof. We didn't say a word. We just swayed there, like, oh, I don't know like what, like nothing most people ever get to experience, I guess.

"You changed the deal on me, Ned. You son of a bitch."

"I know." I held her close. "I'm sorry."

"I love you," she said.

"I love you, too," I replied.

We sort of rocked there for another second in the suddenly quiet night. Then Ellie said softly, "You're going to jail, Ned. A deal's a deal."

I wiped a tear off her cheek. "I know."

Part Seven

MEET DOCTOR GACHET

Chapter 112

EIGHTEEN MONTHS LATER . . .

The gate of the federal detention center up in Coleman buzzed open, and I walked out into the Florida sun a free man.

All I carried with me was my BUM Equipment bag containing my things, and a computer case slung over one shoulder. I stepped out into the courtyard in front of the prison and shielded my eyes. And just like in the movies, I wasn't exactly sure what I was going to do next.

I'd spent the past sixteen months in Coleman's minimum-security block (six months reduced for good behavior) among the tax cheats, financial scammers, and rich-boy drug offenders of the world. Along the way, I had managed to get most of the way to a master's degree from the University of South Florida in social education. Turns out I had this talent. I could speak to a bunch of juvies and social misfits about to make the same choices I had, and they actually listened to me. I guess that's what losing your best friends and your brother and sixteen months in federal prison give you. Life lessons. Anyway, what the hell was I going to do with myself? Go back to being a life-guard?

I scanned the faces of a few waiting people. Right now, there was only one question I wanted answered.

Was she there?

Ellie had visited regularly when I started serv-ing my term. Almost every Sunday she'd drive up, with books and DVDs and cute notes, marking off the weeks. Coleman was only a couple of hours' drive from Delray. We made this date: Sep-tember 19, 2005. The day I'd be getting out. *Today.*

She always joked she'd come pick me up in a minivan, like the day we met. It didn't matter that I was going to have this record and she was still working for the FBI. It would distinguish her, Ellie said with a laugh. Make her stand apart from the organizational clutter. She'd be the only agent dating a guy she had put away.

You can count on it, Ellie said.

Then the Bureau actually offered her this pro-motion. They transferred her back to New York. Head of the International Art Theft office there. A big move up. A lot of overseas travel. The vis-its started going from every week to every month. Then last spring, they sort of came to a stop.

Oh, we e-mailed each other a few times a week and talked on the phone. She told me that she was still rooting for me and that she was proud of what I was doing. She always knew I'd make something of myself. But I could detect a shift in her voice. Ellie was smart and a winner and had even been on the morning news shows after the case. As September grew close, I got this e-mail that she might have to be out of the country. I didn't want to push it. Dreams change. That's what prison does. As the days wound down I decided, if she was there, well, that's where I would pick up from. I'd be the happiest guy in south Florida. If not . . . well, we were both different people now.

There was a taxi and a couple of cars parked in the waiting area in front of the prison. A young Latino family stepped forward excitedly for someone else.

No Ellie. I didn't see a minivan anywhere.

But there was something parked just outside the fence at the end of the long drive that did cause me to smile.

A familiar light green Caddie. One of Sollie's cars.

And leaning on the hood was a guy with his legs extended and crossed, wearing jeans and a navy blazer.

Orange hair.

"I know it's not exactly what you were hoping for, mate," Champ said, smiling contritely, "but you look like a guy who could use a ride home."

I stood there looking at him on the hot steaming pavement, and my eyes started to well. I hadn't seen Champ since I'd gone inside. He'd spent six weeks in the hospital. A punctured spleen and lung, only one kidney. The bullet had ricocheted off his spine. Ellie had told me he'd never race again.

I picked up my bags and walked over. I asked, "So, just *where's home?*"

"The Kiwis have a phrase: home's where the women snore and the beer's free. Tonight, we're talking my couch."

We threw our arms around each other, gave each other a long embrace. "You look good, Champ. I always said you cleaned up well."

"I'm working for Mr. Roth now. He bought this Kawasaki distributorship on Okeechobee. . . ." He handed me a business card. GEOFF HUNTER. FORMER WSB WORLD CHAMPION. SALES ASSOCIATE. "If you can't race 'em, you might as well sell the damn things."

Geoff took the bag from me. "What do you say we boogie, mate? This old bus here gives me the willies. Never did feel safe driving anything with a roof and four wheels."

I climbed in the front passenger seat as Geoff tossed my bags in the trunk. Then he eased his still-stiff body behind the wheel. "Let's see," he said, fiddling around with the ignition key, "I have a vague recollection how this is done. . . ."

He revved the engine hard and pulled away from the curb with a start. I turned and found myself looking through the rear window one last time, hoping for something that I knew wasn't meant to be. The towers of the Coleman Detention Center receded, and with them, part of my own hopes and dreams.

Champ hit the gas and the twenty-year-old Caddie revved into some new gear that had probably lain dormant for a long time. He looked over and winked, impressed. "Whadya say we hit the turnpike, mate? Let's check out what this old bird can really do."

Chapter 113

SOLLIE SENT FOR ME the next morning.

When I got to the house he was watching CNN in the sunroom off the pool. He looked a little older, a little paler, if that was possible, but his eyes lit up brightly when he saw me come in. "Neddie . . . It's good to see you, boy."

Though he never visited me in Coleman, Sollie had been watching out for me. He set me up with the dean of graduate programs at South Florida, sent me books and the computer, and assured the parole board I'd have a job with him, if I wanted it, upon my release. He also sent me a nice note of condolence when he heard my dad had died.

"You're lookin' good, kid." He shook my hand and patted me on the back. "These institutions must be like Ritz Carltons now."

"Tennis, mah-jongg, canasta . . . ," I said. I tapped my behind. "Skid burns from the water-slide," I said with a smile.

"You still play gin?"

"Only for Cokes and commissary vouchers lately."

"That's okay." He took my arm. "We'll start a new tab. C'mon, walk me out to the deck."

We went outside. Sol was in a white button-down shirt tucked neatly into light blue golf pants. We sat at one of the card tables around the pool. He took out a deck and started to shuffle. "I was sorry to hear about your dad, Ned. I was glad you got to see him that time before he died."

"Thanks, Sol," I said. "It was good advice."

"I always gave you good advice, kid." He cut the deck. "And you always followed it. Except for that little escapade up on the roof of the Breakers. But I guess everything worked out fine. Everyone got what they wanted in the end."

"And what was it you wanted, Sol?" I looked at him.

"Justice, kid, just like you." He slowly dealt out the cards.

I didn't pick them up. I just sat there, staring at him. Then I put my hand on his as he went to turn over the play card. "I want you to know, Sol, I never told anyone. Not even Ellie."

Sollie stopped. He tapped his cards and pressed them, facedown. "You mean about the Gaume? How I knew all that stuff was written on the back? That's good, Ned. I guess that sorta makes us even, right?"

"No, Sol," I said, looking at him closely, "not even at all." I was thinking about Dave. And Mickey and Barney and Bobby and Dee. Murdered for something they never had. "*You're* Gachet, aren't you? *You* stole the Gaume?"

Sol stared at me with those hooded gray eyes, then he hunched his shoulders like a guilty child. "I guess I owe you some answers, don't I, son?"

For the first time I realized I had totally underestimated Sollie. That comment he made once, about Stratton believing he was the biggest fish in the pond but there always being someone bigger.

I was staring at him now.

"I'm going to show you something once, Ned," Sol said, putting down the cards, "and for your silence ever after I'm going to pay you a lot of money. Every penny you thought you were going to make that day when you went to meet your friends."

I tried to remain calm.

"That's a million dollars, Ned, if I remember right. And while we're at it, how about another for your friends, and another for Dave. That's three million, Ned. I can't repay you for what happened to them. I can't bring back what's been done. I'm an old man. Money's all I have, these days. . . . Well, not entirely . . ."

There was a sparkle in Sol's eyes. He got up from the card table. "Come on."

I got up and Sol led me to a part of the house I'd never been in before. To an office off his bedroom wing. He opened a plain wooden door I never would've figured was more than a closet. But it faced another door. A keypad on the wall.

With his skinny fingers, Sol punched in a code.

Suddenly the second door slid open. It was an elevator. Sol motioned me in. Then he punched in another code. The elevator closed and we began to go *down*.

A few seconds later the elevator stopped and the door opened automatically. There was a small outer room with mirrored walls and another door, solid steel. Sol pushed a button and a metal shield slid back, revealing a small screen. He placed his palm onto the screen. There was a little flash, then a green light, and the steel door buzzed.

Sol held my arm. "Hold your breath, Neddie. You're about to see one of the last great wonders of the world."

Chapter 114

WE STEPPED INTO a large, beautifully lit room. Plush carpet, gorgeous molding on the ceiling surrounding a recessed dome. The only furniture was four high-back leather chairs in the center, each chair facing a wall.

I couldn't believe my eyes.

There were paintings on the walls. Eight of them. *Masterpieces*.

I was no expert, but I could tell the artists without having to look in a book. Rembrandt. Monet.

A Nativity scene. *Michelangelo*.

Images indelibly imprinted in my brain. All priceless.

One of the last great wonders of the world!

"Jesus, Sol," I said, looking around wide-eyed, "you *have* been a busy fucking bee."

"*C'mere* . . ." Sol took me by the arm. On a wooden easel, set in the center of the room, I saw what I had only heard described before. In a simple gold frame. A washerwoman in a gray dress. At a basin. Her back to the viewer. A ray of gentle light illuminating her as she worked. I noticed the signature at the bottom.

Henri Gaume.

In every direction there were masterpieces. Another Rembrandt. A Chagall. I shrugged at Sol. "Why this?"

Sol stepped over to the painting. He gently lifted the canvas. To my shock, there was another painting hidden behind it. Something I recognized. A man sitting at a table in a garden. Fuzzy red hair peeking from under his white cap, sharp blue eyes. There was a thin, wise look on his face, but his eyes were cast in a melancholy frown. My own eyes stretched wide.

"Ned," Sol said, and stepped back, "I want you to meet Dr. Gachet."

Chapter 115

I BLINKED, fixing my eyes on the sad, hunched man. It was a little different from the likeness I had seen in the book Dave left me. But it was unmistakably a van Gogh. Hidden, all this time, beneath the Gaume.

"The *missing* Dr. Gachet," Sol announced proudly. "Van Gogh painted *two* portraits of Gachet in the last month of his life. This one he gave to his landlord, and it spent the last hundred years in an attic in Auvers. It came to Stratton's attention."

"I was right," I muttered, anger building up in my chest. My brother and my friends had died for this thing. And Sollie had it all along.

"No," Sol said, shaking his head, "Liz stole the painting, Ned. She found out about the phony heist and came to me. I've known her family a long time. She intended to blackmail him. I'm not sure she even knew what was important about it.

Only that Dennis treasured it above all else and she wanted to hurt him."

"Liz?"

"With Lawson's help. When the police first responded to the alarm."

Now I was reeling. I pictured the tall Palm Beach detective who Ellie thought was Stratton's man. "Lawson? Lawson works for *you*?"

"Detective Vern Lawson works for the town of Palm Beach, Ned," Sol said, shrugging. "Let's just say now and then he keeps me informed."

I stared at Sollie with a new clarity. Like someone you thought you knew but now saw in a different light.

"Look around you, Ned. You see that Vermeer. *The Cloth Weavers*. It's thought to have been missing since the 1700s. Only it wasn't missing. It was just in private hands. And *The Death of Isaac,* that Rembrandt. It was referred to only in his letters. No one's even sure it exists. It sat undetected in a chapel in Antwerp for three hundred years. That's the ultimate beauty of these treasures. No one even knows they're here."

I couldn't do anything but stare in amazement.

"Now the Michelangelo over there . . ." Sol nodded approvingly. "*That* was hard to find."

There was a space on the wall between the Rembrandt and the Vermeer. "Here, help me," Sol said, and lifted the Gachet. I took it from him and hung it on the wall between two other masterpieces. We both stepped back.

"I know you won't understand this, son, but for me, this completes the journey of my life.

"I can offer you your old job back, but as a man of some means now, I suspect there're other things you want to do with your life. Can I give you some advice?"

"Why not?" I said with a shrug.

"If I were you, I would go to the Camille Bay Resort in the Cayman Islands. There's a check for the first million dollars waiting for you there. As long as this remains our little secret, they'll be another check every month. Thirty-five thousand dollars for five years wired to the same account. That should last longer than me. Of course, if you have second thoughts and the police happen to find their way down here, we'll consider our accounts cleared."

Then the two of us didn't say anything for a while. We just stared at the missing Gachet. The swirling brushstrokes, the sad, knowing blue eyes. And suddenly I thought I saw something in them, as if the old doctor were smiling at me.

"So, Neddie, whaddya think?" Sol stared at the Gachet, his hands behind his back.

"I don't know. . . ." I cocked my head. "A little crooked. To the left."

"My thoughts exactly, kid." Sol Roth smiled.

Chapter 116

THE FOLLOWING DAY I caught a plane for George Town on Grand Cayman Island. A blue island taxi took me along the beach-lined coast to the Camille Bay Resort.

Just as Sollie said, there was a room reserved in my name. Not exactly a room, but an incredible thatched-roof bungalow down by the beach, shaded by tall, swaying palm trees, with my own little private pool.

I put down my travel bag and stared out at the perfect turquoise sea.

On the desk, my eye came upon two sealed envelopes propped against the phone with my name on them.

The first was a welcome note from A. George McWilliams, the manager, with a basket of fruit, advising me that as a guest of Mr. Sol Roth, I should feel free to call on him at any time.

The second contained a deposit slip from the

Royal Cayman Bank in my name for the sum of one million dollars.

A million dollars.

I sat down. I stared at the slip and checked the name one more time, just to make sure I wasn't dreaming. Ned Kelly. A bank account made out to my name. All those beautiful zeros.

Jesus, I was rich.

I looked around, at the breathtaking view and the lavish room, at the basket of bananas and mangoes and grapes, at the expensive tiled floor, and it sort of hit me: I could afford this now. I wasn't there to clean the pool. I wasn't dreaming.

Why wasn't I jumping for joy?

My mind drifted to being in my old Bonneville two years before, after triggering those alarms. I was about to make the biggest score of my life, right? I was dreaming of sipping orange martinis with Tess on some fancy yacht. A million dollars in the bank.

And now I had it. I had my million dollars. More. I had the palm trees and the cove. I could buy that yacht, or at least rent one. In a twisted, ironic way, everything had come true. I could do anything I wanted in life.

And I didn't feel a thing.

I sat there at the desk, and that's when my eye fixed on something else right in front of me.

Something I'd been staring at, more like staring *through,* next to the ripped-open envelopes. Hesitantly, I picked it up.

It was one of those old Matchbox toys, a replica of a car. Except this one wasn't a car at all. *It was a little Dodge minivan.*

Chapter 117

"YOU KNOW HOW HARD it is to find a *real* one of those down here?" Ellie's voice came from behind me.

I spun around. She was standing there, nicely tanned, in a denim skirt and a pink tank top. She was sort of squinting into the sun that was setting behind me, her freckles almost bouncing off her cheeks. My heart flared, like an engine starting to rev.

"The last time I felt like this," I said, "an hour later, my whole life fell apart."

"Mine, too," Ellie said.

"You didn't come," I said, pretending to be hurt.

"I said I was going to be out of the country," Ellie said. "And here I am." She took a step toward me.

"I had to ride two hours back to Palm Beach with Champ doing wheelies in a classic twenty-year-old Caddie. You know what torture that is? Worse than prison."

She took another step. "Poor boy."

I held out the little minivan in my palm. "Nice touch," I said. "It, uh, just doesn't go anywhere."

"Oh, yes, it does, Ned," Ellie said, her eyes liquid and wide. She cupped her hands over her heart. "It goes right here."

"Jesus, Ellie." I couldn't hold back any longer. I reached out and put my arms around her. I hugged Ellie as tightly as I could. Her heart was beating like a little bird's. I bent down and kissed her.

"This isn't going to play very well with the Bureau," I said when we came apart.

"Screw the Bureau," Ellie said. "I quit."

I kissed her again. I stroked her hair and pressed her head close to my chest. I wanted to tell her about Sol. What I'd seen at the house. His masterpieces. The missing Gachet. It was killing me. If there was anyone on this earth who deserved to know, it was Ellie.

But as Sol said, I was good at taking advice.

"So, what're we going to do now?" I asked her. "Bank on my master's degree?"

"Now? Now we're going to take a walk on the beach, and I hope you're gonna do something romantic, like ask me if I want to marry you."

"Do you want to marry me, Ellie?"

"Not here. Out there. And then maybe we'll talk a bit about how we're gonna spend the rest of our lives. Straight talk, Ned. No games, not anymore."

So we took a walk on the beach. And I asked her. And she said yes. And for the longest time we didn't say another word. We just walked in the surf and watched the setting sun in paradise.

And the thought crept into my head that it might be pretty cool for a guy like me to be married to an ex–special agent of the FBI. . . .

Of course, I was thinking Ellie might be thinking the same thing, about Ned Kelly . . . *the outlaw*.

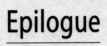

Epilogue

Chapter 118

TWO YEARS LATER . . .

The ring of the phone caught me just as I was rushing out the door. I had ten-month-old Davey the Handful in my arms and was about to plop him, all twenty-two pounds, into the waiting arms of Beth, our sitter.

Ellie was already at work. She opened up a gallery. In Delray, where we settled in a quaint little bungalow a couple of blocks off the beach. She specializes in nineteenth-century French paintings and sells them in New York and up in Palm Beach. In our living room, over the mantel, we even had a Henri Gaume.

"Ned Kelly," I answered, cradling the receiver in my neck.

I was late to work. I still took care of pools. Except this time, I bought the company, Tropic Pools, the largest in the area. These days I serviced all the fanciest ones from Boca to Palm Beach.

"Mr. Kelly," an unfamiliar voice replied, "this is Donna Jordan Cullity. I'm a partner at Rust, Simons and Cullity. We're a law firm in Palm Beach."

I mouthed to Beth under my breath that Ellie would be back around 4:30. "Uh-huh," I said into the phone receiver.

"You're acquainted with a Mr. Sol Roth?" the lawyer inquired.

"Uh-huh," I said again.

"Then I'm sorry to inform you that Mr. Roth has died."

I felt the blood rush to my head, my stomach plunge. I sat down. I knew Sol had been ill, but he was always making light of things. I'd gone to visit him less than a month before. He joked that he and Champ were gearing up to crash a Harley roundup near the Grand Canyon. I felt as shocked and weak-kneed as when my own father had died. *"When?"*

"About a week ago," Ms. Cullity said. "He knew he had cancer for a long time. He died peacefully in his sleep. In accordance with his desires, he didn't want anyone but his family to know."

"Thank you for letting me know," I said, this empty feeling crawling inside. I flashed to the image of the two of us standing in his vault, staring at those paintings. God, I was gonna miss Sol.

"Actually, Mr. Kelly," the lawyer said, "that's not why I called. We've been retained to handle some of Mr. Roth's wishes, in the matter of his estate. There are some issues that he didn't want publicized. He said you would understand."

"You mean the payments he's been making into a Caymans account?" I could understand why Sol wouldn't want that to come to light. Now that he was dead, I guessed the balance would be paid in full. "You can handle it any way you like, Ms. Cullity. I'll always be eternally grateful to Sol."

"Actually," Cullity said after a pause, "I think we should meet, Mr. Kelly."

"Meet?" I leaned back against the wall. "Why?"

"I don't think you understand, Mr. Kelly. I'm not calling about any payments. It's a matter of Mr. Roth's estate. There's an item he wanted you to have."

Chapter 119

SPLIT ACES, wasn't that what I called it a couple of years ago?

No, it's a helluva lot more than split aces. . . . It's like hitting the lottery, mate, as Champ would say. It's like the kick that wins the Super Bowl with no time left. You kick it over and over. The ball sails through. You can't miss.

What do you do when the most valuable piece of art in the world falls into your hands?

Well, first you stare at it. Maybe a million times. A man in a white cap with his head tilted at a table and a melancholy look.

You stare at it until you know every stab of color, every line of the weary face. Trying to figure out how something so simple could be so magical. Or why it came to you.

Or if you ever wanted that kind of money.

Maybe a hundred million dollars, the lawyer estimated.

Then you tell your wife. You tell her every-thing. Everything you were sworn not to. Hell, Sollie's secret was safe now anyway.

And after she yells at you for a while and wants to punch you, you bring her in and watch her see it for the first time. You see something beautiful in your wife's face amid the astonish-ment and the awe. "Oh my God, Neddie . . ." Like watching a blind man discovering color for the first time. The magical caress of her eyes. The reverence. It takes your breath away, too.

And you bring in your ten-month-old baby and you hold him in front of it and say, *One day, Davey, you'll have a helluva story to tell.*

You just won't have a hundred million dollars, guy.

So it always comes back to that question. What do you do with it? After all, it's stolen, right?

Throw some big Palm Beach bash. Get your face in "The Shiny Sheet." On the *Today* show. Make the *ARTnews* Hall of Fame.

You stare at Gachet's face. And you see it. In the angle of the cocked head. The wise, melan-choly eyes.

Not the eyes of a doctor, sitting there in the hot June sun. But the eyes of the person painting him.

And you wonder: What did he know? Who does this really belong to?

Stratton? Sollie? Liz?

Certainly not me.

No, not me.

I mean, I'm just a lifeguard, right?

Chapter 120

NEXT YEAR . . .

"Ready?" Ellie and I took Davey by the hand and led him down to the sea.

The beach was wonderfully quiet and empty that day. The surf was gentle. A couple of vacationers were strolling by, wetting their feet. An old woman wrapped all in white and wearing a wide straw hat, searching for shells. Ellie and I took Davey by the hand and let him jump off the dune to the surf.

"*Ready,*" my son replied, determined, his mop of blond hair the color of the sun.

"*Here.* This is how it's done." I rolled up a piece of paper and threaded it into the mouth of the Coors Light beer bottle. Coors was always my brother's favorite. Then I jammed the cap back on tightly and hammered it with my palm.

I smiled to Ellie. "That oughta hold."

"I never met him, Ned, but I think Dave would like this." Ellie looked on approvingly.

I winked. "Here." I handed the makeshift bottle to Davey. We walked down to the rippling tide. "Wait for the current to draw back into the sea." I pointed toward the foamy riptide. "You see it there?"

Davey nodded.

"Now," I said, easing him toward the water, *"throw!"*

My twenty-month-old ran pitter-patter into the surf and hurled the bottle with all his might. It went only about three feet but caught the lip of the receding wave and was drawn, gently, by the undertow.

A new wave hit the bottle and it bobbed up high but rode on, as if it knew its purpose, and fell over the crest, farther away. We all cheered. A couple of seconds later, it was like a little craft that had righted itself, successfully riding the waves out to sea.

"Where's it going, Daddy?" little Davey asked, shielding his eyes in the bright ocean air.

"Maybe heaven," Ellie said, watching it drift.

"What's inside?"

I tried to answer, but my voice caught in my throat and my eyes grew a little tight.

"It's a gift," Ellie answered for me. She took my hand. "For your uncle Dave."

It was a newspaper article, actually, that I had stuffed in the bottle. From the *New York Times*. In the past few days, it had also been reprinted in most other major newspapers in the world.

The art world was shocked Tuesday afternoon when a painting donated at a charity auction in Palm Beach, Florida, thought to be a reproduction of a missing van Gogh, astonishingly has been identified as an original.

A panel of art experts, consisting of historians and curators at major auction houses who studied the canvas for several days, authenticated the painting as van Gogh's long-missing second portrait of Dr. Gachet, painted in the weeks before the renowned painter died. Dr. Ronald Suckling of Columbia University, who headed the panel, called its sudden appearance "irrefutable" and "a stunning and miraculous event for the art world and the world at large." He added that no one has "the slightest idea" where the painting has been for 120 years.

More baffling is how the painting suddenly surfaced, and how it was anonymously gifted to the Liz Stratton Fund, a Palm Beach charity set up to protect abused children, a fledgling project of the late Palm Beach financier's wife, who was reputed to be murdered in a tragic series of crimes that struck this fashionable resort town a few years ago.

The painting was part of a silent auction of the inaugural charity event. It was, according to charity spokesperson Page Lee Hufty, "donated and delivered to us anonymously. Never for a second did we actually imagine that it was real."

The value of the piece, thought to be upward of $100 million, makes it one of the largest donations to a specific charity in history.

"What makes the thing all the more incredible,"

Hufty explained, "is the note that accompanied the gift. 'To Liz. May it finally do some good.' The note was signed, Ned Kelly," a veiled reference perhaps to the legendary Australian bandit of the nineteenth century known for his good deeds.

"It's like some crazy, generous, unexplainable joke," Hufty said. "But whoever he is, he's right, this gift will do an unimaginable amount of good."

"Is that heaven?" little Dave asked, pointing toward the horizon.

"I don't know," I said, watching the bottle glint a last time as it melded into the sea. "But I think it's close enough. . . ."

About the Authors

JAMES PATTERSON is the author of the two best-selling new detective series of the past decade: the Alex Cross novels, including the #1 *New York Times* bestsellers *London Bridges,* and *The Big Bad Wolf, Mary Mary,* and the Women's Murder Club series, including the #1 bestsellers *1st to Die, 2nd Chance, 3rd Degree, 4th of July,* and *The 5th Horseman.* He is also the author of the bestselling love stories *Suzanne's Diary for Nicholas* and *Sam's Letters to Jennifer.* He lives in Florida.

ANDREW GROSS worked with James Patterson on the previous bestselling novel *3rd Degree.* He lives with his wife, Lynn, and their three children in Westchester County, New York.

**Get ready for an unbelievable
Alex Cross shocker . . .**

**Please turn this page for
a riveting look at**

Cross

**Available wherever
books are sold.**

**Also available now: James Patterson's
novels featuring Alex Cross in the order
they were written.**

Along Came a Spider
Kiss the Girls
Jack & Jill
Cat & Mouse
Pop Goes the Weasel
Roses Are Red
Violets Are Blue
Four Blind Mice
The Big Bad Wolf
London Bridges
Mary Mary

Prologue

I'm Dr. Ormson, with the Berkshires Medical Center. How many shots did you hear?

Multiple shots.

What is your name, sir?

Alex Cross.

Are you having trouble breathing? Experiencing any pain?

Pain in my abdomen. Feel liquid sloshing around.

You know that you were shot?

Yes. Twice. Is he dead. The Butcher? Michael Sullivan?

I don't know. Several men are dead . . . OK, guys, give me a non-rebreather mask. Two wide base IV lines stat. Two liters IV saline solution . . . Now!

We're going to try to move you, get you to a hospital immediately, Mr. Cross. Just hold on. Can you still hear me?

My kids . . . Tell them I love them.

THE BEST

JAMES PATTERSON

THRILLER EVER!

Please turn the page for
a preview of

Judge & Jury

Available wherever
books are sold.

PROLOGUE–The Wedding

CHAPTER 1

My name is Nick Pellisante, and this is where it started for me, one summer out on Long Island, at "the wedding of weddings." I was watching the bride celebrating at the head of the dance line as it festively wound through the tables. *The tarantella,* I groaned. I hated the tarantella.

I should mention that I was watching the scene through high-powered binocular lenses. I followed as the bride slung her ample, lace-covered rear end in every direction, toppling a glass of red wine, trying to coax up some bowling ball of a relative who was scarfing down a plate of stuffed clams, into the procession. Meanwhile, the grinning, affable groom did his Gowanus Expressway– best just to hang on.

Lucky couple, I winced, thinking ten years down the line. *Lucky me to get to watch. All part of the job.*

As agent in charge of Section C-10, the FBI's organized crime unit in New York, my team was staking out a wiseguy wedding at the posh South Fork Club in Montauk. Everybody who was anybody was here, assuming you were into wiseguys.

Everybody except for the one man I was really looking for.

The Boss. The *capo di tutti capi*. Dominic Cavello. They called him the "Electrician," because he had started that way, doing construction scams in New Jersey, union tampering, extorting builders. But "Electrician" was more a term of endearment now, like saying bin Laden had a personal thing against tall buildings. The guy was bad, terror-level-red bad. And I had a slew of warrants on him: murder, extortion, union tampering, conspiracy to finance narcotics.

Some of my buddies at the Bureau said Cavello was already in Sicily, laughing at us. Another rumor had him in the Dominican Republic at a resort he owned. Others had him in Costa Rica, in the UAR, even in Moscow.

But I had a hunch that he was here, somewhere in this noisy crowd. His ego was too large. I'd been tracking him for three years, but nothing, not even the federal government, was going to make Dominic Cavello miss his closest niece's wedding.

"Cannoli One, this is Cannoli Two," a voice deadpanned in my earpiece.

It was Special Agent Manny Oliva, who I'd stationed down on the dunes with Ed Sinclair. Manny had come out of the projects of Newark, then got himself a law degree at Rutgers. He'd been assigned to my C-10 unit straight out of Quantico.

"Anything on the radar, Nick? Nothing but sand and seagulls here."

"Yeah," I said, dishing it back, "ziti mostly. A little lasagna with hot sausages, some stuffed shrimp and parmigiana—."

"Stop! You're making me hungry down here, Nicky Smiles . . ."

Nicky Smiles . . . That's what the guys I was close to

called me in the unit. Maybe because I was blessed with
a pretty nice grin. More likely, the nickname came from
the fact I knew more about La Cosa Nostra than just
about anyone else in the Bureau. Not just because I'd
grown up with a bunch of them in Bay Ridge, and had
one of those same vowel-ending names myself. More
likely, it was because I was offended by what this scum
had done to the reputations of all Italian Americans:
my own family, friends of mine who couldn't have been
more law-abiding, and of course, myself.

*So where the hell are you, you sly son of a bitch?
You're here, aren't you, Cavello?* I craned the binocu-
lars along the dance line.

The procession had snaked all the way around the
room by now. Juiced-up goombas in tuxedos with pur-
ple shirts and their high-hairdo wives busting through
their gowns. The bride sidled up to a table of old-
timers, *padrones* in bolo ties sipping espresso, trading
old tales. One or two of the faces looked familiar.

That's when the bride made her mistake.

She singled out one of the old men, leaned down,
and kissed him on the cheek. The balding man was in
a wheelchair, hands on his lap like he'd had a stroke.
He had on thick black-rimmed glasses, no eyebrows,
like Uncle Junior on the *Sopranos*.

I stood up and focused the lens on him. I watched her
take him by the hands and try to coax him up. The guy
looked like he couldn't pee upright, and could barely wrap
his feeble arms around her, never mind get up and down.

Then my heart slammed to a stop.

You arrogant son of a bitch! You came!

"Tom, Robin, that old geezer with the black
glasses? The bride just gave him a kiss."

"Yeah," Tom Roach came back. He was inside a van

in the parking lot watching pictures sent from cameras planted in the club. "I got him. What's the problem?"

I took a step closer, zooming in with the lens.

"No problem. *That's Dominic Cavello!*"

CHAPTER 2

This is a go!" I barked into the mike attached to my shirt collar. "Target is a bald male in black glasses, seated in a wheelchair at a table on the left-hand side of the room. It's Cavello! He is to be treated as armed and likely to resist."

From where I was, I had a firsthand view of the next few minutes of action. Tom Roach and Robin Hammill jumped out of the van in the parking lot and headed for the entrance.

We had manpower and backup all over the place, even agents posing as bartenders and waiters on the inside. I had a Coast Guard cutter half a mile off shore, with an Apache helicopter that could be mobilized if necessary.

Not even Dominic Cavello would turn his brother's daughter's wedding into an ugly firefight, right?

Wrong.

A couple of hoods in light-blue tuxedos were taking a smoke outside when they spotted my team coming out of the van. One headed back inside, while the other blocked their approach. "Sorry, this is a private affair . . ."

Tom Roach flashed his shield. "Now it's open to the public. *FBI.*"

I zoomed back to the other wiseguy hurrying out to the wedding party on the verandah. He ran up to the crippled old man in the wheelchair.

I was right! It was definitely Cavello! But our cover was shot.

"We're blown!" I yelled, fixing on the commotion on the verandah. "Everybody close in on Cavello! Manny, you and Ed stay put and cover the dunes. *Taylor,*" I called out to an agent posing as a waiter, "wait for Tom's crew."

Then Cavello jumped out of the wheelchair—suddenly the healthiest guy in the world. Steve Taylor put down his serving tray and pulled a gun from under his jacket. *"FBI!"* he yelled.

I heard a shot and watched Taylor go down, and stay down.

Chaos erupted. A few of the heavy Mafioso honchos were scurrying all over the verandah, some shrieking, others ducking under tables. A few of the heavy honchos were hurrying toward the exits.

I zoomed back to Cavello. He was hunched over, slinking through the crowd, still in disguise. He was making a path toward the beach.

I took out my Walther and hopped off the ledge. Then I ran for the clubhouse along the shore road.

I stayed near the white clapboard clubhouse, then hoisted myself onto the deck of the restaurant. The verandah was built out over a ledge, propped over dunes, some thirty feet above the beach.

I could still see Cavello. He had peeled off his old man's makeup and black glasses. He shoved an old woman out of his way and leaped over the wooden fence—then he was running toward the dunes.

We had him!

CHAPTER 3

Manny, Ed, he's headed toward you!"

I saw where Cavello was going. He was trying to get to a helicopter up on the point, obviously *his* helicopter. I pushed my way inside the restaurant and out onto the verandah deck, shoving people out of the way. At the edge of the deck, I looked down.

Cavello was stumbling over the grassy dunes, making his way along the beach.

Then he ducked behind a tall dune and I lost sight of him.

I shouted into the radio, "*Manny, Ed, he should be on you any second now.*"

"I got him, Nick," Manny squawked.

"*Federal agents . . .*" I heard Manny shout through the radio.

Then there were shots. Two quick ones—followed by three more in rapid succession.

My blood turned to ice. *Oh, Jesus.* I ran out of the club, leaped over the fence, stumbling down the dunes toward the beach. I lost my footing and fell to one knee. I righted myself and hurtled forward in the direction of the shots.

I stopped.

Two bodies were lying face-up on the sand. My heart was pumping. I ran to them, sliding in the sand, which was stained dark with blood.

Oh, dear God, no.

I knew that Manny was dead. Ed Sinclair was lying there, gurgling blood, a gunshot wound in his chest.

Dominic Cavello was fifty yards ahead, limping, but getting away.

"Manny and Ed are down," I yelled into the mike. "Get help here now!"

Up ahead, Cavello was running toward the helicopter. The cabin was open. I took off after him.

"Cavello, stop!' I shouted. "I'll shoot!"

Cavello looked back over his shoulder. He didn't stop though.

I squeezed the trigger of my gun—twice. The second bullet slammed into his thigh.

The Godfather reached for his leg and buckled. But he kept going, dragging the leg, like some desperate animal that wouldn't quit. I heard a *thwack, thwack, thwack* and saw the Coast Guard Apache coming into sight.

"That's it," I yelled ahead, aiming my Walther again. "You're done! The next shot goes through your head."

The Mafioso pulled himself to an exhausted stop. He put his hands in the air and slowly turned.

He had no gun. I didn't know where he'd thrown it, maybe into the sea. A grin was etched on his face.

"*Nicky Smiles . . .*" he said, "If I knew you wanted to be at my niece's wedding, all you had to do was ask. I woulda sent you an invitation. Engraved."

My head felt like it was going to explode. I'd lost two men, maybe three, over this filth. I walked up to Cavello, my Walther pointed at his chest. He met my eyes with a mocking smile. "You know, that's the problem with Italian weddings, Pellisante, everybody's got a gun."

I slugged him and Cavello fell to one knee. For a second I thought he was going to fight me, but he just shook his head and laughed.

So I hit Cavello again, with everything I had left in me. This time, he stayed down.

PART ONE-The First Trial

CHAPTER 1

In his house on Yehuda Street in Haifa, high above the sky-blue Mediterranean, Richard Nordeshenko tried the King's Indian Defense. The pawn break, Kasparov's famous attack. From there he had dismantled Tukmakov in the Russian Championships in 1981.

Across from him a young boy countered by matching the pawn. His father nodded, pleased with the move. "And why does the pawn create such an advantage?" Nordeshenko asked.

"Because it blocks freeing up of your queenside rook," the boy answered quickly. "And the advance of your pawn to a queen. Correct?"

"Correct," Nordeshenko beamed at his son. "And when did the queen first acquire the powers that it holds today?"

"Around fifteen hundred," his son answered. "In Europe. Up until then it merely moved two spaces up and down. But . . ."

"*Bravo*, Pavel!"

Affectionately, he mussed his son's blond hair. For an eight-year-old, Pavel was learning quickly.

The boy glanced silently over the board, then moved his rook. Nordeshenko saw what his son was up to. He had once been in the third tier of Glasskov's chess academy in Kiev. Still, he pretended to ignore it and pushed forward his attack on the opposite side, exposing a pawn.

"You're letting me win, Father," the boy declared, refusing to take it. "Besides, you said just one game. Then you would teach me . . ."

"Teach *you* . . . ?" Nordeshenko teased him, knowing precisely what he meant. "You can teach *me*."

"Not chess, Father." The boy looked up. "*Poker*."

"Ah, *poker*?" Nordeshenko feigned surprise. "To play poker, Pavel, you must have something to bet."

"I have something," the boy insisted. "I have six dollars in coins. I've been saving up. And over a hundred soccer cards. Perfect condition."

Inwardly, Nordeshenko smiled. He understood what the boy was feeling. He had studied how to seize the advantage his whole life. Chess was hard, solitary. Like playing an instrument. Scales, drills, practice. Until every eventuality became absorbed, memorized. Until you didn't have to think.

A little like learning to kill a man with your bare hands . . .

But poker . . . poker was liberating. *Alive*. Unlike chess, you never played the same. You broke the rules. It was an unusual combination that was necessary. *Discipline and risk*.

Suddenly, the chime of Nordeshenko's mobile phone cut in. He was expecting the call. "We'll pick it up in a moment," Nordeshenko said to Pavel.

"*But, Father . . . ?*" the boy whined, disappointed.

"In a moment," Nordeshenko said again, picking up his son by the armpits, spanking him lightly on his way. "I have to take this call . . . not another word."

"Okay . . ."

Nordeshenko walked out to the terrace overlooking the sea and flipped open the phone. Only a handful of people in the world had this number. He settled into a chaise. "This is Nordeshenko."

"I'm calling for Dominic Cavello," the caller identified himself. "He has a job for you."

"*Dominic Cavello . . . ?* Cavello is in jail and awaiting trial," Nordeshenko said. "And I have many jobs to consider."

"Not like this one," the caller said. "The Godfather has requested only you. Name your price."